Sa

Book One

*For Andrew, whose support is unwavering,
as always.*

*And for Sarah, who gave me the confidence to keep
writing.*

Copyright © 2014 by Ann Serafini Woods

All rights reserved. No part of this book (whether print or electronic edition) may be reproduced in any form without the express written consent of the author

This book is a work of fiction. Names, characters, places and incidents are either the product of the author's imagination or are used fictitiously. Any resemblance to actual persons, living or dead, business establishments, events or locales is purely coincidental.

Prologue

June, 1924
Port of Galway, Ireland

The ocean liner was the biggest boat Asiah had ever seen in all her twelve years. The main deck towered overhead as she mounted the gangplank for the transatlantic voyage. The ship gleamed with a new coat of white paint, and she could see the name of the ship carefully stenciled in black letters near the bow. Overcome with wonder, she leaned her head back as far as she could to marvel at the great smokestacks, and stumbled backward into her brother, Monty.

"Oi! Careful, Cricket, or you'll be lunch for the sharks!" Monty chuckled.

"Will not!" Asiah retorted hotly as she regained her footing. "I can swim just fine. The sharks couldn't catch me!" She stuck her tongue out at her older brother.

"Ah, but the giant squid could!" Monty threatened, throwing his arms around his baby sister and squeezing tightly. "Once they get their tentacles around you—"

"Put the lass down, Montgomery," their father's voice boomed from behind them.

Monty released Asiah and tugged on her braid instead. "C'mon, Cricket, let's go look off the bow of the ship and see if we can see America!"

Asiah nodded excitedly and skipped up the ramp, followed closely by her twin sister, Merica.

"Do you think we can see the Statue of Liberty?" Meri asked.

"I dunno," Asiah replied. "Might be too far away."

Meri took her sister's hand and squeezed. "I can't wait!"

She won't be so excited once we're underway, Asiah thought, recalling her sister's tendency toward motion sickness. Meri and their older sister, Maryn, had always had trouble riding the ferry from the mainland to Inishmor, their island home off the west coast of Ireland. Asiah had never felt seasick a day in her life and seemed to have the "sea-legs of a pirate captain," according to her father. She loved the sea. She couldn't understand how one could grow up on a stormy island in the North Atlantic and not love the ocean.

Patrick O'Connor was a fisherman on Inishmor, as was his father before him. At nineteen, Monty didn't have much choice but to do the same, but Asiah got the feeling that Monty craved a more exciting life than that of a fisherman. The O'Connors were leaving Ireland today because Patrick had recently decided that there was more opportunity in America than on their little island, so he packed their meager possessions and bought them all third-class tickets aboard the *Mermaid* set to sail for Boston. Asiah knew that her father had spent all he had for tickets for a family of six to cross the sea, and she hoped that he'd be able to find work soon so they wouldn't be living on the street when they reached America. A poor life on a stormy island was better than sleeping in the gutter in a strange new land. The thought made Asiah's insides queasy.

As much as the voyage to America excited her, Asiah was loath to leave her remote island home. On Inishmor she did as she pleased – much to her mother's chagrin. Asiah and her siblings had never attended a proper school, and were taught to read and write at home. They learned about history and mathematics, but what Asiah was really interested in was science. She wanted to know everything that couldn't be easily explained by her mother's favorite phrase: "That's just the way things are." Asiah wanted to know why the tides came in and went out and why the moon changed shape every night. She wanted to know why the grass was green and how caterpillars became butterflies.

Aileen O'Connor was a no-nonsense Irishwoman who worked tirelessly to raise four children, three of whom were girls and three of whom behaved as well-mannered children should. She didn't know much about science, and focused her teachings instead on other subjects that she considered useful to children. When she wasn't doing her studies at home, Asiah learned everything she could by observing nature. She would lie on her back for hours looking at different types of clouds. While most children would look for animal shapes in the clouds, Asiah would draw them as they were and include notes on her sketches about how high she thought the clouds were or if they were likely to mean rain.

Her mother didn't seem to mind her wanderings, but was never too pleased when Asiah would bring home tokens from her adventures like frogs or large beetles. Meri never joined Asiah on her excursions, instead played with her dolls and practiced being a "fine lady." She took much delight in tattling on Asiah whenever she was up to no good. Their father would just shake his head and say how he never would have had another child if he'd known twin girls were on the way.

Asiah hoped that in America she'd be able to attend a proper school – one that would teach her more about science and nature and the world she lived in. Sometimes she thought there just wasn't enough room in her brain to soak up all the information she wanted to know. She also hoped her family would live in the countryside so she could go exploring. She'd been to Galway a few times, and from what she'd seen of living conditions in the city for people like her family, she didn't like the look of it. Her mother hadn't taught her much about America yet, but it was widely known to be a land of opportunity.

The blaring sound of the ship's horn sounded as the *Mermaid* slowly navigated out of the harbor, and Asiah felt the familiar sea breeze ruffle her hair. She untied the ribbons securing her braids and let the wind take hold of her long, chestnut tresses. The sun was out today, which was a nice change from the usual clouds she was used to seeing this time of year, and Asiah closed her eyes, basking in the myriad of sensations. She only had a moment to enjoy the feeling before her mother scolded her for removing her hair ribbons.

"I suppose you want a rat's nest on your head, child?" Combing her fingers through her daughter's thick hair, Aileen efficiently plaited it into two braids and tied them tightly with blue ribbons. "That's better, then! Now go find your berth with your sister!"

"I want to watch as we cast off!" Asiah complained. Just because Meri was going to have a rough time on the voyage didn't mean she had to stay below with her.

Aileen cast her gaze skyward and mouthed a silent prayer before turning her stern countenance on Asiah. "We've cast off already and I don't want any back-talk from you, young lady! Your sister can't be left alone down there. Now go on!"

"I'm *not* a lady," Asiah muttered.

"What was that?" Aileen raised her eyebrows in challenge.

"Nothing, Mam." Asiah trudged off toward the stairwell that led down to their cabin and stole one last glance over her shoulder at the endless sea ahead of them. In that instant she felt a strange surge of sensation pass through her, almost like she'd been struck by lightning. It stole her breath and made her knees wobble. Asiah reached for a nearby railing to steady herself as she peered at the horizon, desperately trying to understand what she'd felt. As she watched, a flash of green illuminated the sea, only for an instant, then the feeling subsided. Her mother was scolding her again, but her voice sounded distant and insignificant.

Asiah smiled to herself and continued down the winding staircase. She knew what that feeling meant: that something amazing lay ahead, just out of reach. And she was determined to discover it.

Chapter One

September, 1931
Chicago

The wind was especially gusty the afternoon Asiah's life changed forever. It wasn't a special day, or even a good day; in fact, she was under more stress than usual and was counting the hours until she could go home. A violent gust nearly blew her into the street as she hurried east down North Avenue carrying a stack of books for Mr. Kelsey, the druggist. A particularly virulent flu season was in full swing and Mr. Kelsey had Asiah running around like crazy in an attempt to collect as much information from libraries and doctors as she could to help the people afflicted with the virus. Traditional medicines didn't seem to help, but Mr. Kelsey was known for his effective home remedies.

Asiah had been working for the druggist since last summer after she finished high school. She had tried desperately to save enough money to go to college, but only a handful of schools accepted women into their science programs and not one of them was in Chicago. She'd been accepted by a school in Missouri, but a last-minute tuition increase left her with no options. Frustrated with her bad luck, Asiah took a job with Mr. Kelsey, who proved in the end to be a valuable mentor with his extensive knowledge of chemistry and medicine.

When her dream of attending college fell through, Asiah's parents made several attempts to marry her off to wealthy businessmen. Asiah turned down every offer and dodged every dinner invitation her parents set up for her. She knew they only wanted her to marry for money so they could benefit as well. The Depression had hit her family harder than most. The men her parents introduced her to were all scoundrels to boot. Many of them offered marriage the moment they saw Asiah's photograph, without ever having met her. Asiah knew they were only interested in acquiring a beautiful wife, but she refused to be some rich man's trophy.

    People often told Asiah that she was pretty, but she never took much stock in the words of strangers with wandering eyes. She assumed that's what people said when they had nothing substantial to add to a conversation. Many women spent hours making themselves beautiful, but Asiah never wasted a moment on her appearance. She kept her long chestnut hair in a braid most of the time so it would be out of the way, and dressed conservatively in plain dresses or even trousers if she could get away with it. Her eyes were light brown, almost golden in the right light – not at all alluring in her own opinion – and she was tall and gangly at five feet, nine inches, with a slender figure. She definitely didn't have the voluptuous curves that were coveted by most women. She wondered sometimes why anyone would give her a second look.

    A strand of hair came loose from her braid and tickled her nose as she ran down the street, and she loosened her grip on the stack of books just long enough for one of the tomes to slip. Before she could adjust her grip, the entire stack came tumbling down and loose pages began to blow down the street in a flurry of little white squares. Thankful that at least she wasn't wearing a billowy skirt on a day like this, Asiah dropped to her knees and began scooping books and papers into a haphazard pile. With one arm covering the pile to keep stray pages from blowing away, she attempted to sweep up the loose pieces with her other arm. Soon she was practically lying flat on the ground with her arms spread-eagled between two piles of paper, trying desperately to bring them together against the punishing wind. She looked bleakly down the street ahead as several pages were lost in the gale.

Just as she thought she might have to let go of one stack and hope for the best, a pair of scuffed jack boots appeared inches from her face.

"It would appear that you need a hand," a deep, accented voice said from above.

Conceding that the wind had beaten her, Asiah nearly wilted in relief. "Y-yes, I would appreciate that, thank you," she stammered.

One of the boots moved to hold down one stack as she gathered the other stack into her arms and stood up awkwardly. It took Asiah several minutes to organize her pile, yet the man helping her had somehow gotten his pile into a neat stack with much less effort. When he rose to hand her the stack, her gaze met the most intense green eyes she'd ever seen. Her mortification tripled and she felt her face turn fire-engine red. He must have thought her such a foolish girl to be carrying a pile of loose papers in such a windstorm.

"Oh!" she stammered. "I ... I ... I mean, that is ... ummm ..." She couldn't seem to remember how to speak coherently as those olivine eyes bored into her.

"Come inside my shop; it's just here. You may organize your things there." The man gestured to a dark doorway behind him.

Asiah looked into the unsettling gloom of his shop, then back to her piles of paper. With great force of will she reached down into her memory and remembered how to speak English. "Thank you for your help, sir, but I really should be getting back. My employer will wonder what happened to me." She let out a nervous giggle, then immediately blushed a deeper shade of red.

The man looked at her for a moment, seeming to see right into her soul. It almost felt as if something were tingling in the back of her brain. She shifted uncomfortably and looked over her shoulder. She'd thanked the man already, but couldn't seem to make her feet move away from him.

"Nonsense!" he finally spoke. "You won't get far with everything here in disarray, especially in this wind. Come inside and I'll help you put everything right again." He smiled, showing perfect white teeth.

Asiah almost forgot herself again after that smile, and she straightened her back and stuck out her chin, doing her utmost to hide the strange fluttering in her stomach. She wasn't about to let this shabby-looking shopkeeper invite her inside some strange, mysterious place. There were too many downtrodden that had turned to thievery during the Depression, and she couldn't trust just anyone on the street, however handsome he may be.

She spoke more firmly, "Thank you, but I really must be getting back to my job. I do appreciate your assistance." Asiah stepped forward and clumsily stacked her pile on top of his before she carefully pulled the mess from his hands and clutched it to her chest. As she did, her hand brushed his. A strange electric spark ignited between them, like static electricity, but strangely different, almost ... pleasant. Even after she'd stepped back her hand tingled a bit where it had touched his.

Stranger still was that he seemed surprised by the feeling, like he'd never felt it before, either. He'd jumped just a tiny bit, but recovered quickly glancing away and muttering, "I'm sorry, too." He looked back into her flustered gaze for a moment longer then turned and strode into the dark doorway to his shop, slamming the heavy door behind him.

Completely bewildered, Asiah stared after him wondering what on Earth had just happened.

Chase cursed himself the moment he let her walk away. Was he mad? What if she was the one he'd been searching for? Seven hundred years was a long time for him to remember the task he'd been given by a dying man, and he'd all but given up the search when he came to Chicago a decade ago. He'd read enough prophecies saying that he would eventually find the girl, so it seemed fruitless to keep moving around and looking in different places. The girl he was supposed to find would find him. And he had a sneaking suspicion that she just had.

He'd opened an antique knife shop on North Avenue to keep himself busy, but found it tedious and boring despite his fascination with blades of all kinds. Life in general was becoming tedious. Waiting endless years for a prophecy to come true was no way to live. With only a handful of customers over the years, he had plenty of time to pore over the old texts, scrolls and prophecies he had collected over the past seven centuries. Even these didn't hold his attention anymore. If the girl he'd met outside truly was the right girl, his long life would soon be blissfully over. And he'd let her walk away.

Chase's parents had died the day he was born, his mother during childbirth. His father was crushed by a falling tree while running through a violent storm trying to get help for his dying wife. Chase was raised by a man named Tojen, who was his father's uncle. It was by his Great-Uncle Tojen's teachings that Chase learned to control matter and energy. Sorcery, they called it then, or magic. When Chase was 25, his great-uncle called him to his bedside where he lay dying. He told Chase that he had but one purpose in his life, which was to find his daughter. Confused, Chase asked why it was so important. The old man told Chase a story of a people whose very existence was in jeopardy, and that the only person who could save this world from ruin was his daughter.

Chase asked Tojen where he could find this woman and the sorcerer replied simply that she hadn't been born yet, and may not be born for many years, but when the people of this world needed her most, she would come to them. With his dying breath Tojen made Chase promise to find her and teach her how to set humankind on the right path again.

Chase found it difficult to believe that the woman meant to save all of mankind was just sprawled in the street in front of his shop. It might not even be the right woman. The feeling he felt when their hands touched was familiar to be sure, but it could have just as easily been static electricity.

Even if the girl in the street was who he thought she was, Chase wasn't sure he *wanted* to find her. Her mission was to save humanity from self-destruction, but he had long believed that people were inherently evil – hardly worth saving. Rarely did he see selflessness, love, or kindness anymore. For this reason, he kept his distance from society, but whenever he did venture out, he was often treated as the outcast he was. The people of this world deserved the devastation they were bringing upon themselves.

His strange experience with the girl outside motivated Chase to consult one of his ancient scrolls. The wrinkled parchment he removed from a shelf filled with similar scrolls was just one of many pieces of a puzzle he couldn't solve. By the light of a single candle, his eyes now scanned the browned parchment covered in the scribbled words of a lost language. The words before him meant nothing to Chase. His great-uncle had made it clear that he would never be able to read them, only his daughter would. It hadn't stopped Chase from examining the document thoroughly hundreds of times. He picked up the candle, holding the flame closer to the page and hoping for something new to appear that he'd never noticed before. But, as always, the page remained a mystery to him.

Sighing in resignation, he rolled up the scroll hastily and tossed it aside. He held up his hand and examined his fingers where she had touched him, almost expecting to find some sign of who she was. The jolt he felt when they touched was something he recognized, but the last time he experienced that feeling was ages ago. In seven hundred years he'd never come across another who made him remember the strange sensation. Whether this was the girl or not, he had to try to find out more.

With renewed purpose, Chase pulled a large leather-bound volume from a dusty shelf and dropped it on his oak table. A cloud of dust swirled up to settle on the book and he used his sleeve to brush it from the cover. He started to open the tome, then paused, moving his hand about a foot over the book's cover. He closed his eyes, imagining the passage he wanted to read. The volume flew open and the pages fluttered wildly as if a strong wind had blown through the shop. Finally, the book became still, open to the very passage he'd envisioned. Chase dropped heavily into his chair and began scanning the open page.

Aside from the ancient scroll that only the right woman could read, there was also supposedly a map. According to the archaic texts, she would carry the map with her always, never parting with it for any reason. Chase had no idea what the map led to, but it seemed a fairly simple thing to ask a person whether they carried a map with them at all times. When the page before him revealed nothing more than what he already knew, he slammed the book shut. If he'd stumbled upon the woman he'd been looking for today in the street, then their paths were inevitably destined to cross again.

Chapter Two

Asiah nearly collided with Richard Kelsey, the aging pharmacist and owner of the North Avenue Drugstore, as she burst through the door amidst a flurry of loose papers.

"Slow down there, Asia Minor!" Mr. Kelsey scolded, but his eyes were smiling. Asiah had earned the nickname "Asia Minor" because she was the youngest in her family, and Mr. Kelsey had known the O'Connors since they'd moved to Chicago six years earlier when Asiah had indeed been the smallest of the bunch. Taking the top half of her teetering pile in his own hands, Mr. Kelsey guided Asiah to the counter and helped her release the mess into a crinkled stack.

"I'm so sorry I'm late, Mr. Kelsey," Asiah began. "I dropped a book a few blocks from here and everything fell and a man helped me pick it up and I hurried as fast as I could!" Her words came out in a rush making her feel like a foolish child.

"No harm done, sweetheart, but it looks like you have some organizing to do now. I'll fix you a soda and you can start working on this mess." He busied himself behind the counter and began rattling off something he'd read in the newspaper about the Capone case. The old druggist was fascinated with the notorious gangster.

As Mr. Kelsey rambled on, Asiah tuned him out and turned her thoughts to the mysterious man on the street and the strange feeling that had passed between them when their hands touched. The feeling was so intense that she was almost afraid to think about it. Then again, it was so fleeting that maybe there wasn't actually anything there to think about. It must have been static electricity, like the kind found in her bedsheets on hot, dry summer nights. She also couldn't rule out that her overactive imagination had invented the whole thing.

Asiah focused her attention on the mess of books and papers in front of her. She pulled a blank page out of the pile and began making a list of the texts she had collected: *Herbs and Fungi with Medicinal Properties*, *Healing at Home*, *A Beginner's Guide to Herb Gardening*, *Amazing Emerald Eyes* ...

Wait, that's not in the pile, Asiah thought. She shook her head to clear it. He was just a man on the street – no one of consequence. Why couldn't she get him out of her head?

She decided that if she thought about him just for a minute, then she could write it off as a chance meeting and get back to work. She closed her eyes and summoned an image of his face to the front of her mind. The first things she remembered were his eyes. Such a brilliant green, like the Irish hills, and deep and still like the lochs she had visited as a child in Scotland. His hair was thick and dark, not quite black, falling in unkempt curls to his shoulders. He hadn't had a shave in a few days but the stubble didn't hide his razor-sharp jawline and dimples she'd seen briefly when he smiled. He'd had nice teeth, which were scarce where she came from and uncommon even in America. He was taller than she was by about six inches, and seemed to tower over her. From what she could tell he was muscular, like he'd done a lot of hard labor in his life. His clothing was strange and looked like it was from medieval times: a belted tunic over fitted trousers. Lastly, she remembered that he wore matching silver bracelets on each wrist.

"Quite the little sketch artist, aren't we?" Mr. Kelsey's voice jarred Asiah from her thoughts. She looked at him questioningly and he gestured to the paper on which she had been making her list of books. On the page was now sketched the face of the man she had met, in perfect detail. She had never been much of an artist, but this was an impeccable likeness. She stared at the page in shock. Her eyes had been closed; she hadn't even realized she was holding her pencil.

"Who is that fella? Some new beau of yours?" Mr. Kelsey wondered with a wink.

Feeling confused and disoriented, Asiah scrambled to collect the books into a pile again and tossed them onto a shelf behind the counter. "I-I'm sorry Mr. Kelsey, I'm not feeling well, I need to go home." She collected her belongings quickly and bolted from the drugstore before her employer could stop her.

Asiah ran all the way home and went straight to the bedroom she shared with her twin sister. Meri worked as a secretary for a law firm downtown and wasn't home. Asiah's struggling family knew Meri was incredibly lucky to have a job at all so no one complained when she came home late each evening after her long walk home. Their father didn't approve of a young woman walking alone in Chicago at night, but the O'Connors could barely afford the apartment they had and weren't able to move closer to downtown. As with Asiah, Patrick and Aileen had also tried to pair Meri up with eligible men, but as soon as potential suitors got a look at Asiah, they focused their attention on her instead, despite the twins' insignificant differences in appearance. Meri ended up confused and heartbroken while Asiah was just plain irritated.

Patrick had found work as a fisherman on Lake Michigan when they moved to Chicago six years earlier, but during the stock market crash he'd lost his job. He'd done odd jobs here and there over the years, but the family depended on Asiah and Meri the most. Their eldest sister Maryn had left home at eighteen and moved to San Francisco. Asiah knew Maryn had been desperate to make a life for herself away from her penniless family. Maryn's letters were full of positive words describing a bright future, but when Asiah read them she detected an undertone of anxiety in her sister's words.

Monty worked the bar at a speakeasy on the west side of town, and lived in a boarding house nearby. Patrick disapproved of what Monty did for a living, especially when his only son claimed he didn't make enough to help support his family. Asiah had seen her brother's fancy suits and shiny shoes, and knew he could afford whatever he wanted, which was only to help himself. She suspected that her father was more upset by the fact that Monty's speakeasy was run by some of the most dangerous men in Chicago.

Asiah stayed in her room until suppertime, trying and failing several times to get the mystery man out of her mind. When supper was over and she once again found herself with nothing to distract her wandering thoughts, Asiah lay on her bed and practiced a calming technique she'd taught herself. She imagined a lush, green forest with tall trees covered in moss, dense undergrowth of ferns and ivy, a deep, earthy scent, and distant bird whistles and chirps. The Forest was the place she visited in her daydreams, a place where she felt very connected not only to nature, but to her inner self. She'd always felt that the Forest was a real place, even if she could only see it in her mind.

After several minutes passed she was still unable to free herself of his image, and she reached for her sketch of the man. With one final inspection of his face, she took the sketch to the kitchen, crumpled it up and tossed it in the stove.

༄

The standing stones loomed before Chase just like they always did at the beginning of his dreams. He rarely had a different dream than this one, and it was always here, in this place. It was nighttime, as always, and a bright moon threw silver light into the circle of stones, casting long shadows over the surrounding labyrinth. Without wasting a moment, Chase exited the circle and headed into the maze.

The great network of endless pathways was quiet tonight; there was no wind whistling through the cracks in the stones. The stillness was unnerving, and Chase began to wonder if something would actually be different in this dream that he'd had a thousand times before. His feet knew the way through the labyrinth and he made no wrong turns as he quickly navigated through to the other side, into his subconscious realm.

The moor was bathed in moonlight when he emerged, tiny silver lights glinting off the dew in the grass. He trained his eyes on the rocky cliffs in the distance and spied his quarry: a faint, blue light glowing atop the highest cliff. It was a long trek to the cliffs from the moor, and after what seemed like hours he reached the long, winding stone staircase that reached from the valley bottom to the rocky cliffs above. He leaned his head back as far as he could to make sure the blue light was still there. Most nights it was, but occasionally he walked all the way across the moor to find it had gone out. Chase didn't know what the blue light was or why he continued having this dream, but he knew that it had something to do with his lifelong quest. He believed the blue light represented the Shade and if he could catch up with it in his dream, it meant he was getting closer to finding the woman herself. At least that's what he told himself.

Loose gravel on the steps made the going slow, and Chase forced himself to ascend slowly; if he fell, he would wake up and lose his chance to reach the top. When he was ten steps from the top of the staircase, he paused. Something *was* different this time, he could feel it. Mounting the last steps silently, Chase was greeted by a blue glow emanating from behind a rock, and he took a hesitant step toward it. He'd never been this close before. Three more steps and he'd see exactly what had been taunting him all these years. With a fortifying breath, he rounded the rock and saw her.

She was about thirty yards away with her back to him, sitting on a rock next to a stream, and she was naked. Chase couldn't see her face, but her skin glowed with the ethereal blue light that he could see from the moor below. Her hair was long and dark, reaching all the way down her back and barely obscuring her wings, which were folded against her back. Even without seeing her face, he could tell she was breathtakingly beautiful.

Chase's breath caught in his throat. It was *her*. The Shade he'd been searching for. He didn't know how he knew it, but it was definitely her. Why else would he be having this dream? He took a tentative step forward and his boot crunched on the stony ground. She turned halfway so he could see her profile, but only for an instant before she spread her great wings and vanished in a flash of light. An unseen force propelled Chase backward and his feet scrambled for purchase on the rocky ground. The next thing he knew he was thrown over the cliff's edge, spiraling through the air as the moor rushed up to meet him.

Chase shot straight up in bed, gasping for air. He'd seen her face. The same face he'd seen earlier in the street in front of his shop.

༄

"Excuse me, miss?"

Asiah jumped. She must have been drifting off; it was a slow day at the drugstore. She turned her attention to the man at the counter with a sheepish look.

"I'm sorry, sir, what can I do for you?" she asked with a forced smile.

"First of all, you can grace me with another of those beautiful smiles," a clean-cut gentleman with sandy hair and gentle blue eyes said smoothly.

Asiah felt her face grow hot. Compliments always seemed to catch her off-guard. She smiled again, then covered her mouth self-consciously, feeling like a complete idiot.

"Aw, c'mon now, don't cover it up!" the stranger said, eyes twinkling. "I don't s'pose Mr. Kelsey is available?" He had a southern drawl, perhaps from Louisiana, Asiah guessed.

She glanced down to the other end of the counter where Mr. Kelsey was engaged with an elderly woman in a scarf, speaking loudly so the woman could hear him. "He might be a little while," Asiah said apologetically. "Is there something I can do for you?"

The gentleman leaned his elbows on the counter. "Well, darlin', I'm a physician, you see, and this flu goin' around is just a doozy. I can't seem to find anythin' that helps my patients feel better. I heard about Mr. Kelsey here and his remedy that seems to be doin' a heckuva lotta good. I'm wondrin' if I might could get my hands on some."

Asiah brightened. "We have it available in single-ounce vials for purchase. One vial seems to last about a week, which is enough for most people. How much do you need?"

"How much you got?" he replied.

She glanced down at her receipt book for the day. "I'll have to check our stock. Can you wait here a moment?"

"Take as long as you need, darlin'."

As she walked to the stockroom, she could feel the man's eyes following her. She shook off the disconcerting sensation as she began counting the vials in the cabinet. Reminding herself not to act like a simpering fool in front of the handsome customer, she returned to the front to find him patiently examining Mr. Kelsey's selection of soda flavors.

"We have about thirty vials in stock, and we will need to keep a few on hand for emergencies until I'm able to mix up some more," she explained.

"You make this stuff yourself?" he asked, turning his blue gaze back to her face. "Impressive."

Asiah shrugged. "I compound it, yes, but the recipe is Mr. Kelsey's."

"What's in it?"

She listed the ingredients off on her fingers. "Mint, agave nectar, ginger, lemon, olive oil, chilies, and a splash of bourbon."

"What d'ya know? A girl pharmacist!"

She blushed again. "I wanted to be a doctor, but medical schools don't usually take girls, even with an impeccable school record."

"Well I'll be. So you're smart, to-boot. Say, if you ever fancy learnin' a thing or two, you're welcome to come observe at my office sometime," he offered.

Asiah raised her eyebrows in surprise. "Thank you, but I'm pretty busy around here. I don't know when I'd have a chance to get away." Even as she said the words, she realized she was passing up an amazing opportunity.

"Do you dance?" he asked, completely changing the subject.

"Dance?" she asked, blinking in confusion.

"Yes, dance. The Lindy Hop? The Balboa?" he clarified.

"Oh, yes ... I mean ... I'm not much of a dancer," she said. It was an understatement; her long legs and clumsiness were a fatal combination on the dance floor.

"Why don't you let me be the judge of that? Say, eight o'clock?" He raised his eyebrows.

"Ummm ... alright ..." He'd caught her so off-guard she couldn't think of a reason to refuse.

"Fine, just fine. Why don't you box up twenty of them vials for me and I'll pick them up tonight when I pick you up?" he said with a wink.

Asiah could only nod. Had she really just accepted an invitation from a gentleman to go *dancing*, of all things?

He donned his fedora as he turned toward the door. "Until tonight, darlin'," he said, touching the brim of his hat before he walked out.

Asiah stared after him, speechless. Never before had she had trouble refusing a man's advances. But never before had a doctor offered to let her observe in his office, either.

What a strange couple of days she'd had. Yesterday was the incident with the man in the street, which was completely unnerving, and today she'd acted completely out of character and accepted a man's invitation. She had to admit she was intrigued by the doctor. It *would* be valuable experience if she could manage to spare some time to observe him at work.

She was still having trouble today getting the man from yesterday out of her head, and Asiah decided that dancing – however clumsily – with the doctor would be a welcome distraction. He hadn't even told her his name, but she found she was already looking forward to the evening's activities.

Chapter Three

Asiah returned from dancing with Walter just before midnight to find Meri trudging up the stairs to their apartment at the same time. Knowing that her lovelorn twin would only be discouraged to hear the details of her evening, Asiah didn't tell Meri where she'd been. Unfortunately, Meri was astute enough to figure it out.

"That's Mam's dress!" she cried, pointing at the frilly gingham number Asiah's mother had lent her to wear. "The one she saves for special occasions!"

Asiah tried to act nonchalant as she mounted the stairs. "So it is."

"And it's very late for you to be out wearing it. Where were you?"

She looked away. "Just out."

"With a gentleman?"

Asiah sighed. "We only went dancing."

Meri burst out laughing. "You are a terrible dancer! Are you going to tell me his name?"

"Walter."

"And what does he do? Is he rich?"

She lifted a shoulder. "I don't know. We didn't discuss his finances. I met him today at the drugstore. He's a doctor."

"Do you think he'll ask you to marry him?"

"Meri!" Asiah admonished. "I've known him less than a day!"

"Mam and Father will be very pleased."

Asiah rolled her eyes. "They're over the moon."

"Well, it's about time you went out with a man. The sooner you get married, the sooner I can."

"I'm not holding you back," Asiah pointed out.

"Maybe you don't see it that way," Meri sighed. "One of the lawyers at my firm did wink at me today," she said hopefully.

"See?" Asiah said, retrieving her key to unlock their door. "You'll be married in no time."

Patrick and Aileen had waited up for Asiah and pounced on her the moment she walked through the door.

"Tell us everythin'!" Aileen prodded in her thick brogue.

"Is he well-to-do? Will he provide for ye?" Patrick asked. "Tell us, girl!"

Meri scampered off to their room, leaving Asiah alone to deal with her parents.

"I had a very pleasant evening," she said with finality. "But I'm very tired—"

"Asiah," her father said in a demanding tone. "Does the lad have money?"

Suppressing a groan, she said, "I'm sure he does, Father, but I've only just met him. There's no need to plan the wedding yet."

"Oh! Did you hear that?" Aileen squealed. "A wedding."

"No—" Asiah tried to correct her, but Aileen and Patrick were already discussing what they would do when their daughter was married off to a rich gentleman doctor. "Well, goodnight then," she muttered, lifting the hem of the ridiculous pink dress and taking a step toward her bedroom.

"Wait, child," Aileen called.

Asiah stifled a groan of frustration and plastered a smile on her face. "Yes, Mam?"

"On your way to work in the mornin', I was wonderin' if you might drop off my kitchen knives at that shop on North. They're plenty dull and we've not a whetstone."

"What shop?" Asiah asked, confused.

"It's 'bout a block down from the drugstore, love," Patrick clarified. "Owned by a Limey fella, I think. He sells knives so I assume he can sharpen 'em too."

Asiah's heart lurched. An image of the man who helped her on the street two days ago appeared in her mind. It couldn't be the same man who owned the knife shop, could it? But then there weren't many British immigrants who owned shops near the drugstore, either. It had to be the same man. The thought of seeing him again when she hadn't yet found a way to forget about him sent an unexpected shiver down her spine.

"Al –alright …" she stammered weakly. "I'm going to bed." She hurried from the room before her parents could harass her any further.

※

Chase awoke to the sound of a timid knocking on the shop door, echoing clearly through the dusty shop. He had fallen asleep while reading at the table, something not at all uncommon these days. His candle had burned all the way down to the scarred tabletop, leaving a puddle of wax behind. Wan sunlight streamed through the dingy windows near the door, and Chase shook his head to clear it. He pulled out an old pocket watch and squinted at the time. It was just after seven in the morning. The knocking came again, more insistently this time. Chase shoved back from the table, still rubbing sleep from his eyes, and stormed to the door fully intending to teach the caller a lesson about waking a man at such an obscenely early hour.

"How dare—" He threw open the door with a thunderous gaze, and stopped short. The girl he helped two days earlier with her books stood wide-eyed on the stoop looking as if she might flee. She was dressed plainly in a simple plaid frock under a navy pea coat, and her shoes were worn and scuffed as if she only owned the one pair. She carried a small roll of cloth under one arm.

Her countenance wavered under his piercing gaze. "I-I'm sorry, I didn't mean to ... I'll come back later. I'm sorry!" she said quickly and turned to hurry away down the street.

It's her! Chase thought as he lunged after her. "Wait!" He reached for her hand before he realized what he was doing.

The jolt was stronger this time, like being struck by lightning. And Chase actually knew what that was like, having been in the wrong place at the wrong time a couple centuries back. The girl wrenched her hand from his grasp and whirled to face him, terror etched on her beautiful face.

"Please don't ... don't touch me," she ground out, obviously trying to keep her voice from shaking. "It makes me feel, um, strange," she finished lamely.

Chase raised his hands in front of him in surrender. "I'm sorry. I forgot about that, I just didn't want you to run away again. If it makes you feel any better, I feel the same strange feeling."

Her eyes were still wide in fear and Chase took a moment to examine them more closely. They were brown, not too dark, with gold flecks that complemented her long, dark brown hair, which was pulled back severely into a French braid. She narrowed her eyes when she noticed him scrutinizing her.

"Then it would seem we shouldn't touch each other," she said, all traces of fear gone from her voice. "I didn't mean to come here so early. It was a mistake. I have to go." She turned away once more.

"Why did you come?" he asked, not daring to hope it was for the same reason he'd longed for her return.

"I've got my mother's kitchen knives that need sharpening and, well, this is going to sound silly ..." she began, her gaze darting right and left anxiously.

He raised his eyebrows in encouragement.

"I can't stop thinking about you," she said quickly, and immediately scrunched her face into a grimace as if she'd mean to say something else entirely. "That is, I'm bothered that it feels so strange to touch you. And I like to know *why* things happen. Especially unusual things," she added. "And I can't think of a single explanation."

Chase smiled. She was intelligent, and interested in the way the world worked. He had yet to see concrete proof that this was the right girl, but every sign pointed to it, including his illuminating dream from the other night. "Would you like me to explain it to you?" he asked, keeping his tone causal when nothing but alarm bells sounded in his head.

She glanced down as if just remembering why she'd come. "No, no. I mean, thank you, but I really must be getting to work. I would appreciate it if you could sharpen these for me." She stepped forward awkwardly and shoved the roll of cloth into his hands before backing away again. "And I'm sorry for waking you." Her eyes darted to his hair and he raked his fingers through it self-consciously.

She hurried away and Chase closed his eyes, pictured her face and blurted out the first name that came into his mind: "Asiah! Please wait!" he called, wishing his voice didn't sound so desperate.

The girl spun around, obviously irritated. "How do you know my name? Have you been following me? Did Mr. Kelsey tell you my name? Well?" Her golden brown eyes burned into him and he detected a hint of brogue in her voice.

Chase cursed his quick tongue. He couldn't very well tell her that he'd just read her mind to learn her name. His only thought was to keep her from leaving. In a burst of inspiration, he blurted out, "Would you like some breakfast? I'll cook. I promise not to touch you again, I just want to talk. Afterward, if you wish, we can part ways and you'll never see me again. Agreed?"

The girl named Asiah looked deep in thought for what seemed like ages even to an old conjurer like Chase. Finally, she seemed to come to a decision. "Very well. Just breakfast, then I have to go to work." She paused a moment longer.

"And you *will* explain to me the reason for this ..." — she waved her hand in the air — "feeling."

"Indeed I will," he promised. When she didn't move to go inside he asked, "What is it? I promise not to poison you." He smiled shakily at his ill attempt at humor.

"You haven't told me your name, even though you seem to know mine."

Idiot! He cursed himself. "My apologies. I'm Chase. Chase Brandon." He held out his hand and she jumped back with a glare. Realizing his mistake, he jerked his hand back with a nervous chuckle. "Right. Well, we can skip the handshake then, I suppose."

"Asiah O'Connor," she said. "But you already knew that. I hope you cook better than you introduce yourself." She pulled her wool coat a little tighter around herself and nodded at the door behind him. "Shall we?"

"Of course, please come in." Chase turned and awkwardly held the door open so she could enter. He was completely bewildered by this woman. One moment she was ready to run for the hills, the next she was staring him down like a tiger eyeing its prey. It made him feel flustered and off-kilter. If she was the one he'd been looking for, he'd have to pull himself together or she'd eat him alive.

Chase guided Asiah to the small kitchen located at the back of his shop, shoving crates and piles of miscellaneous rubbish out of the way. As she gingerly sat down at the small table, he busied himself with making tea. "Asiah is a beautiful name, what does it mean?" he asked over his shoulder.

"When my twin sister and I were born, my father said he wanted to give us the world, so he named us after Asia and America, representing the two ends of the Earth."

She has a twin! he thought jubilantly. Another piece of the puzzle had fallen into place. "Your sister's name is America?"

"Merica. We call her Meri." She paused. "You never said how you knew my name."

"No, I didn't." Chase wasn't quite ready to answer that question truthfully yet, so he changed the subject, remembering the books he'd helped her with. "Are you studying to be a chemist?"

She was having none of it, and eyed him suspiciously. "Aren't you going to tell me?"

"What? If you're studying chemistry?"

"Tell me how you know my name! *I've* never told you and we've only met once before. Unless you've been following me." She glared at him in challenge.

Chase sighed, there was no point in dragging it out. If she was the right girl, nothing he could say would scare her. Without looking at her he said simply, "I haven't been stalking you. I read your mind."

She scoffed, "Are you a fortune teller or something?"

Cleary she didn't believe in *that* sort of nonsense. He slanted a glance at her. "Not exactly."

"Then how did you read my mind?" she asked.

"It's difficult to explain," he evaded.

"Try," she said evenly.

He sat down across from her at the table. "People's minds are like safe havens for their thoughts," he began. "Each mind is a sacred space that is as unique as the person who created it. Some people, like myself, possess the ability to see into other people's sacred spaces and learn things about that person, although generally it's not polite to do so without permission." He paused, assessing the incredulous look on her face. He looked her right in the eye knowing the next thing he planned to say would be much more convincing. "Your mind is a dense forest, with tall trees that almost completely block the sun's light. Ferns, ivy, thousands of birds calling each other from far away. It's very beautiful. It suits you." He broke her gaze to trace the wood grain on the table absently. "The breeze in the trees seemed to whisper your name."

Asiah's expression was unreadable and Chase had no idea if she believed him or not. She looked down at her hands, as if searching for something to say. Finally, she whispered, "Who are you?"

Chase closed his eyes and ran his hands through his hair in relief. They'd come this far and it was time to find out how open-minded she could be. She might think he was crazy and run out of the shop, but that might just mean she wasn't the person he thought she was. She also might stay, wanting to know more, as she had done so far. What if all his searching for hundreds of years ended today? He had to find out.

Taking a deep breath, he met her gaze and held it. "I am what you would call ... a sorcerer."

Chapter Four

Asiah blinked at him. A *sorcerer?* Was he mad? She started to doubt her reasons for agreeing to breakfast with him. He was just another crazy person who should be locked away in one of those awful asylums. She considered leaving right then, but remembered what he'd said about her mind. The Forest. No one could have known about that; she'd certainly never spoken of it to anyone. What if he *had* seen into her mind? He was looking at her with his intense emerald eyes and she realized she'd been quiet for a long moment.

"As in ... magic?" she asked in disbelief. "There's no such thing." Asiah believed in scientific study, physics and chemistry. She had a hard time believing that someone could just see into another's mind and read their thoughts, even if it had just happened. There was always a scientific explanation for the seemingly inexplicable.

"I know it sounds unbelievable, but I promise it's all true." Chase looked around, as if trying to find a way to explain. His face suddenly brightened. "Would you care for some tea?"

She furrowed her brow. "Is it magic tea? Will it convince me of your sanity?"

Chase paused as a pained look crossed his face. Asiah immediately felt ashamed for the insult. Perhaps some tea would help calm her nerves. "I'm sorry, I would love some tea."

He seemed to accept that and fetched two chipped teacups from a small cupboard. After scooping some tea leaves from a jar into each cup, he poured cold water over the leaves.

Asiah looked from the cups to his face, confused. "Don't you think you should boil the water first?"

"Aha!" he said excitedly, as if she'd asked exactly the right question. He smiled that brilliant smile that somehow seemed to make her feel much better. "That is an excellent point." He passed his hand over the two cups and immediately the water steamed and darkened as the tea began to steep.

Asiah thought her eyes might pop out of her head. Had she really just seen him heat water by waving his hand over it? It had to be a trick. The water must have already been warm, or ... she couldn't think of any other way he'd done it. She'd seen illusionists do tricks like that at the carnival, but there was always an explanation. This was ... unbelievable. His rumbling chuckle pulled her from her state of shock.

As he strained the leaves from the tea, Chase glanced at her face, waiting for her reaction.

She finally found her voice. "H-how did you—" She gestured at the cups while searching for something coherent to say, "—do *that?*"

Chase smirked, "How do you think I did it? You said you don't believe in magic."

"I didn't say that. I said there's no such thing."

"What if I told you there was? That it's not as far-fetched as you think?"

Asiah gingerly picked up her teacup and inspected the dark liquid inside. "Everything in the universe must have a scientific explanation," she began. "Even this. It's some kind of chemical reaction. It may look supernatural, but in the end, everything can be explained by science."

Chase beamed at her. "You are correct. Everything we know is subject to the same physical laws, but what you don't yet know is how your mind is capable of so much more than what you currently use it for. The laws of physics don't have to be thrown out the window just because some people use more of their brain power than others. The things I do I can do because I'm able to manipulate the energy and electromagnetic forces around me."

This was too much information. Asiah struggled to organize all the questions that had suddenly rushed forward in her mind. She didn't know what to ask first, so she asked the first question that fell out of her mouth. "Are there others like you?"

"There have been in the past, but that number has dwindled down to one, perhaps two." He was looking at her a little too intently.

"Just you?" She felt uncomfortable with the direction the conversation had taken.

A faraway look crossed his face. "When I was taught how to use my abilities there were many. Most could not keep their gifts to themselves and were executed for witchcraft. Others struggled with immortality and either took their own lives or chose to age and die as other humans do. Eventually, I was the only one left."

"Are you ... immortal?" She felt incredibly foolish asking this.

"At the moment, yes, although I grow weary of this world. I've seen much more sorrow and death than any man should see in his lifetime." His eyes seemed to dim at his words.

Asiah wasn't sure how to ask the next question or if she even should, but she couldn't hold it in. "How long have you, that is, when were you ..." She trailed off, too afraid to hear the answer.

"How old am I? Is that what you'd like to know?" A little energy had returned to his gaze.

She couldn't look him the eye. "I'm sorry. You don't have to tell me. It's a disrespectful question."

He seemed amused at her embarrassment. "I am 750 years old. Last May."

She jerked her head up, sure he was putting her on. He looked no older than Monty. "No person can live that long! What about the physical laws we didn't throw out the window?"

"Still in place, love. I told you I can control certain forces around myself, including those in my own body. It's a matter of slowing or even stopping the processes of aging. It's actually pretty easy compared to other tasks."

"So, no magic, just physics?" She might actually be able to believe that, although she still didn't have proof that he wasn't playing a trick on her.

"Just physics, forces of nature. Which brings me to the question that brought you here today: what did we feel when our hands touched?"

She'd completely forgotten about that. "If everything you've told me is true then it must have been some sort of energy transfer or something, like an electric shock. It could happen between any two people."

"Not any two, just the right two. I said that I can control energy, but when we touch the energy between us is out of my control. And there's only one reason I'm not able to control the energy around me." His gaze locked to hers.

Asiah's mouth went dry. "What reason is that?" she squeaked out.

He looked at her a moment longer before he said, "I'm unable to control energies around me when I make physical contact with someone who is trying to control the same energy at the same time. Sometimes this happens without a person even realizing that they are doing it."

Asiah felt dizzy. She absently rubbed her temples trying to clear her head. "What exactly does that mean, 'control the same energy'?" It sounded like someone else's voice.

Chase looked unsure of what to say next. "You see, Miss O'Connor, when two people—"

"Stop," she said, suddenly feeling very woozy. "I can't think about this right now. I have to go to work." She stood and immediately regretted it. Everything swam in front of her and a sparkly cloud obscured her vision. Then it all went black.

∽

Chase hadn't expected her to faint. She certainly didn't strike him as a girl with a delicate constitution, prone to swooning, but apparently he'd overloaded her with information. In a flash he was behind her, catching her under her arms as she sagged against him. Thankfully, she still wore her pea coat and the thick wool layer prevented him from feeling the jolt he felt when their hands touched. He lifted her easily into his arms and cast about for a place to take her. He kept a sleeping mat in the loft above the shop, and it would be as good a place as any. He climbed the steps to his small, cluttered living area. A sleeping mat and bureau took up most of the space in the loft and various items of clothing were strewn about haphazardly. He preferred his cabin in the woods southeast of the city and rarely slept in the loft unless he was too tired to go home. He could transport himself home instantly through a process he called "channeling" where he condensed his entire being into a small ball of light that could travel anywhere in the world in a matter of seconds. It was his preferred method of travel but it also consumed a great deal of energy. Something he didn't always have these days.

He knelt and gently laid Asiah on the mat, tossing pillows and clothing out of the way as he did. He cradled her head in his hands and felt the tingly sensation of her inner power tickling his palms. The feeling wasn't as intense as before, perhaps due to her unconsciousness or because he was prepared for it this time. Apparently it wasn't enough to wake her. He found it somewhat difficult to extract his fingers from her soft hair, realizing that he was starting to enjoy the sensation of touching her. The thought startled him and he quickly removed his hands, but not before he brushed a strand of loose hair from her forehead.

Suddenly, he remembered what he'd read about the map. Everything pointed to Asiah being the right girl, so presumably she would have this mysterious map with her. Chase leaned forward and gently eased her out of her pea coat, making sure not to wake her. After a thorough search of her pockets, though, he found nothing but a small orange, a brass key and a few hairpins. He frowned, seeing no pockets in her plaid frock. Perhaps she kept it tucked away somewhere more private, but he wasn't about to start searching her undergarments when he could just as easily ask her about the map when she woke.

Chase leaned back and crossed his arms over his chest. What was he going to do with her until then? She mentioned something about going to work, and he assumed from the chemistry notes he'd helped her with that she worked for the druggist down the block. He should go tell the man that she wouldn't be in today, but he also didn't want to leave her side in case she woke up and assumed that Chase had kidnapped her.

He stood up and groaned, raking his fingers through his hair. He stopped suddenly and strode quickly to the mirror on the bureau. He stared open-mouthed at his reflection. His hair hung wildly about his shoulders, he hadn't had a shave in days, and he was still wearing his clothes from yesterday, which were covered in dust from an excursion to the attic. No wonder the girl thought he was crazy. He *looked* like he should be in an asylum. He rubbed his hand across his stubbled jaw and decided that he could do with a bath. Perhaps if he had time afterward, he would pop down to the drugstore and tell Asiah's employer that she wasn't feeling well.

Satisfied with his plan, he knelt next to Asiah once more and held a finger just above her forehead. Bracing himself for the sensation, he gently drew his finger down her forehead to the space between her eyebrows, mumbling a few ancient syllables as he did. Her breathing slowed, and he knew she'd sleep comfortably for at least an hour, giving him a chance to clean up. Hopefully, by the time she did wake he'd know what to do next, because right now, he had no bloody idea.

※

The Forest was a little brighter than usual. More sunlight was filtering through the trees and everything seemed to have an ethereal glow around it. Asiah gazed about in confusion, wondering why she was here. She only visited this place when she needed to collect her thoughts, or was feeling too much pressure from the world around her. She tried to remember what had prompted her to take solace here, but couldn't come up with anything.

The Forest was strangely quiet, too. The birds were in the trees around her; she could see them sitting on the branches, silently watching her. Maybe it was a dream. Asiah could never remember her dreams. She knew that she had them and that they were vivid and rich, but in the morning she couldn't recall what they were about. If by some bizarre sequence of events this *was* a dream, it was far from normal.

Asiah scanned the clearing around her, looking for anything out-of-place. The birds followed her with their small black eyes, not making a sound. She wandered toward the tree line, walking in no direction in particular. She thought she could hear the sound of running water and headed toward the sound. The trees opened a few yards later into another clearing at the base of a high cliff. A waterfall cascaded down the cliff face, falling hundreds of feet into a deep, clear blue pool. She stepped out onto a rocky outcropping over the water and looked down at her reflection. She'd certainly never been to this place before, and hadn't known it even existed.

As she gazed into the pool's depths, a shadow moved behind her reflection and she jumped back from the edge, whirling around in alarm. As before, nothing moved in the

Forest. She edged closer to the water again and peered in, bracing herself. Behind her reflection stood a man. He was tall with dark hair and green eyes that seemed to penetrate her soul. His gaze was trained on her reflected image and she turned around again, fully expecting to find him there next to her. He was terribly familiar, but again she couldn't seem to remember much about her life outside this realm of consciousness. She looked back at the reflection and watched as he raised his hand to touch her cheek.

The jolt of his touch caused Asiah to sit up with a gasp. Chase jerked his hand back from her face, where he had just brushed her cheek with his fingertips.

"Wh-what are you doing? Where am I?" Asiah looked around at the unfamiliar surroundings, frantically trying to remember where she was.

"You're safe, I'm here." Chase's brow was furrowed with concern. He was crouched next to the mat on which she was seated, surrounded by pillows and wrinkled blankets. The smell of bergamot oil greeted her and she realized that he'd cleaned himself up. He had washed his hair and pulled it back with a black ribbon, and he'd shaved the scruffy stubble from his face. He'd changed into a loose-fitting linen shirt and clean trousers that looked like they been recently pressed. How long had she been out?

"Where's 'here' and what time is it?" she asked, edging away slightly. His spicy scent was slightly overwhelming.

Chase pulled out an antique pocket watch. "You're in the loft above my shop and it's nearly ten."

"Ten! Mr. Kelsey will be furious with me!" She scrambled to her feet and scanned the loft for her coat, which Chase must have removed after she fainted. She found it draped over a chair, and grabbed it as she made a dash for the narrow staircase.

Asiah heard Chase mutter a curse as she launched herself down the steps. On the bottom step her heel caught on a broken board and she cried out as the floor rushed up to meet her.

Firm hands grasped her waist and pulled her back from the brink of disaster. Chase hauled her back against his chest, still holding her waist. *How did he get down here so fast?* But Asiah didn't have time to consider it because at that moment he bent his head so his lips were an inch from her ear.

"You need to stop running away, love," he murmured, "or I won't be there to catch you when you fall."

A shiver went down her spine at his ominous words. She wasn't sure if it was because she could vaguely feel the tingly sensation of his hands on her waist or if it was the unnerving feeling of his warm breath on her neck. Either way, it was more than she could handle. She carefully stepped out of his grasp and turned to face him.

"Why didn't you wake me sooner?" she demanded.

He blinked at her. "I thought you needed time to process—"

"Because I'm some kind of delicate flower who faints at the slightest provocation?"

"Well, no, but—"

"There's something wrong with me," she continued belligerently. "I faint all the time and I don't know why. I think it's my heart because it doesn't beat the same as everyone else's. But I am *not* weak."

"I never meant to imply otherwise," he said softly. "I'm sorry I didn't wake you."

Asiah crossed her arms and looked away. "I don't know what you want with me, but I'm no one special. I have no special powers, and I can't read minds. I'm just a poor girl trying to support my family in this awful Depression, and now I've probably lost the only job I'll ever have because *you* are trying to convince me that magic exists and that *I'm* some kind of ... that I'm ... like you!" she finished angrily. "I'm leaving now, please don't try and stop me." With that, she turned on her heel, snatched her knives off the counter and stormed out, slamming the door behind her.

Chase wanted to scream in frustration. She was the one, he was almost sure. Her face was the one he'd seen in his dream. If only he'd had a chance to show her the scroll and ask her about the map. Then he'd know. He stood fuming and staring at the spot where she had just stood and berated him. Twice he took a step toward the door, but knew he couldn't go after her, not now. She'd been through enough today. As much as he wanted to run after her and drag her back here, he knew that if she truly was the one, she would eventually come back on her own. If only he had enough patience to wait that long.

Chapter Five

July, 1933
Chicago

"Marry me, darlin', and you'll make me the happiest man in the world." Walter was down on one knee next to their table at Jackson's Chophouse holding a gold ring with a beautiful diamond.

Asiah didn't know what to say. This was the last thing in the world she'd expected. Walter was a good man, but Asiah saw him as more of a mentor than a love interest. They'd been dancing a few times, but Walter had quickly learned that Asiah really could *not* dance. He took her to dinner sometimes after she helped him at his office downtown one afternoon a week for no pay, but she never thought he would propose. She *was* learning a lot about medicine. She still hoped that someday she might be able to attend medical school.

Clearly, Walter had taken a shine to Asiah since their very first meeting in the drugstore, and he was everything a woman could ask for in a husband. His practice was successful and she knew he would always be able to support her, but she couldn't ask him to support her family as well. Patrick still didn't have a job and her family's financial situation was increasingly dismal. Asiah couldn't be sure, but she had a feeling that her family didn't want her to marry someone unless she would still be allowed to work to support them, or her new husband would support them instead. Walter had made it clear several times over the past two years that no wife of his would work for a living. He wanted children and felt it was his wife's job to raise them. He supported Asiah's desire to learn about medicine, but she knew he believed, like most men, that it was *men's* work.

Therein lay her dilemma: Marry Walter and ensure financial security for her family, while never achieving her life's dream, or turn him down and continue supporting her family herself until the day she died, an old maid working in a drugstore. At least if she married Walter he would have the money to send her to college. Maybe he would come around to the idea of letting her work in the medical field in some way. She needed more time to consider his proposal.

"Oh, Walter! I don't know what to say! This is so sudden," she evaded.

"Say yes," he prodded, still on one knee.

"I ... I need to think about it, if that's alright," she said hesitantly. "I'm so pleased you asked," she added when she saw the hurt look on his face.

He sighed. "A man don't wait around forever, darlin'."

She wanted to point out that he'd taken two years to ask for *her* hand, but decided it would be in poor taste. "I know. Please just let me have a day to think about it. I'll give you my answer tomorrow. I promise." She took his hands and pulled him back to his chair, planting a kiss on his cheek.

That seemed to mollify him a bit. He put the ring back in his pocket and drummed his fingers on the table. After a moment, he looked up at her. "You know that I love you, dontcha?"

He'd actually never said as much, but Asiah nodded, trying to hide her discomfort. "I do know." She also knew that she wasn't in love with him. He would make a fine husband, she was sure, but she wasn't even sure she wanted to marry. Not if every man she met believed that she was only good for bearing children. Perhaps she would grow to love Walter if she accepted his proposal. Was his love for her enough of a reason to say yes?

Walter walked her home after dinner and paused outside her apartment door, searching her eyes for an answer that wasn't there. He lifted his hands and tucked her hair behind her ears. "Say yes," he whispered. Tilting her chin up, he kissed her gently, letting his lips linger on hers for just a second longer than Asiah was comfortable with. "Say yes and I'll make all your dreams come true."

If only that were true, she thought sadly. "Until tomorrow, then," she said with as much cheer as she could muster.

Asiah waited until Walter had descended the stairs before entering her apartment. Her parents were fond of Walter, and the last thing she needed was for them to accept his proposal without her. Patrick and Aileen were sitting in their tattered chairs by the window, enjoying the evening summer breeze and listening to the sounds of children shouting in the street below. They used to sit outside their small cottage in Ireland every night after dinner, listening to the waves lap at the shore. Once in a while Patrick would sing a sea shanty, and all the children would listen. He never sang anymore.

"Why so glum, Cricket?" Aileen asked as Asiah trudged through the door.

"Walter asked for my hand," she replied dully, knowing there was no reason to keep the truth from her parents. They'd wheedle it out of her eventually.

"You should be celebratin' then!" her mother chirped.

"I haven't accepted yet. He won't let me work anymore after the wedding. And I won't ask him to support you and Father, either. We have more pride than that."

"Whyever not?" Patrick demanded. "If a man offers to marry you and help your struggling family, it would be rude to turn him down!"

"And it would be disingenuous for me to accept when I don't love him!" Asiah shot back.

"Watch your tongue, girlie," Patrick warned. "Love's got nothin' to do with it, and you know it."

"Didn't you and Mam love each other when you were wed?" she asked.

"O' course we did, be even if we hadna' we still woulda tied the knot. Our duty to our families, it was."

"And what about your duty to *this* family?" Asiah snapped before she could stop her quick tongue.

"Asiah Máire!" Aileen scolded. "Your father's done more for this family—"

"Has he?" she shouted, all her anger about Patrick's unemployment and drinking coming to the surface. "If you mean he's driven us to the welfare lines, then yes, he has done that. But as one of the only people still providing for this family, *I* will decide my own future."

"Ye'll be out on the street!" Patrick raged, his face turning red as he rose from the chair.

"And you'll lose what little income I bring in!" Asiah replied hotly.

When neither of her parents had a response to that, she stomped off toward her bedroom. "Don't ever accuse me of not doing my *duty*," she called over her shoulder, and slammed the door behind her.

⁂

The two years that had passed between Chase's last meeting with Asiah had felt like an eternity. Every day he grew more and more impatient and more and more sure that she was the one. Every time the bell above the door in his shop rang, his heart flipped over in anticipation, but it was never her. Once or twice he'd even gone down the street to the drugstore, if only just to see her face. He'd look through the window and talk himself into returning to his shop without speaking to her. She still worked there, and that was enough for now. He often wondered if perhaps he'd finally gone completely mad and was stalking the wrong girl, but it didn't matter. Something about her told him she'd come around sooner or later.

But today his patience had run out. She couldn't possibly still be angry with him for letting her sleep off her fainting spell. Obviously she hadn't lost her job because of it, so no harm was done. It was likely that she'd written Chase off as the crazy shopkeeper from down the street. If that was her perception, she'd need a life-changing event to occur before she'd come back on her own. Perhaps it was time for Chase to take matters into his own hands.

Just like the one on the door to his shop, a tiny bell tinkled when Chase entered the deserted drugstore. Along the right wall was the soda counter, behind which several brightly colored bottles stood in a row against a long mirror. At the very back of the store Chase could see rows and rows of shelves through a window where the druggist was busy counting tiny brown bottles.

Chase didn't see Asiah at first, seated at the end of the soda counter with her nose buried in a large book. Upon closer inspection Chase could see that it was a medical book, and Asiah was closely examining a diagram of a dissection of the human torso. She didn't seem to notice his approach as her eyes flitted over the graphic illustration.

He cleared his throat and Asiah nearly dropped the book in surprise. Her gaze rose to meet his and she stumbled backward off her stool and skirted quickly around the end of the counter.

"You!" she gasped, her eyes widening anxiously.

Chase smiled and touched his chest with his fingertips. "Chase."

"I remember," she snapped. "What are you doing here?"

Hesitant to tell her the truth, he gazed about until his eyes landed on the soda machine. "It's very hot today, isn't it? I think I'll have a soda."

Asiah eyed him suspiciously. "A soda?"

"Yes, please."

"What flavor?"

Chase lowered himself onto a stool and leaned his elbows on the counter. "What flavor do you like?"

She crossed her arms over her navy frock and lifted an eyebrow. "I don't see how that matters."

"I'm just curious," he said. "You can tell a lot about a person by their preferred soda flavor."

Both brows shot up. "Is that so?"

He grinned. "Would you believe it?"

"Not for a moment." She looked him over with a skeptical eye and he was glad he'd thought to shave that morning. "Why don't you just read my mind to find out what flavor I like?" Her voice held a slight mocking tone.

He shrugged and looked over her shoulder at the colorful array of bottles, pretending to mull it over. "Cherry?" he guessed.

"No," she said, a triumphant glint sparkling in her eyes.

"My first instinct was to guess raspberry."

Her eyes widened, just for an instant. "We don't have raspberry here," she said to cover her reaction.

Chase idly drew circles on the counter with his fingertip. "Is that why you go down to Tilly's Soda Shoppe once a week?"

Asiah's jaw fell open, but she quickly recovered. "You *have* been following me!"

He chuckled softly. "I promise I haven't been. I just wanted to get your attention."

She backed away from the counter, leaning against the shelf behind her. "You've got it."

Hope swelled in his chest. "I want to ask you something that may seem a little strange."

She rolled her eyes. "Shocking."

Ignoring her derision, he pressed on. "I'm looking for a certain map. You don't happen to carry a map around with you, do you?"

"What kind of map?"

"I'm not sure," he hedged. "But it's very important that I find it."

"Why?"

"I will tell you, but I must find it first."

"Well, I don't have a map. And *you* don't even know what kind it is or what it's for."

His heart sank. "You're sure? There's no way it could be hidden?"

She frowned. "I think I'd know if someone had hidden a map in my things."

Chase sighed, unsure what to do now. The ancient writings had been very clear that the Shade would have a map. Even so, he wasn't ready to give up on Asiah yet. He could still show her the scroll.

"I was wondering if you might stop by my shop sometime," he said, practically pleading her with his eyes.

Asiah groaned. "This isn't because you think I'm magical again, is it?"

He laughed nervously. "I just want to show you something."

"I'm sure you do. But I'm afraid I must decline."

"Please, Asiah. Give me another chance. I made a mistake before, and if you faint again, I promise to wake you immediately."

"It's not about that!" she snapped. "You want to talk about second chances? Mr. Kelsey gave me one that day, and I promised never to let him down again. I think the best way to do that is to stop listening to *you*." She started to walk away and Chase reached across the counter and grabbed her hand to stop her.

The mirror behind the counter exploded into a million shards, followed by the flavor bottles and soda glasses. Chase threw his arms up to shield his face as Asiah cried out and ducked behind the counter. The front windows of the shop blew outward onto the street, blanketing the sidewalk in glass. Chase could hear the glass medicine bottles in the back popping one by one as Kelsey let loose a stream of curses. It was over a moment later, but the entire shop looked as though a wild animal had been released inside. Sticky liquid dripped down the shelves and a sparkling layer of glass splinters covered everything in sight. A crowd had gathered in the street wondering just what had happened in the shop.

Asiah rose slowly, her gaze riveted on her shaking hands. She looked up at Chase in horror.

"That was me," she whispered. "I did this."

Her words were only partly true. She *did* possess some sort of power, but she didn't know how to control it. In her heightened emotional state, she released some kind of energy pulse when Chase had touched her. It was *his* fault for touching her when he wasn't aware of the consequences. Somehow, she'd known that the pulse had come from her own body. Unfortunately, none of this could be easily explained to the red-faced druggist or the crowd of onlookers outside.

"What in tarnation is going on out here?" Kelsey demanded, his loafers crunching on the broken glass beneath his feet.

Asiah looked lost for words, still staring at her trembling hands.

"It was a drive-by," Chase said quickly. "Men with machine-guns—"

"Now, son, there's no cause to making up stories. There aren't any bullet holes and they wouldn't have reached all the way into the stock room from the street," the druggist said irritably. "Now tell me why my shop is in ruins before I call the police!"

"It was my fault, Mr. Kelsey," Asiah said, her voice barely above a whisper. "I'm so sorry."

Kelsey looked Chase over suspiciously, then glanced back at Asiah. "And how exactly did *you* break everything in here?"

"I-I ... I don't know," she stammered.

"This is unacceptable, young lady," the druggist scolded. "I'll have to speak to your father about this."

Asiah seemed to realize suddenly that her job was in danger. "I'll clean it up straightaway, sir. Please don't say anything to my father," she begged.

Chase could hear the desperation in her voice and stepped in to take the blame. "Excuse me, sir, but the truth is—"

"My sincerest apologies, sir," Kelsey interrupted him. "But it appears we will be closed for the foreseeable future. May I direct you to Miss Tilly's down the street?"

"Thank you, but—"

"Off you go, then," the man said as he shooed Chase toward the door.

Chase had a mind to stand his ground and ensure that Asiah didn't unnecessarily lose her job, but just as he opened his mouth to protest, he heard Asiah's voice in his mind, pleading with him:

Just go. Please. Don't make it worse.

Understanding that she didn't want his help, Chase took a step toward the door, wishing he could do something to help the situation. Seizing his last opportunity to reach out to her, he spoke into her mind as she had just inadvertently done to him.

I can help you. Please give me a chance.

Asiah sucked in a breath as she heard the words in her head and Chase walked out, certain this time that he hadn't seen the last of Asiah O'Connor.

※

An hour later Asiah sat on the park bench across the street from the North Avenue Drugstore watching the interaction between her father and Mr. Kelsey in silence. Mr. Kelsey had his hands on his hips and was shaking his head. Patrick was clutching his hat to his chest, probably begging the man to give Asiah her job back. Mr. Kelsey held out his hands, palms up and shrugged, gesturing to the broken glass that still littered the area around the store. Still shaking his head, he turned away from Patrick and disappeared into the back room. Patrick stood looking after him for several moments before he hung his head, slowly put his hat on and tugged at his scarf. He turned slightly to look at her from the doorway of the drugstore and shook his head in defeat, then turned and walked briskly down the street toward home.

 Asiah clenched her hands into fists in her lap. That good-for-nothing Brandon had cost her her job! He didn't have to ambush her at the store today, spouting his nonsense about wanting to help her. Why couldn't he just stay away? She'd told him two years earlier that she'd wanted nothing to do with him. She was so angry she was shaking. But it wasn't entirely Chase's fault, otherwise she'd have let him take the blame for the shattering glass. No, something strange had happened when they'd touched. Asiah felt as if her insides had become electrified, like she herself was made of electricity. And suddenly that feeling had shot out of her, reverberating through the shop like a shockwave and breaking everything in sight. It had come from *her*.

 That was one reason she knew she'd have to face Mr. Brandon again. She'd almost believed him before when he'd described the Forest in her mind, but this time there was no logical explanation for what had just happened. If there was, *he* would be the one to give it.

 The second reason she knew she'd see him again was because she was now without a job. Her family depended on her. She knew she shouldn't confront the man when her emotions were so raw, but she had no choice. Her family wouldn't starve because of the crazy shopkeeper, she'd make sure of that.

 The musical tinkle of the bell above the shop's door made Chase jump, just as it had every time it had rung in the last two years. The sound was followed by the door slamming shut.

"We're closed!" Chase shouted from the loft. After the day he'd had, he was in no mood to help anyone shop for antique knives. The next thing he heard surprised him.

"Mr. Brandon, I need to speak with you." Asiah's voice was shaking, just barely, like she was struggling for control.

Chase went to the railing at the loft's edge and looked over, unable to believe that she would actually have come already. When he saw her face he couldn't stop himself from smiling at her. "Miss O'Connor! What a surprise! To what do I owe the pleasure of your return?"

Her eyes blazed. "Would you care to explain just what happened today?"

Chase made his way down to the shop floor, taking his time. "What do *you* think happened?"

"You touched me again, after I specifically told you not to. And I lost my job because of it!"

He felt a little ashamed that his presence in the drugstore had led to the loss of her job, but the fact that she was here was surely a good omen. He sauntered over to where she stood with her hands balled into fists at her sides and cocked an eyebrow at her. "Surely you didn't lose your job simply because I touched you." He was probably enjoying this a little too much.

"You caused something disastrous to happen! Something I couldn't explain."

"You could have blamed me for the mess, you know."

Clearly frustrated, she glowered at him. "I don't blame others for my problems."

"How very noble of you. But didn't you think this time should have been an exception?"

She crossed her arms and looked away. "Maybe."

"Then why wasn't it?" he asked, already guessing her answer.

"Because that glass broke because of me," she whispered. "There's something wrong with me." She raised her tortured gaze to his.

The hurt in her eyes nearly undid him. "No, Asiah. You mustn't believe that. There's *nothing* wrong with you," he said gently.

Some heat returned to her gaze. "I'm sure that's what you want me to believe. But it doesn't matter anyway. I lost my job because you couldn't leave me alone! You knew how important my job was to my family! What am I supposed to do now?" Her voice cracked on the last word.

"I can help you—"

"The only way you can help me is by giving me a job." She stared him down and dared him to deny her.

Chase suppressed a grin at her boldness. "I assure you, that's not all I can do."

"That's all I need. If I can't provide for my family, we'll be out on the street. You owe me this."

He chuckled and shook his head. "I'm not sure I do, but I suppose I could use an assistant." *Or an apprentice.* "I suppose you'll expect to be paid as much as the druggist paid you?"

Asiah's eyes flashed. "Actually, I'll expect 50 cents more per week than Mr. Kelsey paid me." He raised an eyebrow. "For having to put up with *you*," she finished.

He could tell she would be a handful, but he'd expected as much. A shy, soft-spoken ingénue would never make a good Shade. He wasn't worried about paying her, he had plenty of money. It was easy to become rich if one had several centuries to save. He remained silent for another moment, enjoying her discomfort. Finally, he put her out of her misery. "Fine. You'll start tomorrow. I'm sure eight o'clock isn't too early for you?"

Relief flooded her face, but her voice still held a challenge. "As long as it's not too early for *you*." She turned to go and stopped, turning back to face him. "Thank you," she said softly.

The grateful look in her eyes lasted only a long enough to make his mouth go dry. He could only nod before she turned and walked out of the shop.

Aileen was just finishing the dishwashing when Asiah trudged through the door.

"And just where have you been?" She asked in her thick brogue. "Your father said you lost your job today, so I know you weren't working to put food on this table!"

It had been such a long day Asiah didn't feel like arguing with her. Her parents had been short with her ever since her biting outburst the night before. She hung her coat on the rack next to the door of their small apartment. "Where is Father?" she asked, avoiding her mother's question.

"Your father, Lord bless him, is at your brother's pub, probably pissed to high heaven by now." Aileen's eyes held an accusatory glare.

Asiah groaned. She didn't want to confront her father when he was drunk. He was never a drunkard in Ireland; he still went to the pub every night with his fellow fishermen, but only ever had a pint or two before coming home. After the Crash, Asiah noticed he spent more and more evenings across town in the basement speakeasy of Moe's Dance Hall, drowning his sorrows. His visit there tonight likely also included him asking Monty for money.

As if on cue, Patrick staggered into the small kitchen and dropped into one of the spindly chairs at the table. He fixed Asiah with a harsh stare, which might have been more intimidating if he didn't look so tired. When he spoke his words were clear, not slurred. Asiah's heart sank. Things were really bad when her father skipped the drink altogether. "I think you have some explainin' to do, Cricket."

The endearment only made Asiah feel worse for putting him through this. Her family called her Cricket from the time she was a toddler because she never could keep still. At least she might be able to ease some of his suffering with her news.

"I'm sorry, Father. I made a mistake, but I do have some news that might make you feel better." She peeked up at him, gauging his reaction.

His face was stony. "Unless you've procured another job for yourself already, which I doubt, no news will be good enough to save us."

"Well, actually—" she began.

His head jerked up. "You don't mean it, girl!"

She couldn't tell if he was happy or just in shock. "I do, and it pays better than the drugstore."

Patrick shook his head. "You mean to tell me that I've been bustin' me arse for nigh on four years lookin' for a decent gig, and you've found another, *better* job in two hours? What's the job, love?"

Asiah blushed, remembering how Mr. Brandon had used the same endearment earlier. "I'll be working for the shopkeeper of the knife shop on North."

Patrick's expression hardened. "Aye? What exactly will you be doin' for this shopkeeper? Do you even know the first things about blades?"

"Well, no, but the shop's pretty dusty, so I'm sure I can help keep it clean and tidy," she hedged.

"Can I meet this mysterious shopkeeper, make sure he's runnin' a reputable business? How do I know this ain't some sort of scam?" Patrick was incredibly paranoid when it came to his daughters.

The last thing Asiah needed was for her overprotective father to meet the suave Chase Brandon, of whose sanity she still wasn't certain. He'd never let her take the job there, even if it meant keeping a roof over their heads. She skirted the truth for now; she could handle the man in the knife shop. "He will be in Peoria the rest of the week. That's why he took me on with such short notice. He needs someone to watch his shop."

"You said you'd be mostly cleanin'." Patrick narrowed his eyes.

She snorted, "It will take months to clean that place! Besides, there aren't that many people interested in antique knives."

"It's a wonder he can keep his shop open in this Depression with only a few customers. Aileen, love, did you hear about the McKenzies down on Walton Street? Marion's expectin' again! How they feed all those babes I'll never know..."

Asiah watched as her father visibly relaxed into conversation with her mother. She slipped away to her room and flopped down on her bed, letting out a frustrated groan as she realized she hadn't answered Walter's proposal today like she promised. It was late now and she had only ever seen him at his office and had no idea where he lived. If he was so anxious to hear her answer, why hadn't he come to her apartment tonight? Surely her mother and father would have mentioned it if he'd been to see her. For that matter, they would have accepted his proposal *for* her.

She rolled onto her side and hugged her pillow to her chest. It was hard to imagine that only yesterday she'd had a good job and a chance at a future in medicine. Today her entire world had fallen apart. At least she still had all the pieces, she just didn't know exactly how to put them back together yet.

Chapter Six

Asiah raced down North Avenue as she heard the bells of St. Matthew's chime the eight o'clock hour. She couldn't believe she'd managed to be late on her first day. She was the most punctual person she knew, always arriving early for work or appointments. But when she had emerged from her room that morning for breakfast, Walter was waiting for her at the kitchen table.

"Good mornin', darlin'," he'd said with a hopeful smile.

"Walter! I'm glad you're here. I have made my decision," she said, trying to sound confident. She was ready to tell him that she couldn't marry without love.

"Before you tell me, I have something I want to say." He shifted in his chair, looking uncomfortable. "If you won't give up this harebrained idea of becoming a lady-doctor, well, I'll help you. You won't stand a chance of getting into medical school without my help."

Her mouth fell open. "You would do that for me?"

"Yes. And I'll help support your family while you're in school."

She hesitated. She still wanted a love connection. He loved her, and she thought maybe in time she would learn to love him as well. He was helping her achieve her life's dream, after all. "Then my answer is ... yes!" She couldn't believe the words, even as she said them.

He jumped up and put his arms around her. "You've made me so happy, darlin'! Now, I left your ring at home, but

I'll fetch it for you later. Let's go downtown. I'll buy you breakfast to celebrate!"

"I need to go to work," Asiah explained. "Until we're married, I still need to provide for my family."

Walter pouted. "I can't talk you out of it?"

"No, but thank you for the offer."

Walter's presence had made her lose track of time and Asiah hurried back to her room to dress. The dress she'd laid out to wear was missing from the chair on which she'd hung it. Looking around frantically, she found it wadded up beneath Guinness, the lovable stray they'd taken in a year ago. Normally the scruffy mutt slept in her parents' room, but this morning he had chosen Asiah's only clean outfit as his bed. Giving up on looking professional at her new job, she threw on some trousers and a blouse, buckled her scuffed Mary-Janes and ran out the door without even running a comb through her hair.

She reached the door of the knife shop just seconds after the eighth chime. *Maybe he'll still be asleep,* she prayed, thinking about his make-shift bed in the loft. She burst through the door, panting.

Chase stood leaning a hip against the sales counter with his arms crossed over his chest, wearing a smirk. "Good morning," he said, and made a show of pulling out his pocket watch, looking at the time and then back at her.

Asiah drew herself up, tossed her long hair over her shoulder and scowled at him. "Don't give me that look. I'm here, aren't I?"

Chase shrugged and dropped his watch back into his pocket. He was wearing a navy linen shirt, open at the collar with the sleeves rolled up to his elbows, revealing muscular forearms. He still wore matching silver bracelets on both wrists. Asiah also noticed he had polished his jack boots. That seemed odd to her since two years earlier he'd looked like a hobo. When he'd visited her in the drugstore yesterday he'd also looked more clean-cut than she remembered. Why now did he improve on his appearance? It certainly made no difference to her what he looked like. He noticed her examining him and cleared his throat.

Asiah blushed and turned her attention to the various blades adorning the walls. The small room was filled mostly with varying sizes of trunks and glass-covered displays of knives of all shapes and sizes. On the wall behind the sales counter were mounted several swords from different periods in history. She recognized weapons from the American Civil War era from her history studies in high school, but most of the blades looked much older. She wondered how he had come to collect such things. He was watching her with interest.

"This is quite the collection," she commented, hoping it would make him stop looking at her with his intense green eyes.

He pushed away from the counter to gesture at the wall behind him. "These are all from wars I've fought in. Sort of like a journal I keep."

"That's one sadistic journal," she muttered under her breath.

"Did you say something?" he asked, turning back to her.

"I said, 'How many wars have you fought in?'" she covered.

"My last count was seventeen, but I don't think I'll be joining any more armies." A faraway look crossed his handsome face.

"Why did you do it?" she asked, unable to stop herself.

"It was something to do. When you live as long as I have, you look for ways to put your life in the hands of others." It was a dark admission and he looked as if he hadn't meant to say it aloud.

"But you survived them all, why didn't you just ... let yourself age, or whatever, if you wanted to, you know ..." she asked awkwardly, wondering why on Earth it was any of her business what he'd done with his long life.

"Die?" he asked, unaffected.

"Um, well, yes."

"Because I'm on a sort of quest. I made a promise to a dying man. If I die, everything in his life and mine will have been for naught." He was looking at her intently again.

"Listen, Mr. Brandon—" she began, intending to curb any further conversation about her "abilities."

"Chase."

She sighed in exasperation. "*Chase*. If I'm to work for you, you'll have to stop speaking in riddles and staring at me like I'm some ... prize pig at the fair."

Chase laughed out loud at her last statement. "You are a surprise at every turn, Miss O'Connor. Alright, no more riddles for now. That can wait until you're ready to understand."

"If I'm to call you Chase then you might as well call me Asiah." She was surprised that this didn't make her uncomfortable. She usually preferred formality with strangers.

"Very well then, *Asiah*." He said her name slowly, almost luxuriously, and with his English accent it sounded very ... nice. "I don't suppose you'd mind if I asked about what skills you have? To better assign your duties, that is." He smiled, showing her those perfect teeth.

"Only if I can ask you some questions about the job as well." She lifted a brow in challenge.

"I'll allow it," he said in a mocking tone. "What were your strengths in school? Science, obviously."

She nodded. "Science is my favorite. I was also good at arithmetic and history, but I think that's because I'm good at memorizing facts."

"Like what?"

She nodded at one of the swords mounted on the wall from the American Civil War. "I know that sword belonged to an officer and that you fought for the North."

He looked impressed. "That's very good. Do you remember everything you've learned?"

She shrugged. "A lot of it."

He tapped a finger against his lips. "Interesting."

It was her turn to ask a question. "Why do you like knives so much?"

"I'm fascinated that so much care and detail can go into an object that's only purpose is to kill; it's the darkest form of art. What did you do for the druggist?"

"Maintained inventory mostly, ran errands, researched remedies. Do you have a favorite blade?"

"Yes. Did you enjoy your work there?"

"All the way up until I lost my job." She glared at him. "Will you show me this favorite blade of yours?"

"When the time is right. Why are you wearing trousers?"

She shrugged. "Skirts get in the way. If I could wear pants all the time, I would. Have you always worked alone?"

"Mostly, it's hard to build relationships when you outlive everyone you know. You look lovely with your hair down."

"That's not a question."

"That doesn't make it less true." He was smirking at her again.

She'd completely forgotten about her hair. She swiftly pulled it up into a bun and fastened it with the three hairpins she happened to find in her pocket, then fixed Chase with a look of disapproval. "Are we going to stand here and socialize all day or don't you have something for me to do?"

Still smirking, he reached behind the counter and, after some rummaging, found a very old, rarely-used feather duster. He gingerly held it out to her between two fingers. "You may want to take it outside first and remove as much dust from it as you can; otherwise there won't be much use."

Still exasperated at his audacious little compliment, she snatched the duster and headed for the front door.

"Not that way, love," he called. "Best to do the dirty work in the alley." He jerked his thumb over his shoulder toward the kitchen.

Feeling foolish, she avoided his eyes as she hurried past him. She could feel his gaze on her until she was clear of the building. She inhaled deep gulps of fresh air, trying to calm her nerves as she leaned against the brick wall and let the breeze cool her face.

This is going to be harder than I thought.

※

Chase had enjoyed watching Asiah flit around his little shop attempting to "clean" for the past week. There was many years' worth of dust in there, and she'd had to go out to the alley three times a day to clean the duster. Asiah kept busy all the time, never tiring, and only speaking to Chase when she needed another task to do. He mostly just watched her work while he pretended to sharpen or polish his blades, biding his time until he was ready to show her the scroll. Her tenacity was admirable. She probably thought he actually needed her to clean this place when, if he chose, he could simply snap his fingers and collect all the dust into one tiny, dense ball and throw it out the window.

She stopped dusting suddenly and looked at him from atop a rickety A-frame ladder. She turned and sat on the top step and regarded him intently as he polished the hilt of an ancient sword.

"Something I can help you with?" he asked, glancing up.

She furrowed her brow, considering her words. "I thought you had some sort of ability to 'control' things. Energy or something. If that's true, why am I risking life and limb on this clearly unstable ladder to do something you could do with a snap of your fingers?"

His hands stilled on the sword. Had she just read his mind? Was he thinking too loudly? He suspected she could read minds, but he didn't expect her to just do it out of the blue without any training. And not to *him*. He must learn to shield his thoughts around her. It had been too long since he'd been in the presence of another with this ability, although Asiah had no idea she was doing it. She was still waiting for him to respond, eyebrows raised.

"I choose not to use my abilities when the task can easily be done by human hands."

"You mean *my* hands," she grumbled.

"Exactly." He grinned.

She sighed. "So what *do* you use your powers for? Good? Or evil?" She was making fun of him, but not for long.

His eyes twinkled. "A little of both." With that, the ladder step she was sitting on broke in half.

She gasped as she realized she was falling from fifteen feet in the air. She landed with a squeak in Chase's arms.

"You did that on purpose! I could have broken my neck!" Her voice was several octaves higher than usual, and Chase noticed that she didn't move to free herself from his hold.

His voice became serious. "I would never have let any harm come to you."

She opened her mouth to speak then closed it again. Her arms were wrapped around his neck and he noticed that the electric feeling between them didn't seem to bother her as it did before. The feeling was actually starting to feel pleasant. Intoxicating, even.

"You can put me down now," she said, her voice barely above a whisper.

But Chase couldn't seem to let go. It was as if an electric current held them together. With an effort, he gently lowered her feet to the floor, but still didn't fully release her from his arms and she didn't try to extract herself. He'd never been able to study her face from this close before. She had perfect skin and just enough freckles to be adorable.

She bit her lower lip and locked her eyes on his mouth as if in a trance. Her eyes fluttered shut and she leaned her head up slightly.

Chase snapped back to reality. This couldn't happen between them. He didn't even know for sure yet that she was destined to be his student, but if she were, he could never be more than her instructor. Not to mention the fact that he was about seven centuries too old for her. He cleared his throat and forced himself to push her back a step. He took a couple steps back himself to create a buffer between them. He drew a steadying breath to slow his pounding heart and finally glanced back at her face.

Confusion flitted across her features, like she wasn't sure what had just happened. But no sooner did he see it than it was gone. Her holier-than-thou attitude returned.

"Well, so much for dusting the shelves; I think you've rendered this ladder useless," she said, giving it a little shake. The ladder teetered on its spindly legs.

As she did so, Chase subtly waved a finger and the broken rung snapped back together. In fact, the entire ladder straightened and, in an instant, was good as new.

Asiah jumped back in surprise. She whipped around to look at him, her eyes wide in shock. "Did I just...?"

Chase chuckled. "No, love, that was my doing, but it's nice to see you're coming around to the idea of possibly having these abilities."

She dropped her hands to her sides in defeat. "I just ... have a hard time believing in all this. It's not *normal,* you know?"

He came to a decision. Whether she was ready for it or not, it was time to show her the scroll. "Come with me." He strode forward to grasp her hand and pulled her along behind him to the back room. She jumped a little when their hands touched, but didn't try to remove her hand from his.

In the back room, he swept piles of paper and books from the antique oak table. The volumes and pages landed in neat piles on the floor next to the table. He glanced at her. Wide-eyed, she clearly was still not accustomed to seeing him use his powers.

Chase walked to a rickety bookshelf. Instead of selecting from the scrolls piled there, he shoved the bookshelf aside, revealing a hidden panel in the wall. He placed his hand flat in the center of the panel. There was a distant rumble and then the panel slid open an inch. Chase removed his hand from the wall, opened the panel all the way and reached inside. He pulled out a glass tube sealed on both ends with intricate bronze scrollwork.

  He set the tube on the table and stretched out his hands above it, palms down. Murmuring a soft incantation, he watched as the bronze ends of the tube fell away. Inside the tube, the tattered edges of an ancient scroll could be seen and he carefully removed it. Chase stole another look at Asiah. She looked as if she might faint again. He set the scroll down and came around to the other side of the table where she stood, somewhat unsteadily. He summoned a chair from the corner of the room and set it behind her. "Here, love, sit down. I can't have you fainting again." She didn't seem to hear him; her gaze was fixed on the scroll.

  Chase touched her arm and she jumped, awakened from her trance. "Sit," he said firmly, but his touch was gentle as he guided her into the chair. When he was confident she was going to remain upright, he moved back to the other side of the table and carefully removed the scroll from the glass tube. He pulled a small vial from his pocket and sprinkled the oily substance over the edges of the scroll. He began to unroll it carefully, adding a little more oil as he went. Finally, he was able to lay it flat on the table. He placed the vial back in his pocket and contemplated his next move. Asiah looked up at him expectantly.

  Chase took a deep breath and slid the scroll across the table to her. "Now, read."

~§~

  Asiah felt funny. This whole situation was bizarre. She was quite content to dust Chase's shop and help polish his knives, but this was not her idea of honest work. He was talking about magic again, even if he hadn't said the words. She knew just by looking at the scroll that something unnatural was going on here. The back room was dimly lit, but she could tell there was nothing written on the old parchment. Chase's eyes held a look of anticipation and Asiah could see a muscle working in his jaw. What could be so important about a piece of blank parchment? *This must be some kind of test,* she thought. A test she was surely failing, if the look on his face was any indication.

She stalled for time. "Before, you said that everything you do is just a manipulation of physical laws, but a moment ago you said some words. Like a spell or something."

Clearly agitated that she was stalling, Chase pulled a chair up for himself and dropped into it heavily. "The man who mentored me was a great believer in mnemonic devices. Do you know what that means?"

"Of course! I would never have made it through a single science class if I didn't use them."

He nodded, "I might have guessed. Anyway, when you learn to rearrange molecules in a certain way, it helps to have some words associated to that task, to make sure you do it the same way each time. It's part of using more of your brain, like we talked about before. Now, look at that scroll and tell me what you see."

She still wasn't ready. "What words do you say?"

He clenched his jaw momentarily and gave in with a sigh. "Depends on what I'm doing. Not everything requires the words, it's just an old habit. Sometimes it's a Latin phrase, sometimes it's a nursery rhyme. Sometimes it's just nonsense that makes sense only to me. The words don't affect the outcome of the action, but when I haven't performed a certain feat in a long time, it's easier sometimes to say the words. Are you finished interrogating me yet?"

She frowned at him and waved her hand at the scroll. "I don't know what you're expecting me to read, there's nothing written here."

"Are you certain? Look again."

She rolled her eyes in exasperation and looked more carefully at the paper. It was very old, but well preserved. It must have had something to do with the oil Chase sprinkled on the document. None of this changed the fact that there was *nothing* written on it.

Asiah looked back at Chase and shook her head. "I'm sorry, I don't know what I'm doing wrong. I really don't see anything on the scroll."

Chase frowned; clearly he had expected a different result.

"What do *you* see on the paper?" she asked, becoming frustrated with this task.

Chase let out a breath and rubbed his face with his hands. "Nothing," he said, resigned. "I've never seen anything written on it, either. But I was sure that you would."

Asiah leaned back in her chair. "Why would you expect *me* to see something? I'm not like y—"

"You *are* like me!" He raised his voice. "I wish I could prove it to you." He raked his hands through his hair and softened his voice again. "I was told you would see something on the scroll. *He* said you would."

Irritated and confused, Asiah stood up, placed her hands on the table and leaned forward so he had to look up at her. "I've about had it with your cryptic insight. I'm going back out front to do my job. This is enough of your magic nonsense."

He was no longer looking at her. His eyes widened as he focused on something on the table. She looked down at the parchment between her hands. Her thumbs rested on the tattered edges of the scroll – which now had writing on it.

She pulled her hands away with a gasp. The writing vanished. Chase grabbed her wrists and pressed her hands to the paper, his breath quickening in anticipation.

Words scrawled in black ink jumped off the parchment, in a language Asiah had never seen before. It looked more like swirls and dots than words, but somehow she knew that there was a message contained therein. Her heart was pounding and cold sweat began to bead on her forehead.

"Read it," Chase whispered, mesmerized by the scribbles before him.

Asiah stared at the paper, but the ink seemed to blur before her eyes. The paper made her feel strange and she was *not* about faint again in front of Chase. "I-I can't," she whispered, shaking her head. "I can't read this language."

Chase locked his eyes to hers. "You *must*. You're the only one who can," he begged.

"N-no, you're wrong. I can't do this." She felt like crying, but she had no idea why. All she knew was that she needed to get as far away from this paper and its owner as she could. She pulled her hands from where he held them to the scroll, and with one last look into his pleading eyes, she ran from the shop.

Chapter Seven

Asiah stared bleakly at the shot glass of honey-colored liquid in front of her.

"Drink it, Cricket," Monty pressed from behind the bar. "They don't call it liquid courage for nothin'." Monty still retained his brogue from their homeland, while Asiah had all but lost hers. It only surfaced on occasion in certain words or when she was angry.

Asiah swallowed and fiddled with the neckline of her dress in a vain attempt to tug it up a little higher. After abandoning her post at the knife shop three days ago, she had spent every waking hour looking for gainful employment. After three days she'd found nothing, not even in the most dismal workhouses. She wouldn't ask Walter for help. He would support her only after they were properly married, not a moment sooner. She wondered what he would think of her working in a place like this.

It was a difficult decision to approach her brother and ask him for help. In the end, Monty talked to his boss who offered her a job waiting tables in the speakeasy. She was about the clumsiest person she knew, but she wouldn't turn down any job right now. Asiah knew why the club's owner had given her a job after a single glance, without even asking about her experience, but she didn't have any pride left. The only real issue she had was with the flimsy dress they expected her to wear on the job. The dancing girls on stage were scantily clad enough, why did the staff have to dress this way, too? She'd spent much of the afternoon convincing herself that she'd only have to work there a short time. Since she didn't have to work during the day, it left her days open to find a job where she could wear whatever she liked – and not put her livelihood in the hands of a mobster.

"Go on, then. Boss wants you on the floor," Monty urged. He tossed his bar cloth over his shoulder and moved down the bar to help another patron.

Asiah was no stranger to alcohol; her mother used to put a drop of whisky in some warm milk to help her sleep. On the other hand, she'd seen what drink could do to a man when taken in excess. Gritting her teeth, she threw her inhibitions out the window and tossed the shot back. It burned her throat all the way down to her stomach. Her head spun ever so slightly for just a moment, and the feeling passed. She adjusted her dress once more, picked up her serving tray, took a bracing breath and turned to face the crowded room.

~

Chase removed his fedora as he approached the man next to the door labeled "Private Party." The man was sitting in a chair much too small for his portly frame, smoking and reading a newspaper by the light from a dim bulb over the door. He barely spared Chase a glance.

"Password?" he grumbled.

Chase stroked his chin and considered the man for a moment. "Lucky Lindy?" he guessed.

The man merely grunted his assent and jerked his thumb toward the door.

Chase shed his overcoat and handed it with his hat to a boy of fourteen or fifteen standing near the coat room at the bottom of the entry stairs. Chase was dressed in the current American fashion as part of his cover for getting in, but he much preferred a loose-fitting linen tunic to these uncomfortable suits American men wore now. It wouldn't be so bad if he would just go to a tailor and have a suit custom-made for his large frame, but he rarely had an occasion to dress this way. For now, the slightly-too-tight clothing would suffice.

He had been following Asiah from a distance for the past three days. Ever since she was able to activate the scroll, he wasn't about to let her out of his sight. Yesterday he'd followed her here. She'd gone inside looking about as despondent as ever. But when she came out, there was a spring in her step. He assumed she'd gotten a job, although he worried about what it entailed. This dancehall was controlled by the mob, and Chase didn't like the idea of Asiah working in close proximity with dangerous men. It might make him a hypocrite, he thought, since he led a dangerous life himself. The difference was that he would never hurt Asiah; she was too important. He knew if he were ever in a situation where it was his life or hers, he would gladly die for her. Especially after he'd lived so long already.

He looked around the smoky basement room, keeping to the shadows. It wouldn't do for Asiah to recognize him. At the far end of the low-ceilinged room was a stage upon which three nearly-naked women were dancing a can-can. The only light in the room came from the stage and the tiny candles on each table. To his left was a long bar manned only by a young blond fellow efficiently filling glasses from one end of the bar to the other. Chase couldn't see Asiah anywhere, but his instincts told him she was nearby.

Chase strolled up to the bar, tugging anxiously on his tie. Patrons on either side of him moved to let him take a seat. Chase smiled as he thought about how Asiah would disapprove of him using his powers to get a good seat at the bar. As if he'd summoned her, she appeared near the far end of the bar carrying a precarious tray of drinks. Chase couldn't believe his eyes. *What is she wearing?* He made an effort not to stare at her. She wore a low-cut red silk dress edged in black lace that left little to the imagination. The wispy fabric clung to her body in ways that made him feel strange. Her hair was piled loosely on top of her head instead of in the tight braid she usually wore. His mouth suddenly felt very dry, and he was thankful that the barman chose this moment to serve him.

"Gin," he managed to choke out.

"Ah, Limey are ya?" The bartender smiled. "From the Emerald Isle, meself. Guess we're both foreigners on this side o' the pond, eh?"

An Irishman who didn't hate the English? Chase nodded and sipped the clear liquid the man set in front of him. He turned his gaze back to the girl in the red dress slipping between the tightly-packed tables. He felt the Irishman's gaze and turned back to face him. With his best dirty-scoundrel grin he asked, "What time does that one get off?" He nodded in Asiah's direction.

The man's eyes became like shards of ice. "That *one* is me baby sister, and you'll not be layin' a finger on her if y'know what's good for ya." He opened his vest an inch to reveal the butt of a revolver.

Chase held up his hands in surrender. "Didn't mean anything by it, forgive me." *Now he's got a reason to hate the English.* He stood and with a slight bow to the barman, made his way to a table in the back, well-ensconced in shadow. The man was her brother? It made sense why she would have come *here* to look for work. At least he felt a little better about her safety. Still, her brother was behind the bar, and much too distracted to keep an eye on her. The randy patrons of establishments like this one were likely to throw her over their shoulders and disappear before the man could make his way out from behind the bar. No, this was no place for her.

He watched her serve drinks as tirelessly as she'd dusted his shop. Each time she ventured near his table, he knocked a glass over somewhere else in the room so she'd have to run to clean up the spill. She smiled at each customer as if he were the only man in the room, and Chase noticed that many of them started paying less attention to the dancers on stage and more attention to the new waitress in the red dress.

Chase's apprehension mounted. He sensed a tension in the room. He cracked his knuckles under the table, every muscle in his body tensing, ready to come to her rescue. He forced himself to take a deep breath. He was being paranoid. Nothing was going to happen to her. He was letting jealousy get the better of him. *Jealousy?* How could he be jealous of these clods? He had no more claim to her than they did. He sighed aloud. This was unhealthy. He shouldn't even have been there, stalking Asiah like Jack the Ripper. She was safe; if her brother worked for the mob, then surely she was under their protection as well. If all was well, why did he still feel this sense of unease?

⁓

Asiah could feel the eyes of every man in the room follow her with every step she took. She figured she'd learn to ignore the gawking patrons eventually, but this feeling wasn't just the lascivious stares of scoundrels. She felt like *he* was here, watching her. It was a foolish thought, she knew. What reason could he have to follow her? Had she not made it clear that she wanted nothing more to do with him? Still, she had a strange feeling that he was looking right at her. She scanned the room every chance she got, which wasn't many; she was much too busy to worry about whether Chase was stalking her. Besides, her brother was here to watch over her, and he had a *gun*. Much better protection than magic tricks and old knives.

She made a quick inventory of her tables. She knew she was neglecting one corner of the room, but every time she tried to make it over there, someone would spill his drink and she had to go clean it up. It seemed odd to her that this had happened four times already, but she didn't think about it too hard. Drunken men spilled their drinks sometimes. She glanced to the far corner of the room where she hadn't been able to take orders, hoping the patrons there were getting their own drinks from the bar. A lone figure sat at the farthest table and his candle had gone out. The poor man was sitting completely in the dark. He probably couldn't even see his drink! She groaned. Part of her job was keeping the candles lit. They were the only light source in the room after all. She dug in her apron pockets for her matchbook. Unable to find it, she leaned over to the patron nearest her.

"Hey sugar, got a light?" She felt extremely uncomfortable flirting with the customers, but Monty told her that her job depended on it.

"Sure do, sweetheart. Question is: what have you got for me?" The man slid a beefy hand up the side of her thigh to squeeze her backside.

Asiah didn't immediately register what happened next. She knew that she was thrown back against a table, which toppled, and she fell hard on her wrist. She watched in disbelief as a tall man tackled the offending patron, slammed him down on a table and held him there with a very wicked, very *ancient-looking* knife to his throat. The entire room was silent as a tomb. Then she heard *his* voice.

"Do *not* touch her again. Understand?" She'd never heard Chase sound so menacing.

The man squeaked out an unintelligible reply that Chase must have taken for a "yes." Chase dragged the man to his feet, still holding him by his shirt collar. The knife had vanished; the only sign that it been there was a small red scratch on the patron's neck.

"What's going on here?" Monty appeared at her side. "Cricket! Are you hurt?" He reached for her to help her up and accidentally grasped her hurt wrist.

Asiah cried out in pain, and Chase released the man and whirled around to see her sprawled on the floor. He moved to help her up, but Monty recognized him.

"Oh, no ya don't, ya filthy Brit!" Monty pulled his revolver out and leveled it at Chase, forcing him to back up a step.

"Let me help her," Chase implored him.

"I'm sure that's exactly what you want: to 'help' her." Two more men with guns appeared at Monty's side. "I think this one's had enough to drink. Why don't you show him out, boys?"

The men took a step toward Chase but stopped when he fixed them with an icy glare.

"I can show myself out." He turned to Asiah, still sitting on the floor. "Will you be alright, love?"

She nodded mutely, still in shock.

"She's not yours to worry about," Monty said, stepping between them. "Now get out."

With a look of regret, Chase turned and headed for the door as the other patrons gave him a wide berth.

When he was gone, Monty crouched to help her up. He gently touched her wrist and she winced in pain.

"I think it's broken, Cricket. We should get you home." He helped her stand and guided her to the back room where she could change. "If you wait here a tick, I'll walk you home meself. Alright?"

She nodded and sank into a chair. Monty stroked her hair for a moment then strode briskly from the room. She heard him barking orders at his men and the dancers, telling everyone to get back to work. She dropped her head into her good hand. *What just happened?* She tried to recount the events of the evening. Obviously Chase had been there the entire time, watching her. She should have guessed. She didn't know why he attacked that man, though. It was very impulsive of him. He always seemed to consider his actions carefully, but not this time.

An hour later Monty hadn't returned. Asiah had already changed into her trousers and button-down shirt and pulled on her pea coat, wrapping it tightly around herself. Right now, she could not wear enough clothing. She shivered as she remembered how the man had touched her so inappropriately. Was it possible Chase attacked the man out of some misplaced sense of gallantry? She shook her head to clear it. Thinking about the man's touch was making her feel queasy, and she decided she couldn't stand to be here anymore.

She opened the door a crack just in time to see Monty toss back a shot of liquor. He'd probably forgotten all about her. He was a good man, her brother, but his own needs always came first. She waited until his back was turned and slipped out of the back room. The nearest exit was the back door in the dancers' dressing room and she headed there quickly, keeping her head down.

The dancers were taking a break, laughing and smoking while they gave their feet a rest. When she entered they stopped their conversation to regard her in silence. She stood awkwardly for a moment before she remembered why she had come this way. As she started for the door, one of the girls said, "You should have kicked him in his misters, honey." The other two screeched with laughter.

Asiah slammed the door behind her and slumped against it. Tears blurred her vision and she slid down the door until she reached the ground, pulling her knees to her chest. She wished she could just disappear right then and there. Leave all this and go back to Ireland where she'd been happy. Everyone was happier in Ireland.

"There, there, love, don't cry," she heard distantly.

She raised her head to see a handkerchief being held out to her. It bore the initials *C.B.* She looked past the offered cloth into Chase's eyes, full of concern.

"You shouldn't be here," she sniffled, taking his handkerchief.

"It takes more than a couple of gangsters with guns to scare me off," he said with a smile.

"Why did you attack that man?"

His voice held an edge. "He touched you in a way he shouldn't have."

"That's what the men here do. They don't mean any harm." She didn't really believe her own words. If that's what she'd have to put up with every night she worked here, she wouldn't last a week.

"It may not seem harmful until they take it too far. *He* took it too far." Chase was getting agitated.

"Well, I appreciate the gesture, but I don't need you to protect me. My brother can do that."

"He bloody well didn't show it tonight."

She pushed herself up the wall with her good hand and stood shakily, wondering if this night would ever end. "I need to go home. It's been a long night." She took a step and stumbled.

Chase grabbed her arm to steady her and she grimaced. He pressed two fingers to her neck under her jaw and shook his head.

"You're hurt and you're in shock, and your home is on the other side of town. Let me get you somewhere safe where you can recover." His eyes were asking her permission and she felt too weak to resist. Chase had never given her any reason to think he'd cause her harm. If anything, she was disturbed by how comforting his presence was. She gave a weak nod. "Good. Now love, I need you to take a deep breath and hold it in, alright? Hold onto my hand and don't let go."

What a strange request, she thought. She sucked in a breath and felt a strong wind against her face. She closed her eyes and squeezed Chase's hand as she felt the world tilting. She thought she must be fainting again, so she opened her eyes just as her feet connected with solid ground. She stumbled again, but Chase still had ahold of her hand and he pulled her upright before she could fall. She stood facing him, breathless, wondering what on Earth just happened.

Chapter Eight

Asiah looked around wild-eyed at the new surroundings, uncomprehending. Chase gently took her chin between his thumb and forefinger and turned her face toward his so they were eye to eye.

"Look at me, Asiah," he said in a soothing tone. She was still breathing too fast, clearly distressed, and was having trouble focusing her attention on him. Chase did the only thing he could think of to calm her down. He kissed her. She immediately went still as his lips touched hers, just a whisper of a kiss. Time seemed to stand still during their very brief contact, and Chase suddenly wished that he could prolong it, taking far too much enjoyment from the feeling of her lips tingling against his. But he pulled away, still holding her chin and trying to force the memory of her kiss from his mind. "Look at me," he coaxed.

She looked at him, steadily this time, with uncertainty in her eyes.

"Are you alright?" he asked, releasing her chin and taking a step back.

She glanced around, still winded, and nodded.

"I want to hear you say it," Chase said.

"I-I'm alright ... I think." Not the most reassuring answer, but at least she was coherent.

"Come inside and sit by the fire." Chase held the door of his cottage open for her to enter. It was small, but it was his home ever since he'd been in America. He'd had many homes over the years, always preferring the solitude of the forest to living in a city.

He pulled two chairs up near the cold stove, then carefully helped her remove her pea coat and guided her into one of the chairs. He flicked a finger at the stove and flames burst from the cold logs inside.

Asiah's eyes widened but she didn't speak. Chase shed his overcoat, suit jacket and waistcoat. He rolled up his shirt sleeves and unbuttoned the top two buttons on his shirt. He dropped into the chair across from her and held out his hand. "Let me see your wrist."

She'd been hugging her hurt arm to her chest protectively. Now she gingerly extended it to him, blinking at him uncertainly. He took her hand, never taking his eyes from her face. She winced slightly when he touched her wrist. He carefully rolled up her sleeve and traced his fingers over the damaged joint.

"Take some deep breaths, love," he said, then turned his attention to her wrist and placed two fingers on her skin directly above the break. Her eyes went wide with fear. He pressed gently on the joint and she moaned. "Stay with me, Asiah." He began to massage her wrist, moving his fingers in small circles with gentle pressure. He heard her gasp and glanced up at her face. Her mouth was open in surprise. He ensured bones had mended completely and smoothly replaced her hand in her lap.

She looked from his face to her healed wrist and back. "You healed me," she whispered, as if she were afraid to say it aloud. "You mended the bones."

He laughed softly, happy to see some of her spirit returning. "That I did, love. Tea?"

She seemed confused. "T-tea?"

"Yes, tea. You steep it, you drink it, you feel better." He flashed her a smile.

"Oh, yes. But not black tea. I'll be up all night."

"I may have some chamomile," he said and went to a small store cupboard in the corner. He returned with two mugs and a kettle of water, which he hung over the fire.

"You're not going to boil the water yourself this time?" she asked, eyeing him skeptically.

Chase felt immensely better now that she was being herself again. She didn't seem to mind that he'd brought her out to the middle of the woods in the middle of the night. She'd also let him kiss her. He'd have to figure that one out later.

"I usually do let the fire boil the water. Like I said before, human hands." He waved his hands in front of him.

A pregnant silence followed as they sat and waited for the water to boil. Chase didn't want to push his luck by asking her to come back to work for him. For now, she was here and she let him help her, but he didn't know if she meant to give him another chance to train her. She was staring bleakly into the fire as if the answers were written there in the flames.

Chase took a moment to examine her. She really was exquisite. Every feature was perfectly formed, but then, that would be the case. Chase had only ever met one other like her, centuries ago. Last time, *he* was the student. He never envied his mentor, and now he understood why the man always seemed to have the weight of the world on his shoulders. He only hoped he could be half the teacher the Ikhäle was.

He absently fiddled with the buttons on his shirt. There had to be a way to convince her to stay without making her run again. Before he could figure out a way to broach the subject, she spoke.

"Why were you at the club tonight?" Her voice was tired, but her tone held an accusation.

"I wanted to make sure you were safe. That's no place for a girl like you." Might as well be straight with her.

"I'm 21 years old! I'm not a child," she said in an annoyed tone.

"Of course not, I only meant ... there are better ways to use your potential." It was a weak argument. Aside from the fact that she was destined for bigger things, the reality was that he didn't want her near those rogues in the speakeasy.

"Like learning to do what you do?" She considered for a moment. "Can you heal ... anything?"

Chase raised his eyebrows. It was the first time she'd actually seemed interested. "To an extent. Fatal wounds are difficult to heal; they use up a lot of energy. If you'd like, I can show you how to do it." He tried to sound nonchalant, but inside he was begging her to say yes.

"What do you mean when you say it uses a lot of energy?" she asked, genuinely attentive now.

He stared into the fire for a moment before he answered. "If you truly want to know the answers to these questions, you must first accept who and what you are." He fixed her with an intense look. "It won't make sense until you do."

She sighed and looked down at her newly-healed wrist, flexing it. She was quiet for a moment longer, then seemed to come to a decision. "Alright, then. Who am I?"

Chase was so relieved he could have cried.

⚘

Asiah woke to the smell of fresh soda-bread baking. She yawned and stretched. It was her favorite aroma to wake up to. She rolled onto her side and opened her eyes – and shot straight up in bed. *This isn't my bed. Where am I?* She panicked for a moment, struggling to remember where she was and how she'd gotten there.

Sunlight streamed through a leaded glass window to her right. She was seated in the center of a large, brass bed with a down-filled mattress. She still wore her shirt from the night before, but her trousers were draped over a chair next to the bed. She wracked her brain to remember what happened last night. She looked down at her hands and traced her fingers over her right wrist. It all came back in an instant. Chase attacking the man at the club, the dancers laughing at her, the way he healed her wrist simply by gently touching it.

The smell of fresh bread made her stomach growl. She climbed out of the huge bed and donned her trousers, trying in vain to smooth out the wrinkles. She removed her shirt and smoothed her camisole. Her bag was sitting on the chair and she dug inside for anything that might help her appearance. The red silk dress tumbled out. She held the dress at arm's length and examined it with a frown.

"You might as well get rid of it," Chase said from the doorway. "I'm bloody well not going to let you wear it in public again." He leaned against the door frame, arms crossed over his chest. He was dressed in a white linen tunic over fitted brown trousers, looking far more comfortable than he had in his suit last night. A leather belt circled his narrow waist, bearing two daggers in their sheaths. His feet were bare. He noticed her staring at his feet and wiggled his toes playfully.

Her gaze snapped back to his face and she clutched the red dress to her chest defensively. "Don't you knock?" she said, miffed.

He shrugged. "It's my house. I had to make sure you didn't try to escape." He winked at her.

She scowled. "Am I a prisoner, then?"

Chase laughed. "Of course not! I just know last night was very trying for you. I hope you're still considering my offer."

Asiah balled up the red dress and stuffed it in her bag. "I haven't changed my mind." She turned her back to him and pulled her shirt on, acutely aware that he was watching her every move.

"Good. Come have some breakfast," he said and disappeared.

In the daylight, she was able to observe her surroundings more closely. His cottage was small with a low ceiling and exposed wooden beams from which dangled various dried herbs. The walls were lined with shelves packed with books, scrolls and glass vials of various sizes displaying liquids of every color. In the center of one wall was a potbelly stove. There were at least five wooden chests crammed into corners and between shelves, lending to the cluttered yet cozy feeling the cottage provided. A large table took up a third of the room. Vials and papers had been hastily shoved to one end of the table while two place settings occupied the other half. Asiah sat down in front of one of the plates.

The last time he'd invited her to breakfast, she hadn't actually eaten anything. That was clearly a mistake, because Chase could *cook*. Aside from the best soda bread she'd ever had in her life, he'd made her eggs, bacon, fried tomatoes, boiled potatoes and Irish black tea.

"This is a very Irish breakfast," she commented between mouthfuls.

"You are from Ireland, aren't you?" he said.

"Yes, but I haven't eaten like this in years! My family, well, we don't have much." She paused. "How did you know I'm Irish?"

"I assume you've been in America long enough to lose your brogue, although I can hear it sometimes ... when you're angry at me." He grinned. "And I had a chance to meet your brother last night, if you recall."

"Yes. It's probably best you don't meet him again anytime soon."

"Will he worry about where you disappeared to last night?"

"Not likely. Monty only cares about himself. He's fiercely protective in the moment, but as soon as he thinks I'm safe, he goes back to caring about Monty. He probably thinks I went home on my own last night."

"What about your parents?"

"They think I'm staying with Monty. I'm in no hurry to get home, as I have no paycheck to give them this week. Ever since Mr. Kelsey fired me, they don't seem to wonder where I am." Her voice broke, and Chase reached across the table to grasp her hand.

"I'm sure that's not true," he said soothingly. His thumb traced small circles on the back of her hand.

She was becoming accustomed to the strange feeling when they touched, but now, as he held her hand, she felt something else, too. Her insides did a little flip. It was strange; she had never felt anything like that before. She saw him watching her and slowly pulled her hand from his grasp.

Last night, Chase hadn't thought it was a good time to begin her education. She'd been exhausted and had had a long day. He'd said they would get a fresh start in the morning when she was feeling better. Now that it was morning, she was still somewhat apprehensive. She reminded herself that he had healed her wrist in a matter of seconds. There was no denying that it wasn't an illusion. Something more powerful was at play here, and she needed to know what it was, no matter how crazy it sounded.

"So ... what now?" she asked quietly.

"That depends on what you want to know first. I'm sure you have questions."

"Where are we? How did we get here from the club last night?"

"This is where I live, just outside the city. You didn't think I lived in the knife shop, did you?"

"I suppose not. One minute we were in the alley behind the club, and the next thing I knew we were here. Did I faint again?" She truly hoped that she hadn't fainted in front of him again.

"You didn't faint. I brought you here by a method of travel I call 'channeling'." He waited for her to respond.

She stared at him blankly.

"I'll explain channeling to you later. First you need to know who you are and what your importance is." He looked a little nervous, like he wasn't sure how to explain. He cleared his throat and poured himself some more tea. He raised his teacup to his lips then put it down again without drinking. He drummed his fingers on the table.

"Is something the matter?" she asked. Clearly he was uncomfortable about something.

Chase rubbed the back of his neck with his hand. "I've never had to explain this before and I want to make sure ... well, it's very complicated. I want to get all the details right. It's been so long since it was explained to me."

It was Asiah's turn to provide reassurance. "You've got my full attention, although it took some persuasion." She smiled. "Why don't you start at the beginning? The details will come."

Chase nodded and then exhaled. "Please stop me if you have questions." He waited for her to nod before continuing. "Since the beginning of time, there has only ever been one race of sentient beings. The people that became known as the Ikhälean race exist all over what humans call the 'universe.' No one knows who first called them that or why, but they are the only intelligent life in this dimension."

"This dimension?" she asked.

"Yes. There are many dimensions of time and space, but one cannot travel between them in this life. At least I've never known anyone to do it. Many believe that your soul goes to another dimension after death, but no one has ever returned from death to tell the tale."

"These people, are they human?"

"In a manner of speaking. I'm getting to that."

"Oh. Sorry to interrupt you. Go on, please."

"You can stop me all you like, love. I want you to understand this. The Ikhälea are a highly evolved species living in harmony with nature on the many worlds they inhabit. Their highly developed minds are able to predict events far in advance based on past or current happenings so they may avoid any threats to their existence. When one of their populations is in danger of annihilation, whether it be from disease or disaster, the Ikhälea cease reproduction on that world and find another world on which to carry on their existence."

He paused and she nodded encouragingly. He relaxed and warmed to the subject.

"It begins with elemental seeds – what humans know as the primordial soup: bacteria, single-celled organisms and the like. Eventually, after much time has passed, they become fully evolved. Unbeknownst to themselves, human beings are only a link in the evolutionary chain between bacteria swimming in the sea and the Ikhälea. The evolutionary stage at which humans exist on this planet is only a little more than halfway between the elemental seed stage and full development. On most Ikhälean worlds, evolution progresses swiftly and is completed in around three and a half billion Earth years. That is, if nothing interrupts the progress of evolution.

"Once every few worlds, a glitch in the chain of events causes the progression to slow. This can be from war, plague, or natural disasters. Usually the population will correct its course, as it is designed to do. Sometimes, however, the people unknowingly stray too far off course, and assistance must be brought in from the nearest Ikhälean world. Those chosen to travel to the developing worlds are known as Ikhälean Clerics. Because of their advanced brain function, they are able to manipulate energy and matter and even see into the minds of others. Because they can control the rate at which their bodies age, Ikhälea may live indefinitely until they are ready to die, as long as there are other Ikhälea to nourish them. However, when the Ikhälean Clerics arrive on a world that is in distress, they begin to age immediately. This is because a fully evolved Ikhäle does not consume food as humans do. Instead, nutritional value is shared between two Ikhälea during physical contact with each other. This is why the Clerics begin to age on under-developed worlds; they do not have other Ikhälea to nourish them. Are you still following me?"

Asiah was floored by the information he'd given her so far, but somehow it all made sense to her. It certainly answered the question of whether humans were alone in the universe.

"What kind of physical contact do they need to survive?" Asiah wondered.

"Any contact will do, but the more intimate the contact, the better the nourishment."

She blushed. "Oh. It's very strange, isn't it?"

"Only because it is not the way of life you are accustomed to," Chase said. "When survival depends on the sensation of touch between two people, it is difficult for the Ikhälean Clerics to avoid physical contact with others. Only the most disciplined are sent to correct the balance of progression to the fully evolved species. At any level of evolution, a hungry man will find a way to eat, and inevitably the Clerics become intimate with their younger counterparts: human beings. It is a foolish attempt to slow the aging process, for physical contact with under-evolved beings does not satisfy their hunger."

Asiah was sure her face was beet-red by now.

"That's where you come in," Chase continued. "Because they have begun aging, Ikhälean Clerics have a limited amount of time to correct the course of evolution. Often they do not finish the task before them. Ironically, the only saving grace is that most of them do reproduce with the under-evolved people, leaving offspring to finish their work. These offspring are known as Ikhälean Shades. They are not born directly to the Ikhälea but often centuries later, and always one of a set of twins. They are always female and only one is ever conceived by a Cleric."

Asiah's heart began to beat faster.

"Shades have the ability to travel between worlds and survive in any conditions. They may be ageless on all worlds as well. Because their birth, by definition, upsets the balance of evolution, their task to correct the course is that much more difficult. That is assuming the Shade is even aware of her own existence – which now, you are."

"So ... that's what I am? An '*Ikhälean Shade?*'" Asiah was in complete shock. Her eyes were wide and she was breathing too fast again. "And I'm supposed to, what? Realign the evolutionary process so someday we can all evolve into these ... *things*?"

"The *only* True Ikhälean Shade on Earth. And they're called Ikhälea," Chase corrected her. "And I think it's time we took a break. I'm worried I'm giving you too much information too fast." He studied her face. "Tell me how you're feeling about all of this."

She pushed back from the table, stood up and paced the small room. "I think I'm alright. I'm not going to faint, if that's what you're wondering. Please keep going. Tell me how you fit into all this. Are you one of these Ikhälea too?"

"No, I am one hundred percent human flesh." He grinned at her, to which she raised an eyebrow. He cleared his throat. "Yes, I suppose you'd like to know how I can do what I do. I was taught by the Ikhälean Cleric who was sent to Earth many years ago. When the world entered what we now call the Dark Ages, Ikhälea on other worlds saw that humans had taken a wrong turn. My mentor's name was Tojen. When he began raising me he was already an old man; he wasted too much time on Earth abusing his powers, giving 'magic' lessons to anyone with enough gold. I was told that he was my father's uncle, but now I wonder if that had any truth to it. I only have his word. Anyway, he realized that his life was nearing its end and that he had never fulfilled his task. You, of course, had already been conceived, but would not be born for several centuries. His genes first needed to travel through several human generations before you could be born. In his final years he told me his story and taught me what I needed to know and what I needed to do, which was to find and train you. I am what is known as an Ikhälean Conjurer," he finished.

She sat down again, trying to decide whether to laugh out loud or be utterly confused and overwhelmed. The latter won out. She still couldn't be sure she could trust Chase, and if what he was saying was true, she needed time to process it. "You're right, this is a lot to take in. I need to go home, Chase. My family must be wondering where I am."

"Oh, yes, of course." He couldn't hide the disappointment on his face.

"I'm sorry, I just need ... some time," she explained.

"I'll take you home." He shoved back from the table and went to put his boots on.

Chase channeled Asiah and himself to an alleyway near her apartment. When their feet hit the ground she took a step back and pointed a finger at his chest.

"You're going to have to explain *that* ability at our next meeting," she said. She started to turn away, noticing as she did that his expression was one of defeat. He thought he was losing her. Turning back, she stood on her tiptoes and kissed his cheek. "Thank you for healing my wrist."

He nodded, rubbing his cheek as some of the light returned to his eyes.

She turned and started to walk toward the street.

"Tomorrow?" he called after her.

She reached the street and turned back. "We'll see," was all she said.

Chapter Nine

Chase touched his cheek where her kiss still tingled on his skin and then dropped his hand in resignation. He needed to stop letting her affect him so. There could never be anything between them. He should take solace in the fact that he'd found her and, in a few weeks' time, she would know everything she needed to know to set the population of Earth back on the right evolutionary track. After that, he could die in peace and become one with the æthers. His existence had been too long already, and he was ready for this eternity to end. Then why did the thought of dying seem so depressing?

He shook his head to clear it, needing a distraction from his troubled thoughts. He walked toward the street and turned right in the direction of the knife shop. A woman on the street regarded him strangely, trying to hide her observance of his strange clothing. People often gave him strange looks when he appeared in public, usually because of his outdated wardrobe, but he paid them no mind. He learned long ago that the opinions of others meant nothing, but there was also such a thing as keeping a low profile. Something he hadn't been paying much heed to recently.

Chase entered his shop and wondered what to do with himself. The shop was spotless; there wasn't a speck of dust anywhere. Asiah really had done an amazing job cleaning the place. He thought about reading over the prophecies again, but that would only cause him to think about her. He walked behind the sales counter and pulled out several knives from a display under the counter and began sharpening them, even though they hadn't been used since the last time he sharpened them.

  Several hours passed and Chase wondered if Asiah would be ready to learn more tomorrow. How would he know? Would she come to the shop? She didn't know where the cabin was so it made sense she would come here. He groaned in frustration as his thoughts once again settled on her. She was a child compared to him, and he was doing himself no favors by thinking about her in any other way.

  The bell above the door jangled and he looked up, half-expecting Asiah to walk through it. Instead, a young woman with flaming red hair entered the shop. She looked to be around the same age as Asiah and nearly as beautiful. It was strange that a woman would come in here alone; most of his few customers were men. She wore a tattered black cloak that reached to the floor, which was also unusual. It was like she'd stepped out a medieval storybook. Chase put down the knife he was honing and focused intently on his guest. Something was not right about this woman.

  "Something I can help you with?" he asked, trying to sound casual.

  "I'm wondering if you can appraise something for me," she said with a lilting accent. Russian, Chase guessed. She kept her eyes downcast.

  Chase shifted uncomfortably, his whole body tensing. "That depends on what it is."

  She pulled a long, sheathed dagger from beneath her cloak and laid it on the counter, still averting her eyes. Chase stared at the knife. It was very old and somewhat familiar to him. He unsheathed the blade slowly, examining it as he went. The grip was carved onyx with small, black stones inlaid on the hilt. The blade was eight inches long and made of folded steel, with a slight bluish hue. It was an expert design.

  A small engraving at the top of the blade just under the hilt caught his attention. He brought the knife to eye level for closer inspection. It was the mark of the one who forged the blade. He knew that signature; he had another dagger with the same insignia. That meant ...

He lowered the blade to look at the woman. She was looking directly at him now, and he could see her eyes were completely black. Chase's breath caught in his throat. *She can't be ...* He reached for one of the daggers on his belt, but he was too slow. The woman vaulted the counter and slammed him against the wall before he could wrap his hand around the grip. She was very strong. *Too* strong. She jerked him away from the wall and threw him down on the counter. She leapt on top of him, straddling his torso, and pressed her dagger's blade to his throat.

"*Conjurer,*" she hissed, inches from his face, "you've grown slow and weak in your old age."

Chase struggled to free himself but she pressed the blade harder against his throat.

"I wouldn't do that if I were you. A wound from this blade never heals, even with your powers." She reached for his belt and withdrew a similar dagger, inlaid with pearls and sapphires. "But then you knew that, didn't you?" With her free hand she threw his dagger, lodging it in the wooden doorframe. Turning her attention back to him she asked, "Where is the other Shade?"

Other? Only one Shade was ever born of an Ikhälean Cleric, but the way she had said "Conjurer" with such venom led Chase to believe she was not like him. She was something else. *A Phantom Shade?*

"You're no Conjurer. How did you come by that blade?" Chase asked, stalling for time.

"It is not your concern how I acquired this particular dagger. But I'd like to add your blade to my collection, too," she said with a sinister smile, "after you tell me where she is."

Like hell. "I don't know who you mean. If you are a Shade, there can be no others like you on this world," he rasped.

The woman made a small movement with her knife and Chase felt a warm trickle of blood run down the side of his neck. He gritted his teeth against the burn of the alien blade.

She licked her lips at the sight of his blood. "You know exactly who I mean and where she is. You are correct that there should only be one True Shade, a situation I mean to rectify. I have felt the fluctuations in the energy fields around this place. Fluctuations I haven't felt in decades. You've been keeping a low profile. Until now. You've found her and you *will* tell me where she is."

"Or what, you'll kill me? Then how will you find her?" His mind raced to think of a way to warn Asiah.

"I have ways." With that she pressed her palm to his forehead.

A searing white pain tore through his skull. Chase struggled to erect his mental barriers against the psychic attack. She pressed harder, strain showing on her face. Through the lightning bolts of pain, he realized she didn't possess the capacity to break down the walls of his mind. He pushed back with all his might against the invading force. With a final blocking thrust, he shattered her attempt to penetrate his mind and she was thrown back. She fell hard on the floor of the shop. He was on top of her in an instant, his own blade in hand, and now it was his turn to threaten her.

"Leave this place, Phantom." His voice was an ominous whisper. "Or the next time we meet will be your final day on this planet."

She laughed despite the blade at her throat, an evil, rasping sound. "I am called Marysa, and your mercy will be your undoing, Sorcerer. When we meet again you will wish you'd killed me. I will find the Shade, just as you did. You cannot protect her from me. Balance must be restored." At her last words she vanished in a flash of light.

Chase collapsed on the floor, exhausted from both mental and physical battles with her. As he drifted in and out of consciousness, he pictured Asiah's face. *I must warn her ... then the world went black.*

※

If Asiah thought her family didn't care where she'd been all night, she was sorely mistaken. Patrick railed at her for a good hour while Aileen paced the small kitchen, wringing her hands. Apparently Monty *had* noticed she was missing and thought it odd she would try to cross town on her own late at night with a broken wrist. He immediately called the police, but they said it wouldn't do any good to search until the following morning. Monty then set out to find her himself, to no avail. When he turned up at the apartment alone, her parents suspected the worst.

Asiah arrived home the next morning, and her father was fit to be tied. By way of explanation she said she had gone to Walter's where he offered to set her broken bone for her. She said she stayed at his office and walked home the next morning. She hated lying to her parents, but the truth was definitely not an option. She could tell Patrick was skeptical of her story, and he didn't push her, only eyed her disheveled appearance suspiciously. She made sure to keep her hand in her pocket so her father wouldn't ask to examine it.

"The girl I know wouldn't stay out all night and worry those who love her," Patrick said sternly. "And to stay with your fiancé unchaperoned? Disgraceful!"

Asiah gritted her teeth. "Because all men are randy, rutting pigs?" she shot back. "I'm home safe now, you don't have to worry about me anymore."

"I don't want you working at that club anymore. We'll find you another job where men know to keep their ruddy hands off you." With that, the subject was closed.

Asiah went to her room to clean up. She'd slept last night, but between what Chase had told her this morning and her father's scolding, she was completely drained. She pulled the shade on the small window in her room and fell into bed. She was asleep before her head touched the pillow.

The Forest was darker than usual this time. She couldn't see the sky through the trees, but it must have been overcast. There was a chill in the air, and the wind whispered a foreboding omen through the trees. The birds were gone; the wind was the only sound. Asiah shivered, rubbing the goose bumps on her arms. She wore only the ethereal blue dress that she always wore in the Forest, and it was not meant for cooler temperatures. *The weather has been so strange here of late,* she thought. She remembered the last time she was here and how she saw the man in the reflecting pool. *Chase. His name is Chase.*

She needed to know why the sun was gone and why this place that was normally so warm and comforting was now cold and gloomy. She recalled the way to the reflecting pool and started walking that direction. Dead leaves crunched beneath her bare feet. Gone were the soft beds of ivy from the forest floor. The pool was still when she reached it; the waterfall was gone, leaving a bare cliff face. She almost feared to look into the depths. She didn't know what she would see there. Something told her it wouldn't be good.

She made her way to the rocky outcropping over the water and carefully leaned over the edge, peering into the glassy water. She didn't see her own reflection this time, nor did she see any reflection at all. Instead, deep beneath the surface, she could see *him*. He was floating near the bottom of the pool, far beyond her reach. His eyes were closed as if he were sleeping peacefully. His long hair drifted around his face like dark flames. She squinted at his floating form and saw blood clouding the water from a wound on his neck.

Asiah tried to call his name but no sound came out. She moved to the edge of the outcropping, preparing to dive in after him. Her feet wouldn't move. She couldn't leave solid ground. Desperately looking around for a way to help him, she suddenly heard his voice on the breeze. It whispered through the trees and seemed to swirl around her. *Focus, Asiah. This is your mind, you can do anything here.*

She closed her eyes and imagined diving into the still water. She focused all her energy on doing this one task. Before she realized it was happening, she splashed headfirst into the cold water.

Asiah sat bolt upright in bed, gasping. Her sheets were tangled around her and a cold sweat tinged her brow. Through the thin window shade she could see the sun setting. *Chase.* She didn't know how she knew, but he needed help, and she was the only one who could help him.

She leapt from the bed searching for her trousers. Aileen must have taken them to be washed. Throwing open the closet, she shoved her few skirts and dresses aside. Why did women's fashion have to be so impractical when one was in a hurry? She found a pair of Monty's old dungarees in the back and threw them on, hastily tucking her shirt into them. Grabbing her pea coat, she dashed out of the apartment and down four flights of stairs to the street. She heard her father shouting after her, but she didn't stop. She'd have to deal with him later. Once outside, she froze, realizing in despair that she had no idea where Chase was. What if he were at his cottage and needed help? She didn't know how to get there.

He might be at his shop. It was the only lead she had. A young woman running down North Avenue in men's dungarees at night attracted more attention than she liked, but at the moment she didn't care. Breathless, she reached the shop doorway. The windows were dark and there was no other sign that anyone was there. She tried the door. The knob turned, but the door seemed wedged, like something was blocking it. Asiah sat down heavily on the stoop, still breathing hard from her run.

She leaned back against the door, trying to catch her breath and decide what to do next. Chase had said his cottage was outside the city limits. That didn't really narrow anything down; it would take her ages to find the place on her own. "Where are you, Chase?" she asked aloud. As if in response, she heard a muffled groan through the door.

She flew to her feet and pounded on the door. "Chase! Are you in there? Are you hurt?" Silence followed. She rattled the knob again and pushed against the door with all her might. She thought about going around to the back kitchen door and glanced toward the alley to her left. A few vagrants wandered the alley, digging through the refuse there. She knew her odds of making it through the alley to the back of the store unscathed were slim, especially now that the sun had gone down. And even if she made it, that door might be locked as well.

Asiah remembered what Chase had told her by the pond in her dream. It was her mind, she could do anything there. But this was the real world; she could no more control things here than she could avoid the drifters in the alley. But what if she could? Taking a deep breath, she gripped the doorknob again.

She closed her eyes and concentrated all her mind power on opening the door. After a moment, her hand hurt from gripping the knob and the door was still jammed. She was beginning to get desperate. Glancing toward the alley again, Asiah sighed in frustration. That way was blocked. She had to get through this door somehow.

She leaned her forehead against the door in defeat. "Help me, Chase," she whispered. "Help me so I can help you." She had all but given up when she heard a soft scraping sound, as if something had moved just inside the shop.

Asiah leaned back from the door, frowning, and tried the knob one more time. It turned easily in her hand and the door opened smoothly. Throwing the door open the rest of the way, Asiah ran blindly into the dark shop. The light from the street was not enough to illuminate the dark interior and she stopped short just inside the door.

"Chase?" she called, praying he was all right.

She heard a groan from a spot a few feet in front of her. She edged forward, not wanting to stumble over him, were he lying on the floor. Her foot touched something and she reached down with her hands to identify it. She felt the rough leather of a boot. Moving her hand forward she realized there was a foot inside the boot.

She knelt beside his body and searched for something to hold onto: a hand or his face. Blindly searching, her fingers brushed his hair. She held his face in her hands, recognizing the electric charge of her skin on his.

"Chase," she whispered, smoothing his hair back from his face. He moaned softly. She traced her fingers to the side of his throat, feeling for his pulse. His heart was beating normally, but when she pulled her fingers away they were sticky with what she could only imagine was blood.

Asiah needed to assess the damage; he was obviously injured. She didn't want to leave his side, but it was too dark to do anything for him. As she moved to stand, his hand gripped her wrist, gently tugging her back down.

"Don't ... leave me, love ..." he whispered weakly.

She could have cried in relief. "It's too dark. I need to look at your wound."

He swallowed with some difficulty. "Candle ... table ..."

He let her stand this time and she fumbled for the candle on the oak table in the back room. A moment later she'd managed to light it. Fortunately, there had been a book of matches right next to it. She brought the lit candle to where he lay and set it on the floor nearby.

A dark stain covered the skin of his neck and had bled onto his shoulder, staining his tunic. Asiah had rarely seen so much blood.

Chase blinked at her, trying to focus. He lifted a hand to cup her cheek. "I knew you'd find me, Asiah." He attempted to smile, but it was more of a wince. "I was afraid that she—" He stopped abruptly, as if he hadn't meant to tell her what he'd been afraid of.

Asiah took his hand from her face and held it between her hands, glancing fearfully at his neck wound. "You're still bleeding. You need a doctor. You must let me fetch one for you."

"No," he said, shaking his head slightly. "*You* will heal me. Just stay here with me."

"But ... I don't know how!" She was beginning to panic. "Please let me fetch the doctor," she pleaded.

"You are healing me already." His voice was stronger now. "Just don't let go." He squeezed her hand and closed his eyes.

Several moments passed and Chase's breathing slowed. Asiah thought maybe he'd fallen asleep, even though his grip on her hand remained strong. She felt something strange, like something deep inside her was being pulled to the surface.

"Chase ...?" she asked tentatively.

"Hmm?" He opened one green eye and looked at her.

"What are you doing?" she asked.

"I'm letting you heal me."

"But I'm not doing anything!" she said, confused.

He smiled and closed his eye again. "Yes, you are." He squeezed her hand in reassurance.

Another few moments passed and Chase inhaled deeply. He opened his eyes and exhaled forcefully. Letting go of her hand, he pushed himself up into a seated position next to where she was still kneeling. He leaned closer and stroked her cheek, gratitude shining in his eyes.

"I think you just saved my life, love," he said softly.

She bowed her head, fidgeting with a stray thread on her shirt. "I don't know about that."

Chase put his finger under her chin and tipped it up so he could look into her eyes. "I do, and you did." He closed the distance between them and brushed his lips against hers. It was the merest touch, asking permission. He leaned back an inch, gauging her reaction. She didn't know what to say, only knew that she wanted him to that again. She met his gaze and gave him the tiniest nod.

He didn't need any more than that. Sliding his hand around the back of her neck, he brought his mouth down on hers, his lips more insistent this time. His kiss was both passionate and gentle and Asiah had never felt anything like it, even with Walter. She touched Chase's chest, tentatively at first, then clutched at his stained tunic, pulling herself closer. He groaned and deepened the kiss until she was breathless. Breaking away abruptly, Chase began trailing kisses along her jaw. He nipped at the soft skin of her neck with his teeth until she moaned softly.

That seemed to bring him back to reality. His mouth stilled on her skin and he sighed against her neck. He lifted his head and rested his forehead against hers.

"I'm sorry, Asiah." She heard the regret in his voice. "We can't do this, and I shouldn't have kissed you." He sounded like he didn't believe his own words. He pushed himself off the floor and walked a few feet away, his back turned to her.

Asiah could see his anguish in his shoulders, but she was confused and a little wounded by his words. "Why not?"

He was silent for a moment, then said, "I can never be more than your teacher, Asiah. Let's leave it at that."

She didn't want to leave it at that, but she knew better than to push him further. He'd had a rough day, after all. She stood up and walked around in front of him. He looked at her questioningly as she inspected his neck wound. "We need to clean you up," she said matter-of-factly, hoping to change the mood a bit.

He seemed to snap back to reality. "Get some water from the kitchen," he instructed and pulled his tunic off over his head.

Asiah stood frozen, staring at his chest. She'd not seen that many men shirtless, and she was quite sure none of them looked like *this*. All lean muscle and sinew, his body bore the scars of many battles. Several of the scars looked like they must have been life-threatening wounds, and Asiah wondered how many times Chase had had to save his own life on the battlefield. The scars did nothing to quell the unexpected fluttering in her stomach, and Asiah thought that if men were formed in God's image, Chase Brandon was the epitome of that statement.

He noticed her staring at his chest and gently roused her from her reverie. "Asiah? The water?"

She jumped and blushed, scurrying off to the kitchen, returning a moment later with a bowl of water. Chase was sitting at the oak table tearing his ruined tunic into rags. She soaked the torn fabric in the water and wiped away the blood on his neck and shoulder. His eyes followed her every move. When the blood was gone, only a thin white scar remained on his neck.

Asiah realized she didn't even know what had happened as traced her finger over the scar. "Who did this to you?"

He caught her hand in his and placed it in her lap. His face was grim. He looked like he was struggling to control some emotion. Finally, he spoke.

"Things have changed. I thought we would have more time, but it has become apparent that your training must begin as soon as possible. Tomorrow." His tone brooked no argument.

"Oh. Will you not tell me what happened?" What was he keeping from her?

"I will tell you, but not tonight. For now, you need rest. I'll walk you home." He got up and headed for the loft. He returned wearing a clean shirt and jacket. "Come." He held out his hand. She took it and let him pull her out of her chair and lead her out onto the street.

They walked hand-in-hand in silence all the way to her apartment building. Asiah couldn't understand why he felt guilty about kissing her when he clearly had no problem holding her hand as they walked down North Avenue. She decided it wasn't the right moment to point it out, either. She kind of liked the way his large hand felt enveloping hers.

When they reached her building, she stopped him. "Thank you, but I can make it from here." She definitely didn't want to explain Chase's presence to her parents.

He shook his head. "I'm not letting you out of my sight until I know you're safe."

"But—" she protested.

He tightened his grip on her hand and dragged her toward the stairs. "Don't argue, love. I'm coming with you."

They reached her door and Asiah gave him a pleading look to which he shook his head again. She sighed and opened the door, dread filling her heart.

Chapter Ten

Chase and Asiah were met with a flurry of activity as soon as she opened the door. A young woman identical to Asiah rushed forward and wrapped her in a tight hug. Their mother followed, sobbing. Chase stood awkwardly aside waiting for the tide of emotions to ebb while he glanced around the small apartment. The small kitchen took up half the main room, leaving only enough space for two tattered armchairs near the wood stove in the corner. The rug was worn with several holes revealing the splintered floorboards beneath. Two doors led off the main room, presumably one bedroom for Asiah's parents and one for her and her sister. How did someone so important to the world live in such miserable conditions?

When the women had calmed down, it was Mr. O'Connor who spoke next. "Well, let's hear the wild tale of the *cailín* who ran away from her family and returned in the middle of the night with some vagrant in tow." He shot a derisive look at Chase.

Chase frowned at the word "vagrant" but didn't speak. He assumed that Asiah could handle her father.

"Father, this is Mr. Brandon. He owns the knife shop." She didn't explain further.

Chase held out his hand to Mr. O'Connor. "Your daughter is a hard worker, sir."

O'Connor wasn't buying it and ignored Chase's hand. "Don't be smart with me, boy. Asiah left the knife shop three days ago. Now, tell me what's really going on here."

The man was smart and deserved a straight answer. While Chase couldn't tell him the truth, he could tell the man what he wanted to hear.

"The truth is, sir, I'm here to ask for your blessing to court your daughter." He slid his arm around Asiah's waist and heard her give a tiny gasp.

O'Connor stared. "You want to marry her, too?"

Too? What was the man talking about? "Are there others vying for the privilege?"

Asiah shifted away from him uncomfortably. "I told Mr. Brandon what happened at Monty's club, and we decided it would be safer for me to go back to work for him." She paused and looked at Chase. "I didn't know of his intentions to court me."

"I hinted at it earlier," Chase said, dropping his gaze to her lips.

She looked away, her face suffusing with color. "I'm engaged to another."

Her words hit him like a punch in the face. How could she let him kiss her the way he did and not tell him she was engaged? Jealousy threatened to overtake him until he remembered that *he* was the one who stopped the kiss from going too far. And certainly not because he'd wanted to.

A tense silence followed. Asiah's face was still red and she was poking at a splinter in the floor with her shoe.

Her older brother chose that moment to enter the apartment. His eyes grew wide when he saw Chase. "You're that bloody Brit from the club! Get away from me sis!" Her brother lunged for Chase, but Asiah stepped between them. Chase noticed she kept her healed hand in her pocket so as not to arouse suspicion from her brother.

"Move, Cricket," the Irishman growled.

"No, Monty, he's not who you think he is," Asiah said desperately.

"You mean to tell me he didn't cause the biggest ruckus my club has seen in weeks? Asiah, he pulled a *knife* on Johnny Cavendish!" Monty exclaimed.

"The man touched her inappropriately," Chase struggled to keep his voice even. "*Someone* had to do something." He eyed Monty darkly.

"I suppose you think you're the man to do it?" Monty stepped forward in challenge, but the top of his head barely reached Chase's chin.

Asiah stepped between them again, placing a hand on Monty's shoulder. "Monty, Cha— Mr. Brandon did what he thought was right and no one got seriously hurt. Why don't we let him get home and we can all go to bed?"

"I couldn't agree more," Chase said. He needed time to think about what he'd just learned, and he still had to prepare for tomorrow. Asiah would be safe here with her family. With a last look at her, he left, closing the door with a snap. He'd descended five steps when he heard the door open behind him.

"Chase, wait!" Asiah called after him.

He turned and didn't give her a chance to explain. "Why didn't you tell me you were engaged to be married?" he demanded.

She stopped one step above his so they were eye to eye. "I didn't realize it was any of your business." She gave him a defensive glare.

He lowered his voice in case her family was listening through the door. "You should have told me before I kissed you."

Her eyes blazed. "Which you said you shouldn't have done in the first place! And it's not like we had a chance to discuss it beforehand!"

"That's not the point!" he hissed. "I would never have done it at all if I'd known you belonged to another."

"Why *did* you do it then?" She crossed her arms and regarded him defiantly.

Indeed, why? He tried to stare her down, but she was doing a fine job of it herself. Finally he said, "You didn't tell me about your engagement, so why should I tell you why I kissed you?"

She opened her mouth to speak and closed it again with a growl of frustration.

He grinned in spite of himself. Against his better judgment he pulled her close and pressed his lips to her forehead. "Tomorrow," he whispered against her skin, then trotted down the stairs. He could feel the heat of her glare on his back.

He stopped in the street, taking a deep breath to clear his mind. He wasn't sure he had the strength to channel to his cabin, but he needed to make sure he had everything ready to begin Asiah's training. There was so much to prepare, he knew he probably wouldn't sleep tonight. He inhaled deeply again and visualized the cottage in the woods, then vanished in a flash of green light.

※

Asiah saw the green flash outside the window and knew that he was gone. Inside her apartment everyone was arguing at once. She sat numbly at the kitchen table, letting the chaos reign around her. She loved her family, but she realized that she didn't care what they thought of Chase or the fact that she wanted to go back to work for him. It was the only thing they might actually believe. They'd never believe the truth about her. *She* barely believed it herself. She was aware that marrying Walter would complicate things if she was to begin training with Chase. Luckily, the wedding would not be until next spring, so she had time to figure things out.

Chase said he wanted her to be safe. Had someone hurt him to get to her? She couldn't imagine anyone who would want to hurt her. Until that morning she had believed she was no more important than anyone else. She'd slept most of the day, but realized that she was still exhausted. Helping Chase had physically taken a lot out of her and her sleep schedule had been too erratic lately. While her parents continued to argue and Monty tried to raise his voice over theirs, she slipped off to her bedroom.

Meri was sitting up in bed with tearstained cheeks.

"Don't cry, they'll wear themselves out soon," Asiah nodded toward the kitchen.

"It's not that. I thought now that you've accepted Walter's proposal that men would start leaving you alone. I thought that maybe we could both be married together ... but every man in the world wants to be with you, and no one ..." she trailed off.

Asiah had done most things before Meri: walking, talking, learning to read and write, but Meri always had her eye on the boys. Asiah hadn't cared about boys or kissing – that was until Chase had showed her how wonderful it could truly be. Meri had been lovesick over some boy or another since they'd come to America. Asiah realized how much it must hurt her sister to see two men vying for Asiah's attention at once, even if the attention was unwanted.

Asiah climbed onto Meri's bed and held her sister's hands. "Can I tell you a secret, Meri?"

Her twin nodded with a sniffle.

Asiah leaned closer conspiratorially. "Mr. Brandon is tutoring me in science because I can't attend college. I think he just told Father he wants to court me because he thought that's what Father would want to hear. I hadn't told him about Walter."

Meri looked confused. "So he doesn't want to marry you?"

"No," Asiah said, smiling at her sister.

"He's ... available then?" Meri's eyes took on a dreamy quality at her words and Asiah felt an unfamiliar pang of jealousy.

Asiah snapped her fingers in front of Meri's nose and she jumped. "I didn't say that. He's *much* too old for you anyway."

"He didn't look that old."

"Well, he is." *And he's mine.* Where had that unbidden thought come from? Asiah was engaged to Walter, and she mustn't forget that, no matter how much Chase's kisses had made her head spin earlier.

"Is he very successful?" Meri didn't want to let it go yet, apparently.

"I suppose he is. His shop is still open, despite the Depression."

"Well, whether or not you're courting him, he's terribly handsome."

Asiah rolled her eyes and climbed off the bed and sat down on hers. She began brushing her hair, which, as usual, was full of knots. She thought that she really should braid it more often.

Meri was murmuring something about "his broad shoulders and square jawline" and Asiah turned out the light and rolled away from her sister's dreamy musings.

She was nervous and excited about tomorrow. She touched a finger to her lips, remembering the way his kiss sent jolts of blissful electricity throughout her body. Then she remembered Walter, whom she was supposed to marry, but his kisses never made her feel anything like Chase's did. On the other hand, Walter offered her financial security and a chance to achieve her dream. Chase was offering to teach her magic tricks. She smiled in the dark at the ridiculousness of the situation. She'd have to give some real thought to her future now more than ever. Two paths lay ahead of her: the safe road was to marry Walter and maybe go to medical school someday. The risky path was to trust Chase and learn how to do the things he could do. Was there any future in that? He said something about her having to save the world from itself. It seemed too grandiose for a girl from Inishmor. She still wasn't sure Chase wasn't crazy. He had done some amazing things right in front of her eyes, things she couldn't explain by any rational means. She closed her eyes and told herself that in the morning, she'd wake up with a clear head and know exactly what she was going to do. At least she hoped so.

Chase paced the street in front of Asiah's apartment the next morning, debating whether to retrieve her or continue waiting for her on the street. He didn't want to risk upsetting Asiah's family again by appearing at the door, yet he was anxious to get started. He hadn't slept because of all the preparation he needed to do. He spent the majority of the night establishing various electromagnetic fields around his cottage to shield their activities from anyone sensitive to energy spikes in a concentrated area, such as Marysa. If she could sense that Chase had found Asiah, it wouldn't be difficult for the Shade to find out where he was training her.

Chase knew he wouldn't have slept anyway after Asiah's startling revelation. He was inordinately depressed that she was engaged to be married, and had to remind himself several times throughout the night that he had no more claim to her than anyone other than her betrothed. Even so, his mood was buoyant this morning because he'd get to spend the entire day with Asiah. He would get to show her things that made her face light up like it did when he'd healed her wrist.

His spirits dimmed somewhat when he considered that he didn't know how much time he had before Marysa would resurface. He hadn't yet had a chance to figure out where she had come from. It was obvious she was a Shade like Asiah, but in all his readings, nothing was written about there ever being more than one offspring of an Ikhäle. He'd read about Phantom Shades, and the thought that Marysa might be one was enough to set Chase's nerves on edge. Tojen had not said anything about anyone ever being banished to Earth. If she were the offspring of a banished Ikhäle, her sire would have arrived on Earth after Tojen had died. Or had Chase's mentor actually produced two offspring? It didn't matter. Clearly Marysa was evil, which meant she had no plans on helping the human race and must not be allowed to coexist with Asiah.

More often than not, when Shades learned how to use their powers, their greed for power overcame their sense of purpose and doomed the people of the world to extinction. The fully developed Ikhälean worlds were few, hence the drive to create new worlds where their race could evolve and thrive.

Being human, Chase did not know enough about how other worlds of times long past survived their evolutionary journeys, and he suspected that Earth was headed down a very dark path. He'd lived through the Dark Ages, and if any world could recover from something like that and evolve into the perfect world of the future, he'd be very surprised. Even centuries later, one of the most powerful countries on Earth was suffering through a debilitating economic depression, one that it would take quite a while to recover from. He only hoped he could do his part by instructing Asiah in the ways of energy manipulation so she could do her part and save humanity, however lost the cause may be.

Chase was saved from his decision of whether to fetch Asiah as she bounded out the door onto the street a moment later.

"Good morning," she said tiredly. She was wearing her awful trousers again with a gray shirt that looked like it had been handed down from her older brother. After seeing her in the red silk dress at the club, it was hard for Chase not to imagine her in more enticing attire. If he didn't have so many other things on his mind, a lot of his spare time would be dedicated to imagining her in such clothing ... or less.

As wonderful as that thought was, he shook it off and raised a dark brow at her. "Sleep well?"

She shrugged. "Not really. You?"

"Not a wink."

Reaching up with both hands to massage her neck, Asiah bit her lip as if unsure what to say. "Listen, before we get going this morning, I need you to know something."

Chase frowned, certain she was about to call off the training. "What is it?"

She huffed out a breath. "I know I haven't been very receptive to the things you've shown me, but you need to know that I believe everything you've told me is true."

His brows shot up. "How did you come to this conclusion?"

Asiah glanced away, looking frustrated. "Every time I let myself believe in it, it just feels right. I don't know how to explain it, but it's like my mind knows the truth. When I try to find an explanation for why it *can't* be true, I feel ... heavier. Like the weight of the lie is pushing me down." She looked up at him. "Does that make any sense to you?"

"It does," he replied. "I believe that you are correct when you say you mind knows the truth. It makes sense that your entire being would feel better – lighter – when you accept it. You are an intelligent woman, Asiah. You must learn to trust your instincts."

Her mouth curved into a half-smile. "Is that lesson number one?"

Chase smiled and took her hand, pulling her toward the alley. "If you like. How did your parents respond to you coming with me today?"

She shrugged. "They think I'm going to work at your shop."

"Don't they think it's strange since you're to be married soon?"

Her smile faded. "I have to work until the wedding. I can't expect Walter to support me before then."

"Ah. Is that why you're marrying him? For financial support?" Chase hoped his relief didn't show on his face.

She looked torn. "I am fond of him as well."

Chase smiled. "I'm not judging your decision. At least it's a practical one."

"He loves me," she said flatly. "It's not just an arrangement for him."

He nodded, unsure what to say next, so instead he squeezed her hand and pulled her deeper into the alley. "Hold on."

Chase landed on his feet as always, but Asiah hadn't gotten the hang of traveling this way yet. The other times he had channeled with her, he'd steadied her. This time, though, she needed to feel what it was like to land on her own and he released her hand as soon as his feet touched the ground. Chase suppressed a smirk when she stumbled backward, landing hard on her backside.

He stood over her and held out a hand to help her up. "Like everything, channeling takes practice. Landing after channeling takes even more." He smiled at her.

She dusted herself off. "Channeling. So that's what it's called. Let's start with that."

Chase beamed at her eagerness. "Not yet, love. Let's start at the beginning."

∽

That morning, Asiah had woken up feeling more sure of Chase than Walter. She didn't know why, but her instincts told her that Chase held the key to her future. She figured there was no reason she couldn't still marry Walter and work with Chase as well, as long as Chase didn't try to kiss her again.

"Sit," Chase gestured to his large table and disappeared into the bedroom. He returned with a small wooden chest covered in intricate carvings. He set it down on the table before her and took the seat opposite her, rolling up his sleeves as he sat down. "Do you know why I wear these bracelets?"

Asiah shook her head, trying not to stare at his muscular forearms.

"Manipulating force and matter on a molecular level takes immense control and strength. Each atom must be precisely maneuvered. This type of control is very exhausting, and this is why you've never been aware of your abilities to do these things. There are elements and substances on this planet that, like the Ikhälea, have changed and evolved over many, many years and can be used as sources of power for people like us. You know these as gemstones, but they are so much more than just pretty rocks." He removed one of his bracelets by undoing an elaborate clasp. His wrist began to bleed where the bracelet had just rested.

"You're bleeding!" she exclaimed, moving to get up. He stayed her with a look.

He laid the bracelet on the table in front of her. Along the inside of the bracelet were several small green stones: peridots. Attached to the clasp was another peridot. This one was elongated with a sharp point. Asiah could see blood on the tip of the stone.

"The peridot is my power stone. When in contact with my vital source, blood, my power is nearly limitless. This is why I wear these all the time. They also make my eyes green." He blinked flirtatiously and she laughed, enjoying this playful side of him.

"What color are your eyes normally?" she asked.

"It's been so long since I've seen my natural eye color, I've forgotten. Why don't you tell me?" He took off his other bracelet and looked up at her.

His eyes faded to a stormy gray, completely different than the bright green she was used to, but no less appealing.

"Gray," she said, "like the North Atlantic after a storm." She looked down, embarrassed, and heard him snap his bracelets back on. He gave a small groan of discomfort as the stones pierced his skin.

"I'm not sure anyone has ever described them that way to me before," Chase said as he opened the small chest in front of her. It was full of different gemstones of all colors and sizes. There was an emerald, amethyst, ruby, as well as different shades of pearls, turquoise, malachite, carnelian and goldstone. There were a hundred different stones or more inside.

"Give me your hand," he instructed.

She reached her hand across the table. He took it and held it palm up. With his other hand he drew a knife from his belt. Her eyes grew wide and she struggled not to pull her hand away.

"Don't worry. Just a small cut." He drew the blade across the tip of her forefinger, drawing blood. She winced. "Now," he said, "touch each of the stones here to your fingertip until you find your power stone."

Asiah did as she was told, pressing each stone into the cut on her finger. She felt silly, especially after she'd tried about thirty stones and nothing had happened.

"How will I know which stone it is? None of these are making me feel any different," she said.

"You will know." He looked deep in thought, then pulled an onyx from the chest. "Try this one."

She pressed the black stone to her bleeding finger and immediately dropped it. Her finger burned where her blood has touched the stone. She glanced up at his reaction. "Was that it? It burned my finger."

Chase frowned. "No, that's not it, but I think I know which one is." He rummaged through the chest and withdrew a dark blue stone: a sapphire. He dropped it in her hand, then sat back, holding his breath.

Asiah rolled the stone around in her palm, suddenly anxious. She looked at Chase, and he nodded with his thumbnail between his teeth. She held the stone tightly between her thumb and forefinger of her left hand, then, taking a deep breath, touched her right finger to the sapphire.

Stars exploded in her vision, and her heart began to pound. Her breathing became more rapid and she thought she might faint again. It felt like every cell in her body had suddenly come alive with some unknown energy force. She heard Chase's voice distantly, through the ringing in her ears.

"Let go, Asiah. Put the stone down." She felt him pull the rock from her fingers and the feeling subsided. Still breathless, Asiah gulped air and tried to slow her pounding heart.

"W-was that it?" she asked, panting.

"Yes, love, that was it," he said, distracted. "I need to fetch something for you now. Stay here and catch your breath. I'll return in a moment." He walked outside and she saw him vanish in a green flash.

Asiah inspected her finger. The small cut had almost completely healed. That was odd, but then everything she'd been going through in the last week was far from normal.

Chase reappeared a few moments later, covered in dust. His hair had come loose from its tie and hung wildly about his shoulders. He dropped into the chair across from her and pulled a pouch from his belt, shaking its contents onto the table: two jagged shards of blue rock.

"Where did you just go?" Asiah asked, still having trouble wrapping her mind around the concept of channeling.

"Australia," Chase answered. "To a sapphire mine." He ran his hands through his hair and pulled it back into a short ponytail.

Asiah raised an eyebrow at his appearance.

Chase shrugged. "They don't like being robbed." He grinned mischievously, then retrieved another pouch from his belt and pulled out two silver bracelets. He picked up one of the blue shards and examined it. "I'll need to hone these down for better connectivity, but they'll do the trick for now." He inserted the shard through an opening in the bracelet and secured it, repeating the process with the other bracelet. He closed the jewel chest and pushed it out of the way. "Hands," he commanded gently and Asiah stretched her arms out across the table. He slid a silver band over each wrist and pushed the clasps almost all the way closed. Asiah could feel the sharp ends of the rough stones pushing against the skin on the underside of her wrists. Her heart began to beat faster.

"Ready?" Chase asked.

"No," Asiah shook her head, knowing she didn't really have a choice at this point.

"Neither was I," Chase admitted and snapped the bracelets closed.

The feeling she felt before was a drop in the bucket compared to the tidal wave of adrenaline that rushed throughout her body as the sapphire shards plunged into her veins. She thought her head would explode with the bright flashes she was seeing and the roaring in her ears. She squeezed her eyes shut and gritted her teeth. She knew if she just held on a little longer she could make it through this. She thought she heard Chase speaking, but couldn't understand what he was saying. All she could hear was someone screaming and she realized the sound was coming from her own mouth.

A moment later she opened her eyes to see Chase staring at her wide-eyed. He had a death-grip on her hands, probably to keep her from convulsing. She felt slightly dizzy.

"Alright there, love?" Chase's voice was shaking just a little.

She nodded and he reluctantly let go of her hands. She looked around the cottage. Everything was brighter, more vivid. Her body felt tingly all the way to her toes. She looked across the room at the mantel and spied a weevil creeping along the wall. She could hear its tiny footsteps as it crept along.

Her eyes are blue ... and so beautiful ... She heard Chase's voice, but he wasn't speaking. She frowned at him.

"You look beautiful in blue," he said.

"I heard you say that ... just now, before you said it aloud."

His eyes went wide and he looked sheepish. "Didn't I tell you it's not polite to read others' minds without permission?"

"I-I'm sorry! I didn't know I was doing that. I heard your voice inside my head – just like before, when you came to the drugstore and the glass shattered."

He nodded knowingly.

It was the strangest feeling and Asiah was having trouble concentrating on all the things the stones brought into her awareness. "Are my eyes really blue?"

Chase fetched a small mirror from a cupboard nearby. "See for yourself."

She looked at her reflection. Her eyes *were* blue: a dark indigo shade that matched her power stone. She inspected her face in the mirror. Except for her eyes, she looked exactly the same, but now she could see more of herself. Every pore and eyelash was clearly visible in great detail. She put the mirror face down on the table and pushed it away.

Chase laughed. "I didn't want to look at myself right away, either. Too much detail can be a bit disturbing."

Asiah nodded, still not used to the prickly sensation all over her body. She was ready to move on to something else and hopefully take her mind off the pins and needles. "You seemed troubled when I found the right stone. Is it not a good stone to have?"

Chase shook his head. "The sapphire is a very potent power stone. The only power stone that carries more power is a diamond. The sapphire will serve you well. It's somewhat similar to the onyx, which is also very powerful. I met someone once who used an onyx and it tends to lead those who use it down a dark path." He absently touched the scar on his throat.

"But not sapphires?" she asked, fully intending to confront him about the scar again.

"Not to my knowledge, but I've never known a Conjurer who used them." As if he sensed her next question, he quickly changed the subject. "Let's move on to some *real* magic."

Chapter Eleven

It was a breezy, unusually cool August day. *A good day to learn*, Chase thought. He felt guilty for not being forthcoming to Asiah about Marysa. She was onto him, too. She was smart enough to see he was keeping something from her, and he could see she was dying to find out what it was. But it wasn't time yet. Asiah hadn't even had her first lesson. How could she defend herself against a Phantom Shade like Marysa? It was with grim determination that he led Asiah outside. He was going to have to stop being so gentle with her, especially now that she had access to her power. He knew in his heart that she was the answer to the world's problems, he just needed to show her the way.

Standing together in the clearing in front of his cottage, Chase noticed Asiah's hand-me-down shirt again and the fact that it was much too big on her and would be a fire hazard. He reached out and pulled her shirt from where it was tucked into her trousers.

"What are you doing?!" she squeaked, trying to pull away from him.

"Hold still, love. You don't want your clothes to catch fire, do you?" He pulled the loose fitting material tightly around her body and knotted it at her navel. As he tied, his fingers brushed against her flat belly, causing her to shiver. He glanced up at the terrified look on her face. *This woman is going to be the death of me,* he thought, and tugged her into his arms to nuzzle her hair. "You can do this, Asiah. I know you can," he whispered. She remained silent and he released her, looking into her blue eyes. "Ready, love?"

Asiah closed her eyes and took a deep breath. When she opened her eyes again, he could see steely resolve shimmering in their depths. "I'm ready."

Chase smiled wickedly. "It won't be easy and I'm going to push you hard."

She set her shoulders and lifted her chin. "Good."

He nodded and walked about ten paces away. "Now, defend yourself!" he called and threw his hand into the air. She was thrown backward and hit the ground on her back, the wind knocked out of her. It was only a small push, to get her warmed up. "Up!" he shouted. She staggered to her feet, unsure what to do. He hit her harder the second time, sending her flying through the air before she hit the ground. He knew her body could handle the assault, and if she was sore later he'd give her something for the pain.

She got to her feet again, looking a little less bewildered and a little more irritated. *Good,* he thought, *now she'll start fighting back.*

He didn't get a chance to throw another push because she threw first. It was a weak push and he only stumbled backward a step, but a look of triumph came over her face. She'd picked that up more quickly than he'd expected. This time, he heated the air around his hand, creating a ball of green flame. Asiah's look of triumph vanished as he hurled the fireball at her. Instead of blocking the attack, she dove to the side. She rolled to her feet and threw another push, harder this time.

Chase blocked the push and threw two more fireballs, one from each hand. Asiah tried to dodge again just as she was hit in the leg. She looked down in horror at her burning trousers, then looked to Chase for help, her eyes pleading.

It took every fiber of his being not to put the fire out himself as he stood his ground and shook his head. He saw the hurt flash in her gaze a second before she hit the ground and began rolling to put the fire out. He needed her to stop thinking like a human and start fighting like a Shade. At this rate, her clothing would be burned away by the end of the day. *And what's the problem with that?* his subconscious asked. He thrust the thought aside and launched more fire at her.

    She rolled to the side, dodging the onslaught. She pushed herself to her feet, eyes blazing. He opened his hand to create another spark, but this time the air wouldn't ignite. He also suddenly found it was becoming difficult to breathe. He thrust more heat to his palm but still no flame. He began gasping for air and looked across the clearing at her. She stood with her arms outstretched and a look of intense concentration on her face. Sparkles started to flicker in his vision and he realized what she was doing. Asiah was removing all of the oxygen from the air around him. It's why he couldn't produce a flame and why he was about to ...

    Chase opened his eyes to see her face hovering above his. *What a nice way to wake up,* he thought. Asiah looked entirely too pleased with herself. "Have a nice nap, did we?"

    He couldn't let her insolence pass. With an evil grin, he tackled her without warning, pinning her hands above her head with one of his. His other hand pinned her hip to the ground beneath him so she was immobilized. "Now who's lying around?" he said in a low rumble.

    The shock on her face evaporated instantly and her eyes twinkled. She lifted her head off the ground and pressed a soft kiss to his lips. He definitely hadn't expected *that*. She pulled away while he was still reeling and brought her knee up between his legs. Hard.

    Chase howled in pain and released her, seeing stars for the second time that day. He rolled onto his back, trying to use his power to make the pain subside. It wasn't working.

    "Chase!" Asiah shrieked, kneeling beside him. "I'm so sorry! Are you alright? I didn't know that would happen. Tell me if you're alright!"

"I'll be alright in a minute, love," he ground out, taking some deep breaths. "That was a brilliant move, by the way. Where did you learn to do that?"

"The dancers at Monty's club told me I should have done that to the man who squeezed— who touched me."

"Remind me not to let you kiss me like *that* again." He tried to smile but grimaced instead. He slowly pushed himself up into a seated position with a groan. "Since we're taking a breather, maybe we should go over some of the finer points of your assault."

"I won, right?" She still thought she'd gotten the best of him ... and in a way she had. If it hadn't been for that kiss.

Why *had* she kissed him anyway? What about what's-his-name? Walter?

Chase snorted. "You bested me this once, but it won't happen again. I underestimated your ... hatred of men."

"I don't hate men!" Asiah protested.

"You pressed your sweet lips to mine and then did the most heinous thing a person can do to a man, and you don't qualify *that* as hatred?" he teased.

"It *was* effective," she said.

"Perhaps, but there are better ways to best a foe using your powers. I applaud your innovation, especially removing the oxygen from the air ... and your use of your knee," he nodded at her leg. His eyes widened at the sight of her burnt trousers and reddened skin underneath. He cursed under his breath and tore the singed material away. He smoothed his hand along her leg, healing the burned skin with his touch. Perhaps they should have covered healing before fire-throwing, but Chase didn't exactly have a lesson plan. He only hoped he could teach Asiah enough to survive before it was too late.

∽

Asiah bit her lip and let Chase brush his hand gently over the scorched skin. His touch was like a cool cloth calming the angry burn. She hadn't realized how much her leg hurt until this moment.

"Ahh ..." she sighed, and his hand stilled on her leg.

"Does that feel better? You should be doing this yourself," he said and continued to massage her calf.

"You haven't shown me how yet," she quipped.

"You've studied biology, right? You surely know how cell regeneration works." His fingers traced the skin at the back of her knee and her stomach flipped over again.

"Of course. I also learned a lot about anatomy from Walter. Mmm ..." His fingers were incredibly distracting.

He frowned slightly at the mention of Walter's name and continued, "It's a matter of focusing your mind on specific cells and speeding up the process of regeneration. It's easy for things like this." His thumb grazed her inner thigh.

Asiah pressed her lips together to stifle a moan. Whatever he was doing had passed the point of healing and had become something else entirely – and Asiah couldn't bring herself to stop him.

Chase glanced up and gave her a sly smile. "It's more difficult when the wound involves several types of tissue, naturally." His hand stopped moving on her thigh. "Shall I continue?"

Asiah suffered a moment of confusion. Did he mean his explanation or his tantalizing caress of her leg? *What does it matter?* "Yes, please."

Chase gave her a dark, smoldering look that made her melt inside. He dropped his eyes to her lips, then squeezed them shut with a frustrated sigh.

"You tie me up in knots, love," he said, shaking his head.

"I'm sorry." She wasn't sure why she was apologizing. He "tied her up in knots," too.

"No," he placed his finger over her lips, "don't ever apologize for being who you are." He ran his thumb across her bottom lip. "I'm the one who needs to stop taking advantage of you. I have a feeling your fiancé would disapprove."

He looked torn for a moment, and Asiah wondered what he was thinking about. Before she could ask him he let out a groan.

"I just can't keep my bloody hands off you."

He smoothly pulled her to the ground and seized her mouth with his. His kiss was more urgent than before, like he couldn't get enough of her. He pressed his thumb against her chin, opening her mouth wider. He slid his tongue along her lips and boldly explored her mouth before raining kisses down her neck and along her collar bone. He sat up momentarily, holding the collar of her old shirt in both hands. In one swift movement, he tore the fabric down to where it was knotted at her navel, leaving her with only her camisole and half-burned trousers. Asiah opened her mouth to utter a half-hearted protest, but he silenced her with another fiery look. All thoughts of Walter vanished from her mind completely as if her fiancé didn't exist.

Satisfied with his work, Chase continued kissing her collar bone, working his way down to the valley between her breasts. The sensations were too much for her. She thought she might die of pleasure. A tiny voice in her head, most likely her cursed conscience, piped up at that moment to remind her that she was engaged to another and she barely knew this man. This man who was supposed to be nothing more than her teacher – and also happened to be seven centuries older than she was.

"Chase ..." she managed to choke out between sighs.

"Yes, love?" He pulled her camisole down on one side to reveal her breast.

"I ... think we should ..." He captured her nipple in his mouth and sucked. The electric sensation of his touch tripled and her mind went blank.

"Should what, love?" His hand was kneading the other breast. This had to stop.

"S-stop ... Chase ... please ..." She found her voice finally. "Yes ... stop, we should stop this before it goes too far!" She held his head between her hands and lifted his face from his wonderful assault.

Chase glared at her for a moment before his expression softened. He sighed and sat up. "You're quite the voice of reason, aren't you, love?"

"Someone should be." She pulled the scraps of her torn shirt together in a vain attempt to cover herself.

Chase reached for his discarded jacket and draped it over her shoulders. "Come inside, I'll help you mend it."

Asiah wrapped the jacket around herself and stood unsteadily. Chase touched her elbow and steered her toward the small house.

Once inside, he turned his back so she could remove the torn shirt and re-cover herself with his jacket. She sat at the table examining the torn garment.

"Do you think you can mend it?" he asked her.

"Do you have a needle and thread?" she replied, wondering if they were going to discuss what had just happened outside or not.

"I do, but I want you to mend it without those things." He went to a large, wooden chest near the stove and started rummaging through it, humming softly to himself. Apparently they were not going to address the elephant in the room.

"Oh." She peered at the torn fabric again. Her eyes watered for a moment, from the strain, she guessed. She wiped her eyes and looked closer. She could see the individual fibers that had come apart from each other, and placed the torn edges together and focused on re-weaving them together with her mind. She managed to make the fibers wiggle a little, but no more than that. She sighed in frustration. "It's a good thing you're a patient man, because I can't even do the simplest task yet."

She thought she heard him mutter something about running out of time, and decided not to question it. She turned back to the shirt. She placed a fingertip on the tear and closed her eyes. She concentrated as hard as she could with every fiber of her being. She opened her eyes and inspected the fabric again. Still nothing. With an exasperated groan she used the one power she seemed to have mastered to throw the torn shirt across the room and into the fire Chase had just started in the stove.

He lifted an eyebrow. "What exactly are you going to wear home now, love?"

She glared at him, silently cursing her impulsiveness.

He rose and walked behind her chair and began to massage her taut muscles. "You're distracted. Your mind isn't clear before you attempt your task. That is why you fail."

"*You're* the one distracting me!" she burst out. Pushing back from the table, she walked a few feet away from him and his electrifying touch. "I can't focus on anything when you keep touching me and kissing me and ... and ..." She couldn't even form a coherent argument while his intense gaze scoured her body. She turned her back to him to look out the window. "I don't see how this is ever going to work."

He sighed. "You're right. I'm forgetting how important your training is and thinking only of myself and what I want. If there was someone else who could train you I'd send you to them, but I'm the only one who can do it." He was silent for a moment. "I promise not to touch or distract you anymore. There are far more important things to worry about."

Like her fiancé. Whose name she couldn't remember at the moment. She stared out the window for a long moment, trying to rein in her warring emotions. Chase didn't speak, but she could feel his gaze from where he stood behind her. It wasn't only his fault, Asiah realized. *She* had been just as willing to let him touch her in exactly all the right ways. It terrified her to think what it would be like between her and Chase if her mission to save humanity didn't stand in between them. The thought alone made her blush furiously.

"Why don't we try some mind-clearing exercises?" he suggested, and Asiah wondered if he'd seen what had been running through her head seconds earlier.

She nodded awkwardly. "Yes. That sounds like a good idea."

Chase moved the chairs from in front of the stove, creating an open space on the floor. He sat down cross-legged and motioned for her to do the same. She was starting to be too warm in his jacket and she removed it, now wearing only her camisole. She figured he'd already seen everything underneath it, so why shouldn't she be comfortable? His eyes widened when he saw what she was wearing, but he wisely didn't say anything.

When she was seated across from him, he took her hands in his, his touch no longer warm and inviting, but firm and businesslike.

"Close your eyes, lov— Asiah," he instructed. "Go to that forest in your mind where you feel safe and calm. Take some deep breaths with me."

She did as he bade, inhaling deeply through her nose, imagining that one place where she felt safe and in control. Suddenly she was there, more vividly than usual. She could feel her body still sitting on the floor of Chase's cottage, and she could also feel the breeze and the sunlight of the Forest. Something was different here. Not like in her dream when it was dark and dying, but like the dream before, where everything seemed to glow. She touched the trunk of a nearby tree and saw tiny blue stones inlaid in the bark. They twinkled in the sunlight.

"I've never seen someone's mind so beautifully imagined," Chase said. She whirled around and saw him leaning against a tree. He was wearing a black linen tunic and loose-fitting black pants. A thin leather belt circled his waist. His hair was loose and blowing in the breeze. He was barefoot and looked positively delicious.

"How are you ...?" she began, thrusting aside thoughts of Chase's handsomeness.

"Here? Our minds are joined at the moment, we're just using your subconscious as the setting," he explained. "I want to show you some things you don't know about your own mind."

It was strange, having Chase give her a tour of her own subconscious. He showed her the reflecting pool, which she'd already experienced, hidden caves where secrets could be kept, a footbridge that crossed a small stream and led into a dark thicket that Chase said held her memories, and a small brick building that was much larger on the inside than it looked from the outside. The building was a library, housing all the knowledge Asiah had gained in her life. She was embarrassed that there seemed to be only a few books on the shelves. She was only 21, but surely she had gained more knowledge than just a few books worth.

Chase noticed her frowning at the volumes. "What's wrong?"

"I thought I knew more than—" She waved her hand at the few books, "—*this*."

"You will. You are still so young. All this space will be filled before you know it." He gestured to the empty rows of shelves.

"Is your library full?" she asked.

"I'll show you." He walked to a door in the library wall and pushed it open.

On the other side was a vast chamber with ceilings higher than any Asiah had ever seen. *Millions* of books lined the pristine shelves as far as she could see in all directions.

When she recovered from her shock, all she could say was, "You know ... a *lot*."

Chase chuckled. "Seven and a half centuries is a long time to learn about the world."

As she was reminded of the difference between their ages, Asiah couldn't imagine how he would ever find her and her tiny library of knowledge an object of attraction. He must have met so many beautiful women over the centuries. The thought made Asiah feel even smaller.

Chase misread her frown. "Don't worry, you will someday have a library even more vast than this." He led her back through the door.

They stepped outside into the sunlight and he led the way down a winding path toward a small lake surrounded by weeping willows.

"How do you know where everything is in my head?" she asked, bewildered.

"Everyone's minds are structured similarly, plus I popped in once before, remember? To learn your name." He smiled, as if recalling a fond memory.

He stopped when they reached the water's edge and pointed at something in the lake's center. "Do you see that mossy boulder in the middle of the water?"

She nodded.

"*That* is where you go to clear your mind. You will forget everything around you; everything that troubles you or distracts you from your purpose. It is here you must come before you will be able to use your powers to your full potential. Go there now, and I will wait for you on the other side." He squeezed her hand and stepped back from the water's edge.

She focused on the rock in the water and allowed her thoughts to carry her across the water to land on its moss-covered surface. She looked back to see Chase disappearing through the willows and a sigh escaped her lips. Settling herself comfortably on the boulder, Asiah closed her eyes and let the stillness surround her.

∽

Asiah's breathing had slowed and Chase knew she had found the state of tranquility she needed to continue her training. He released her hands and placed them gently in her lap, then leaned back and watched her meditate for a while. Her face was perfectly calm, every feature relaxed. He could have stared at her face forever. *I still can ...* came the unbidden suggestion of his subconscious. No, he'd lived long enough and she'd only just begun to live. She had her whole life ahead of her. She also had a sacred duty that required her full attention, not to mention a fiancé. She didn't need Chase in her life, stealing her away from her obligation – and it was a big obligation.

Still, the thought of leaving her alone when her training was finished only depressed him. The Ikhälea spoke of the glory of becoming one with the æthers, how one could not achieve a higher exaltation after death. It must be quite wonderful if it was better than spending eternity with Asiah. Chase let out a frustrated sigh. He didn't even know how he felt about her. He'd never been in love. In all his years on Earth he'd kept a healthy distance from any emotional ties to mortal humans. Maybe this was that elusive emotion after all. He chuckled to himself. This was more likely a passing infatuation. Then why did the thought of losing her make his chest hurt? He groaned and stood up, looking around for something to distract him from these dark thoughts.

His eyes fell on his satchel, hanging from a chair. He opened it and pulled out the scroll in the glass tube. Using the lubricating oil, he unrolled it and laid it flat on the table. Now that Asiah was more accepting of her fate, maybe she would try reading it again. He didn't know what the scroll said, just that the Ikhäle told him to keep it safe until his Shade offspring could read it. Chase gathered that it stated the Shade's mission and duty to set the human race back on the right track. The writing that appeared when Asiah touched the parchment was just a bunch of swirls and dots, but Chase knew that it was the language of the Ikhälea and that Asiah would be able to read it as soon as she was ready.

He heard her sigh and looked up from the blank paper. She was stretching her arms above her head and arching her back like a cat waking up from a nap in the sun. His mouth suddenly felt very dry. It took every ounce of his control not to vault the table and ravish her right there on the floor. Especially when she only wore that thin camisole, which hid nothing of her charms. She must have felt him undressing her with his eyes because she turned her head slowly toward him with an innocent smile. He shifted uncomfortably in his chair. His trousers felt slightly too tight. She rose and walked to the window, the late afternoon rays glinting golden in her hair.

"I should be getting home soon," she said, almost regretfully.

"Right. Did you learn how to clear your mind properly?"

"I think so."

"You must learn to do it every time you use your abilities." He tried to sound like a stern professor, but even he could hear the longing in his voice.

She only nodded. She crossed her arms over her chest and looked at him awkwardly. "Do you have something I can wear? I can't go home like this."

Happy for an excuse to cover her up he practically bounded into his bedchamber. He returned with a linen shirt he hadn't worn in months because he'd accidentally shrunken it. He handed her the garment and backed away, putting distance between them. He certainly wasn't looking forward to channeling her home and then having to let go of her. Then he was struck by an idea.

"Would you like to try channeling yourself home?" he asked.

"I thought you didn't want to let me out of your sight," she reminded him.

She had a point. He just didn't know if he could touch her again without hauling her into his arms. "I'll follow you, a nanosecond behind, I promise."

"What if I do it too slowly, or get lost, or don't put myself right at the end?"

"There's only one speed at which channeling can be achieved, you won't get lost unless you don't know where you're going, and you know what your body is supposed to feel like, so I'm sure you can right yourself at the end," he said. Chase remembered his first solo channel. He didn't get lost and he put his cells back where they were supposed to go, but still managed to throw up upon landing.

"Alright, what do I do?"

"First, always clear your mind, especially with channeling. Distraction can be dangerous when your bodily molecules are condensed into a small ball of light. Second, picture the place you want to go and the path you will take in your mind. You cannot channel through solid objects, so your path must be clear. We are southeast of the city, so you'll want to focus on traveling northwest from here. Finally, know your body, where every cell belongs and what it does. You know this inherently, even if you are not conscious of it. Trust yourself to put yourself right at the end and you will."

"How do you channel with another person?" she wondered.

"You must make physical contact; holding hands is enough. When you touch them you must learn *their* body so when you land, you can put both of you back together correctly."

Her cheeks pinkened. "So you had to ... learn my body?"

"On a cellular level, yes. It's not nearly as intimate as it seems. You can try it with me sometime." He smiled weakly.

"That sounds difficult. I don't know if I could learn how to do that."

"You can. For now, we'll just work on you transporting you. Someday you will be able to channel with ten people at once."

"You've done that?" She was impressed.

"Once or twice. It's not my favorite thing in the world." He grinned. "Are you ready to try it?"

She shrugged. "You obviously aren't going to take me home so I might as well."

He gestured to the door. "After you." They stood together in the clearing outside the cottage. "Clear your mind, see your destination, trust yourself," he reminded her.

She closed her eyes. He watched her carefully, ready to follow. She took a deep breath and clenched her jaw – and disappeared in a flash of blue light. Chase was so surprised he almost forgot to follow her. He'd failed at least a dozen times before he managed to actually do it the first time. He followed her and landed in the alley just in time to catch her as she fell. He set her on her feet and let go. She stumbled again and he caught her a second time.

"I think you're doing this on purpose," he murmured in her ear.

She giggled, high on adrenaline. "I'm not, I swear!"

He made sure she was stable before letting go this time, and even then it was difficult.

"Congratulations, you've successfully channeled on your own. So it shouldn't be hard for you to meet me at my house tomorrow morning."

"I don't even know where it is!" she protested.

"You found your way here, you can find your way back. Tomorrow, Asiah," he said, and before he did something he would regret, he vanished.

Chapter Twelve

When she reached her door, Asiah realized she was still wearing her bracelets. She removed them quickly; it wouldn't do for her parents to see her with blue eyes. As soon as the power stones left her veins she felt heavier, like a stone had been placed on each shoulder. Everything around her seemed to dim. It was a strange and unpleasant sensation.

Asiah entered the apartment to the silent stares of her parents. They had been giving her a bit of a wide berth since Chase had left last night and she didn't mind at all.

Aileen, on the other hand, didn't like the uncomfortable silence. "Good day at work, dear?" she asked, which was her way of asking if Asiah had brought home any pay.

"Fine, Mam." Asiah said evasively.

"Cricket! Your wrists!" Patrick noticed her puncture wounds before she had a chance to cover them up.

"Oh, it's nothing. You know how it is working in a knife shop. I'll just go get cleaned up." She tried to make a dash for her bedroom, but her father caught her arm.

He turned her hands palms-up to examine her wrists. "How did you get these?" She had to admit that identical puncture wounds on the wrists didn't exactly look good. She hoped he couldn't tell how fast the wounds seemed to be healing.

Asiah pulled her hands back. "They're just scratches. Once I clean the blood away, I'll be good as new." She darted into her room before he could stop her.

In her room Asiah scrubbed the blood from her wrists with a damp cloth. The wounds were now completely healed. There wasn't even a scar left behind. She was amazed that something like that could happen. If she could learn to heal people like Chase could, she knew she could do a lot of good in the world. Maybe that was her true calling. Maybe it was a start, anyway.

Her mind raced as she tried to fall asleep that night. There was so much she wanted to know about herself, about her people, about Chase. She remembered what he'd taught her earlier about focusing her mind and used the technique to calm her nerves. It would be nice to have a full night's sleep after these last few hectic days.

In the morning, Asiah slipped out before her parents were awake, shortly after five. She knew Chase didn't like to be woken early, but she would take his morning grouchiness over the awkward tension with her parents any day. Dressed in her most comfortable trousers and a shirt that actually fit her, Asiah went into the alley nearest her building and walked to the far end, away from the sleeping vagrants. Yesterday was the first time she'd channeled alone, and it had been surprisingly easy. Today she thought back to the path that had led her home. If she traveled in the opposite direction, it should take her back to Chase's house. It was simple enough, but her greatest fear was that she'd somehow put herself back together in the middle of the sky and fall to her death. She'd just have to trust herself not to do that.

She pulled the bracelets with the rough blue stones out of her pocket and fastened them into place with a click. Bracing one hand against the wall of the building, she rode the wave of adrenaline surging through her body. It was the most amazing feeling she'd ever experienced. The only thing that even came close was the tingly rush she felt when Chase touched her, a feeling that multiplied when he kissed her. But she knew *that* couldn't happen again, no matter how enjoyable it was. He made it clear that he had one more job to do on this Earth and then he would be gone forever. Asiah had chosen not to confront her feelings about that yet.

When her heart had slowed to a more normal pace, she pushed away from the wall and stood with her feet in a wide stance, bending her knees slightly with the absurd notion that it would help her stay upright when she landed. Chase would most definitely not be there to catch her this time – that was if she didn't crash through the roof of his cottage and land right on top of him.

Asiah closed her eyes and held her breath. *Clear your mind, see your destination, trust yourself.* Suddenly she was falling. Or was she flying? She couldn't tell, just that the ground was coming toward her very quickly. She braced herself for the impact and released her body back to its normal shape. A second later she felt her body being slammed against a hard surface, then she blacked out.

∾

Chase shot up in bed. *What the bloody hell was that?* An earthshaking *boom* had roused him from a very good dream he'd been having. He couldn't remember what it was about, but the fact that it had ended prematurely didn't help his mood. He threw off the covers and grabbed his dagger from the bureau. Wearing only the loose-fitting linen pants he slept in, he dashed outside to see what had caused the sound. If Marysa had found him ...

He spied a crater in the clearing in front of his cottage. It was about ten feet across and deep enough that he couldn't see what caused it. Unsheathing his knife, he crept toward it slowly and peered over the edge to see Asiah lying in a heap.

Quickly sheathing his dagger, he climbed into the crater and gently rolled her onto her back. She was breathing and didn't appear to have any broken bones. He knew exactly what had happened. She channeled here successfully, but came out of the channel too late and crashed into the ground, knocking herself out. He'd done it a few times in the beginning, too.

He scooped her up and carried her toward the house. She groaned as her eyes fluttered open. "Wh-why are you carrying me?" she asked, confused.

"You were unconscious ... again." He smiled. He didn't mind coming to her rescue like this. It just meant he got to touch her again.

"I must have done something wrong," she said weakly, not fully recovered yet.

He settled her gently in an armchair near the stove and went to fetch the kettle for tea. "You did well, just timed the landing wrong. I told you it takes practice."

"Did I hurt myself?" she asked, pressing hands to her arms and ribs.

"Perhaps," he replied, "but you will have healed already." When the tea was ready, he brought her a cup on a saucer. She took it, looking at him for the first time that morning. Her eyes widened slightly as she took in his attire, or lack thereof, but she recovered quickly, examining her tea leaves instead.

He chuckled, "I would have had time to dress if you hadn't shown up so bloody early and caused an earthquake outside my window."

She blushed. "I-I'm sorry. I had to leave before my parents woke up. We've all been walking on eggshells a bit lately."

Chase immediately felt ashamed for deriding her. "I didn't know things were so strained between you and your parents. I'm sorry."

Asiah shrugged. "Don't be. They take me for granted. No one knew that Meri and I were twins until we were born, then they saw me as the inconvenient second child they didn't plan for. That is, until I started working and bringing home money to support them."

Chase wanted to channel over there right now and give her parents a piece of his mind. How dare they take for granted someone as special and perfect as Asiah?

She noticed him grinding his teeth and changed the subject. "Why don't you tell me what we're going to do today?"

He came back to the present and nodded. "Alright, let me just put some clothes on." He didn't miss the brief look of disappointment that crossed her face at his words.

He returned to his room and dressed quickly in a green tunic, black fitted trousers and his jack boots. He added a leather vest today. He would teach her about one of his favorite things today: knives. It wasn't really in the curriculum, but it would be helpful if she knew a thing or two about weapons. Opening a chest on his bureau, he pulled out several knives of different types and lengths and slid them into the many hidden sheaths built into his vest.

Asiah was braiding her long hair when he came out. It was his turn to be disappointed. He loved how she looked with her hair down, blowing wildly in the breeze.

He took her outside and showed her the basics of knife throwing. He was an expert, even without using any of his powers. He could throw three knives so fast that they would all hit the tree at the same time. He showed Asiah that she could be just as fast and accurate with the aid of her powers, and that with enough practice, she would be able to throw like he could. Once she had the hang of it, he threw knives at *her*, the first few of which she dodged by channeling a few feet to the side. He found this amusing and started anticipating her movements, hurling knives to where she would be. When she learned that she couldn't dodge his flying blades, she began actually trying to stop them midair and, after a while, launching them back at him. He never let the knives hit her, even if there were only a couple times they would have.

Chase had prepared a picnic lunch since the weather was so fine, and at midday they sat on a blanket under the big oak tree in front of the cottage eating sandwiches.

Asiah nodded to a knife strapped to his belt. "You didn't throw that one at me today."

"That one could kill you if it hit you."

"Couldn't they all kill me? They are all sharp, right?" she joked.

"Yes, but this one is not from this world. It's an Ikhälean blade."

"Sharper than Earth blades?"

He smiled but his tone was serious. "Human flesh cannot fully heal from wounds inflicted by an Ikhälean blade. If I threw this at you and you didn't block it, I don't know if you would survive, being half-human."

"Oh. This is your favorite, isn't it? Can I ... see it?" she asked timidly.

He unsheathed it and offered it to her. She marveled at it. He wasn't sure why he didn't figure out sooner what her power stone would be. The knife that would eventually be hers was covered in sapphires. *Just like Marysa's blade was encrusted with onyxes.* He should have known.

"I remember this one. You used it to threaten the man in the speakeasy. It's so beautifully made," she said in a breathy tone.

"It was your father's blade. Not your human father, the Ikhälean one. Someday it will be yours."

"Really? Doesn't it belong to you?" she asked.

"I'm keeping it safe for my great-uncle until it can be bequeathed to you."

"Bequeathed?" she looked distressed.

Chase sighed, not thrilled with the turn the conversation had taken. "Yes ... upon my death."

She opened her mouth to speak, then closed it again. She handed the knife back hastily, troubled by the topic as much as he was. She was silent for a moment, then perked up a little. "I don't see why you can't keep it. You've had it for so long already. I don't see why I'd need an ornate dagger, anyway. It would feel strange for me to take it from you, even if you were ..." She trailed off and hung her head, avoiding his eyes.

He brushed his fingers against her cheek and she raised her eyes to his, brimming with unshed tears. "I've been here too long already. This is my final task. Don't weep for me, love. I'm going to a better place. Besides, you need the blade to achieve your Oneness."

She wiped her eyes with her sleeve. "My what?"

He smiled sheepishly. "Tojen said there isn't a word in any Earth language that translates very well. 'Oneness' is described as you becoming one with yourself and your world. The blade is somehow part of that process, but I don't fully understand how. You won't achieve this for many years, until after your Ikhälean side has reached maturity, so don't worry too much about it right now."

She looked overwhelmed and he was about to suggest they do some more exercises when she found a new topic to question him about.

"So what exactly am I supposed to do after you ... leave me?"

She looked lost and he wished he could kiss her senseless and make her forget about this entire depressing conversation. "Are you sure you want to talk about this now? We could practice throwing knives some more," he suggested.

She shook her head, the tears starting again. "I want to know how I'm supposed to do *all this—*" she waved her hands in the air, "—without you."

Her anguish was killing him. He moved next to her and pulled her into his arms. He smoothed her hair off her face as she cried into his shoulder. It wasn't just the fact that literally the fate of the world was now in her hands that was bothering her. Her family couldn't understand what she was going through, and the only person who could was going to leave her after her training was completed. Chase couldn't blame her for feeling like he was going to abandon her.

"Listen to me, love," he whispered into her hair. "I'm not going anywhere. I will stay with you as long as you need me. I know this is a lot to handle and I'm not going to make you do it alone until you're ready." He ran his hands up and down her back soothingly and kissed the top of her head. "Please don't cry, Asiah. You're getting my shoulder all wet."

She laughed tearfully and sat up. "I'm sorry. I'm not usually so emotional. This is all so *much*." She blew her nose on his proffered handkerchief and stared off into the woods blankly.

"I've always felt like an outsider," she murmured softly. "I don't have any friends and even my twin sister thinks I'm strange. I don't know why being alone scares me so much."

"Much of a Shade's journey is completed alone. That's why you are the perfect person to fulfill that role. You aren't afraid of being alone. You're afraid of losing the only person in your life who understands your purpose." He smoothed her hair away from her face. "But there is a place you can go to learn more about your people and become proficient with your powers. You won't feel so alone there. It's called Ocea, and you will finish your training there before achieving your Oneness," he explained.

"I wish there were another word for that. 'Oneness' sounds so silly. This place – Ocea – where is it?" she wondered.

"It's a very small planet with a similar atmosphere to Earth's. Astronomers here on Earth don't know of its existence, even though it's very nearby. It's hidden by electromagnetic fields put there by the Ikhälea that found it. It's there for people like you to hone your skills and live peacefully until you are ready to fulfill your destiny."

"I wonder how long that will be," she said gloomily.

"My great-uncle said it takes about a century on Earth for a Shade's Ikhälean side to mature."

"Do I have to leave Earth for the entire time?" she asked, looking stricken.

"No, you'll be able to channel back and forth to Ocea. It's meant to be a safe haven for you, so people don't discover what you are doing and attempt to harm you or exploit your powers."

She swallowed at his words. "Where is this place?"

Chase looked at the clear blue sky. "It should be a clear night. I'll show you once the sun goes down."

"Will there be others like me there?"

"It's unlikely. Tojen told me that Earth is fairly far from the other worlds inhabited by Ikhälea or human forms of Ikhälea. Only True Shades are shown where the in-between worlds are, so no, no one else will be there, unless you bring people with you. Although, I would caution against that. It is too great a secret to share with ordinary humans."

She hugged her knees to her chest and rested her chin upon them. "Have you been there?"

He ran a hand through his hair. "No, I haven't, but my great-uncle said it's more beautiful than any place on Earth. I imagine it's like the forest in your mind."

She nodded, seeming to accept her fate a little more than she did an hour before. He knew it would be like this for a while. She would accept little pieces of her destiny at a time, then a few more until she was the woman her ancestors bred her to be.

They finished their lunch in silence. Asiah practiced throwing knives some more and reviewed her other skills before it started to get dark. They went inside and had some tea while Chase showed her the different nuances between each of his knives.

"Are you sure it's alright for you to return home so late? I know things are uncomfortable for you at home, but I don't want to make it any worse," Chase said as they headed outside to look for the hidden planet.

"I don't care," she said in a tired voice.

They stood side-by-side in the clearing, staring up at the sky as the stars came out.

"There," Chase said pointing.

"Which one?" Asiah said, confused.

Chase stood behind her, leaning forward so his cheek rested against hers. He raised her hand and pointed to the heavens. "Do you see that cluster of stars?"

"The Pleiades?"

"Yes. The brightest one is Ocea."

"I thought they were all stars?"

"That is what you are made to believe, but it is a planet with many suns."

"You said it couldn't be seen from Earth," Asiah said, stepping forward, away from the tingle of his touch.

Chase stifled his disappointment. "*We* can see it, ordinary humans can't. Even with telescopes. That is why people believe that it is only a cluster of stars."

"Thank you for showing me," she said turning to face him.

"You're welcome," he said.

They stood and regarded each other for a moment, palpable energy cracking in the air between them. Chase took a tentative step forward.

"I should get home," Asiah said quickly, breaking the spell. She was definitely better at controlling her feelings than he was.

Chase nodded. "Can you do it? By yourself, I mean?"

"I think so. Hopefully I won't create a crater in the alley like I did over there." She pointed to her right.

"I can follow you if you're nervous," he offered.

"No, I think it's time I do more things on my own. I'll have to eventually anyway. Goodnight, Chase." He could see the heartbreak on her face a moment before she vanished.

He lifted his gaze to the heavens and sighed heavily. "Goodnight, Asiah."

༄

After a somewhat smooth landing, Asiah trudged up the stairs to her apartment, dreading that the tension between her and her parents would come to a head sooner rather than later. She wasn't entirely sure why she felt so defiant against them lately. Her parents were very conservative and all Asiah wanted to do was make them happy, but sometimes she felt like they were holding her back. Maybe that's why she was spending so much time with Chase recently. He was showing her a future where she could make a difference – a huge difference, it seemed – and all they wanted was for her to marry a rich doctor so they could live in comfort. Asiah had had three jobs since her father was laid off, so why couldn't he find work himself? Most likely because he drank too much and decided that his daughters should do all the work for him. She felt guilty thinking these thoughts. Patrick had worked hard on Inishmor. She thought that maybe he regretted leaving Ireland after all and now he couldn't afford to go back.

Her parents were sitting near the stove when she entered, apparently waiting up for her. They both looked up at her and Patrick said, "Pull up that chair there, Cricket. We have some news."

This doesn't sound good, Asiah thought. At least they hadn't commented on the fact she was coming home much later than usual. Meri was standing by the window and Asiah could tell she'd been crying. *Oh, no ...* Dragging a chair from the kitchen table, Asiah sat gingerly between her parents, dreading the worst.

"Merica, would you like to join us?" Aileen asked.

Meri shook her head and continued to stare despondently out the window.

Patrick turned his attention to the younger twin. "Your sister, Maryn, wrote us a letter yesterday." He paused and Asiah blinked at him. "She recently started workin' for a shippin' company in San Francisco. She wrote that the company is expandin' and needs able-bodied men with sailin' experience. Apparently the Depression hasn't reached all the way out there yet. There really ain't nothin' here for us, so we leave on the mornin' train tomorrow."

Asiah stared. They were leaving Chicago? Just like that? "What about my job? And Meri's job?"

"*Your* job has barely paid you and Meri won't need to work once I have another job," he said.

"But ... I just started working for Mr. Brandon again. Surely I'll be paid again soon." She hadn't even thought about money since she started training with Chase.

"Oh, you can stay, Cricket," Aileen chimed in. "Dr. Henderson said you could stay with his sister until the wedding. That is, if you still want to marry him."

She blinked at them. Now that they were relocating, it didn't matter to them if she married the wealthy doctor. Obviously they didn't care if she was doing it for any other reason. Like to secure herself a place in the medical field. Marrying Walter was only one reason she wanted to stay in Chicago. She'd just learned that she could do some amazing things with the aid of a small blue stone. How could she quit in the middle of Chase's training? On the other hand, she wasn't ready to say goodbye to her family, either, no matter how much they seemed to resent her.

Everyone was staring at Asiah as if her decision would affect their plans. She couldn't stand their glares any longer and fled, stumbling blindly down the stairs. Outside on the street she struggled to catch her breath. She couldn't choose between Chase and her family. They may be hard to live with, but she couldn't abandon them for a man she barely knew. She also couldn't desert him after everything he'd shown her. She knew now that her destiny and his were intertwined, but there was just no way she could be expected to sever all ties to the only people who had ever truly loved her. It wasn't fair for them to ask her to leave this all behind. And Walter, well, she'd have to sort out her thoughts on marriage later. Her parents didn't know how important she was. Maybe they needed to know.

She forced herself to tromp back up the stairs to the fourth floor. Her family seemed surprised to see her and she held up her hands to silence their questions. "It's time for me to explain something," she said. "It's important and maybe you'll understand what I've been going through."

She told them everything, starting with who Chase was and how he was helping her hone her abilities. She even did her best to relate the story of the Ikhälea and her role in setting the world to rights. She told them all the skills she was learning and how old Chase was and why her clothes were burned yesterday. She said her shirt had also caught fire, not that Chase had ripped it for better access to her body; there was no need to reveal *everything* that she'd be up to. When she finished, an hour later, her mother was near tears and Meri was holding her head in her hands. Patrick stared blankly at the wall. Everyone seemed to be in shock. It *was* pretty shocking information, she just thought they would handle it better.

Aileen came back to life first. "That's all very interesting dear. Why don't you get some sleep? You must have had a hard day." Her tone was overly sweet, almost pitying.

"Don't you have questions?" Asiah wondered. "I know it's all very confusing and shocking—"

"Of course, Cricket, but they can wait until you've had some rest," Patrick chimed in.

She *was* tired. Going to bed sounded just right. Maybe her family just needed some time to process what she'd told them. She couldn't expect them to understand everything right away. It had taken her quite some time, even after Chase had shown her the scroll and channeled with her and healed her wrist.

Asiah awoke a short while later to hear hushed voices talking on the other side of her bedroom door. She strained to hear what they were saying. She caught the words "delusions of grandeur" and "rehabilitation" and started to wonder if maybe her story had not been as well received as she'd thought. Before she could think of a way out, the door opened and Walter appeared, followed by three men in hospital smocks.

Her parents thought she was crazy. Of course they did! She told them a story about wizards and aliens and how she was meant to save the world! Now these men were here to lock her up.

"Walter? What are you doing here?" she asked, forcing herself not to panic.

"I'm here to help, darlin'. These men are going to take you to a place where you can get better." He had a sad look in his eyes.

Asiah had to escape. She'd had her bracelets with her last night, but where had she put them? As the men slowly approached the bed she jammed her hands in her pockets searching frantically for her power stones. Her hand closed over one bracelet. She pulled it out and tried to get it on her wrist before they took her. One of the men mistook her actions and grabbed her hand, turning it palm up. There was dried blood from the puncture wound on her wrist from when she'd removed the bracelet earlier. With her parents' disturbing news, Asiah had completely forgotten to clean the blood from her wrists.

"She's already tried to hurt herself!" the man said, tightening his grip so she dropped the bracelet. He picked it up and inspected it, holding it out so Walter and the other men could see. "Quite the sadistic little vixen isn't she?" he commented to his colleagues.

"No!" Asiah shrieked as he dropped the bracelet in his smock pocket. "I'm not crazy, everything I said is true! Please, Walter!" she pleaded, but he just shook his head and turned away. Two of the men restrained her arms, and without her bracelets, she couldn't fight them off.

The third man approached her with a large syringe. *No, no, no!* Asiah knew that struggling only made her look crazier, but her rational mind was not engaged at the moment. All she could think about was Walter's betrayal and the fact that Chase would never know what had happened to her. The orderly sank the long needle into her arm and she felt the medication burn as it invaded her veins. *Chase ... help me ...* she thought desperately before it all went dark.

Chapter Thirteen

Chase had trouble sleeping that night. He had always been able to calm his thoughts and drift off without a problem, but tonight he was haunted with visions of his blue-eyed beauty. Dreams of Asiah being hurt or captured left him restless and apprehensive. Her training after only two days was coming along better than he'd hoped, even though she still had a long way to go.

For some reason, Chase was certain that Asiah's fiancé had something to do with his strange dreams. Even though he'd never met this fiancé, Chase had a feeling that Asiah was settling for the man when she could have anything or anyone else that she wanted. He knew his jealousy was misguided, and he didn't care. But he couldn't shake the feeling that something wasn't right, and he got out of bed to find some wine. When psychological methods failed, alcohol wouldn't let him down. Perhaps a glass of Bordeaux would help him take his mind off Asiah's relationship, which wasn't any of his business in the first place.

Cloudy, gray light filtered through the leaded glass windows of his cottage, waking him. Chase sat up quickly, wondering why he was sitting at the table and not sleeping in his bed. He spotted the empty wine bottle on the table and remembered his nightmares. He rubbed his stubbled chin with one hand, feeling his pockets for his watch with the other. He spied its chain hanging from his jacket pocket on a chair by the stove. His head ached dully from the wine and rather than get up to retrieve his watch he extended his hand

and summoned it to him instead. He peered at the watch's face. It was midafternoon. He must have overdone it with the wine. He slowly got to his feet and stretched. The ancient scroll was still unrolled on the table, waiting for Asiah to read it today.

He frowned. He'd told Asiah to be here this morning. Maybe she'd had trouble channeling today. That couldn't be it; she'd done it perfectly on the first try, and at least arrived in one piece yesterday. He glanced out the window looking for a new crater. Only the one from yesterday marred the clearing. He remembered how he'd had an uneasy feeling last night and had dismissed it, drowning it in wine. Doubt started to creep in. He went to his room and dressed quickly. He would go to her apartment and fetch her himself. The devil take her family if they wouldn't let her go with him.

Landing in the street, Chase vaulted up the four flights of stairs to her door. His tension mounted when he sensed that there had been a disturbance there. The energy was all wrong. He knocked on the door and found that it wasn't completely closed. He pushed it open all the way and his mouth fell open. Asiah's family had only a few possessions to begin with, but now the apartment was empty. Not a single item was left behind. Chase checked both bedrooms to be sure, but they were gone. Fury quickly replaced confusion. Asiah hadn't even said goodbye. He felt hollow inside, his heart an empty void. As he struggled to slow his breathing, a glimmer of silver caught his attention in one of the bedrooms and he bent to retrieve one of Asiah's silver bracelets from the floor. Of course she'd have left her power stones behind if she didn't ever plan to see Chase again.

Numb, he trudged back out to the kitchen and froze. Marysa stood by the window, staring out at the bleak sky.

"They left hours ago," she said, turning to face him.

His hand flew to his dagger at his belt and she held up a hand.

"That won't be necessary. I should kill you for lying to me, you know, but you're not really worth my time, even if we do want the same thing." Her black eyes glowed with an ominous light.

Chase saw that she didn't wear bracelets as he did. Instead, she wore a sinister-looking necklace with two sharp black stones inserted directly into her jugular veins, held in place by steel hooks piercing her skin.

He did his best to keep his anger from his voice. "What would that be?"

Marysa laughed her evil rasping laugh. "You want to find her, but not for the same reason I want her. You want to find her because you're in love with her."

Chase's head snapped up.

Her eyes glinted. "You Conjurers are all the same: so much power yet so powerless when a pretty girl smiles at you," she mocked.

He took a deep breath and flexed his fingers, fighting the urge to throttle her. "You cannot hurt her. She's much stronger than you."

She laughed again and the sound grated on his nerves. "You cannot lie to me, Sorcerer, I can hear the doubt in your voice. She is no match for me."

Chase gritted his teeth. He'd killed men in war dozens of times, yet never in cold blood. He preferred to expose evil people to authorities and let them handle it. But he would kill this woman in a second if he could keep her from hurting Asiah.

With fire in his eyes he lunged at her, drawing his blade. She sidestepped him, drawing her dagger at the same time. He slammed into her and they tumbled to the floor, each rolling to gain the advantage. By sheer size Chase pinned her with his dagger under her chin. She smiled wickedly and wiggled the point of her blade just under his ribs.

"It looks like we both die today," he growled. "Because I'll not allow you to escape again." He pressed the blade more firmly against her throat, drawing blood, as she had done to him.

Her eyes flashed and he felt the tip of her dagger prick his skin. "Two can play that game, Brandon." She saw the question in his eyes before he asked it. "Oh, I've been learning about you, Chase ... Brandon ..." she spoke his name threateningly. "The last of your kind, yes? You eradicated all the others, didn't you? I'm sure that's not what you've told *her*, but I know the truth."

A pang of regret shot through Chase. While Chase hadn't wielded the death blow in the demise of most Conjurers, he'd had a hand in almost all of their deaths.

"If you know so much about me, then you know I am psychologically *much* stronger than you and will never help you hurt her. Or did you forget what happened last time we met?" He saw a flicker of fear pass over her face momentarily, then it was gone.

"I'd love to see your powers of concentration right now," she pushed the knife a millimeter deeper, reminding him that she held his life as much as he held hers. "But maybe you'd like to see more of me, instead ..."

Chase pressed his knife against her throat, but not fast enough, as she had already moved. In horror he realized she was transforming into her Ikhälean form, something he'd only seen in the sketches in his old books. His psychological superiority counted for nothing against her now. He rolled to his feet and drew another knife as the creature barreled into him, throwing him through the window. One four-story fall and several broken bones later, Chase's vision faded as the creature streaked across the sky, hunting the woman he loved.

~

A crowd had gathered when Chase woke up in the street and the previous evening came back to him in a flash: the empty apartment, Marysa, the long fall from the window. He sat up and groaned, causing half the crowd to jump back in surprise. His bones had mended overnight, but he was still sore and bleeding from where she jabbed the knife under his ribs. At least she hadn't tried to read his mind again. He stood, garnering more gasps from the crowd. They began to murmur, pointing at the window above and his bloody clothes. He didn't have time to deal with these people, nor could he channel away in the middle of a crowd. He shouldered his way out of the throng and began walking briskly down the street.

He had no idea where to go from here. Asiah was gone, her family with her. Someone had to know where they had gone. He paused and looked back toward the apartment building. The crowd was dispersing. With a sigh Chase entered the building again and knocked on the first door he found.

An old man with a Ukrainian accent answered the door. Chase asked him about the family from the fourth floor.

"Irish, right? Left town yesterday, early. Took everything in a big truck."

"Do you know where they went?" Chase asked.

"Left out of here so fast, I was barely out of bed, sorry."

"Did anyone see them leave? Talk to them?" He was getting desperate.

"You ask the other tenants if you want." The man gave him a pitiful look and closed the door.

Chase asked every other tenant in the building and three shopkeepers from neighboring buildings, yet no one knew where the O'Connors had gone. A few had seen the truck and seen the family leaving, but their destination remained a mystery. Chase even asked Mr. Kelsey, Asiah's former employer, and the man was no help. He knew Asiah's fiancé's name was Walter, but had no idea where to find him, or even if the wedding was still on. He had only one other lead.

Chase channeled across town to Monty's club. Maybe the man was still there or, if not, perhaps someone had heard where he'd gone. In the morning hours, no guard was posted outside the door and Chase headed inside and down the stairs. To Chase's surprise, Asiah's blond brother was behind the bar taking inventory. He glanced up from his clipboard and his features hardened.

"You!" he shouted in his brogue. "Ya have a lot o' nerve comin' here!" His hand moved to his holstered gun as he started to move out from behind the bar.

Chase held up his hands. "I mean you no harm, I just want to know where she is. Please, old chap, then you'll never see me again," he pleaded.

Monty took in Chase's bloody clothes, seemed to mull things over, then shrugged. "M'folks packed everythin' up and headed out west. Frisco, I think."

"Why didn't you go with them?"

"Got me own gig here, they don't need me taggin' along."

Chase got the feeling Monty was keeping something from him. Unfortunately, he had no choice but to trust the Irishman.

"You're sure they went to San Francisco?"

"Yes! Now get outta me club!"

Chase didn't have to be asked twice. He put his hands together and gave Monty a little bow in thanks. Back outside he faced west, planning his path. San Francisco was a big city. It could take him months to find Asiah. He refused to believe that she had just left of her own accord. Her family surely spirited her away in a misguided attempt to rescue her from Chase. He didn't care, he would find her. She was too important to the future of the world and to him.

Chapter Fourteen

The lights were too bright. They were always too bright here. Asiah buried her face in the scratchy pillow in a vain attempt to shut out the light. Her shoulders ached, another thing she couldn't control in this place. She hadn't moved her arms in days. Maybe it was weeks, or it could have been only hours, she had no concept of time. Everything blurred together, even her vision, when she was aware of it. In her more lucid moments she saw what she thought were people clad in white milling about nearby. She couldn't understand what they said, as if they spoke in a foreign language. There was pain, she was sure, but it never lasted long. She was vaguely aware that she was unconscious much more often than she was awake. When things did come into focus, she found she was in a small room with green tiled walls. There was a bed, and sometimes she was on it and other times she was on the floor. There was always blood nearby when she was on the floor as if she'd fallen or hurt herself – or someone had hurt her. She couldn't remember. She never remembered her previous waking moments. She wasn't sure she could remember anything before this monotonous fog.

There was an antiseptic smell in this place, like it had been vigorously cleaned. She knew this wasn't true because when she woke up on the floor she could see dirt and grime encrusted in the grout between the floor tiles. There was a drain in the floor and it was stained with blood and other bodily fluids that Asiah didn't want to consider. She didn't like being on the floor, but she couldn't move well enough to get up.

Today, much like every other day, she woke to an intense pounding in her head and the harsh glare of the unnatural lights in her room. The bed was uncomfortable, but at least she wasn't on the floor this time. She must have been trying to speak because two blurry figures entered and began fussing over her in that strange, muted language. She tried to understand their words, and her ears felt like they were full of cotton. Slowly, the people began to become focused and she could hear them more clearly, even though it still sounded like they were talking on the other side of a wall.

"Good morning, sweetheart," one of the men said. "Managed to stay in bed last night didn't we?"

A new blurry person entered the room. She couldn't remember this one. It was a man. He still wore white but it was only a coat, like a doctor or druggist. She thought perhaps she knew a druggist once. She couldn't remember. He touched her face and spoke more clearly than the others.

"How's our star patient? You know you're the only one so far who's survived this drug trial? We have high hopes for you, yes we do."

One of the others in white was holding a syringe. Something in her brain fired and she began screaming. She didn't know how, but she knew that needle had something to do with why she couldn't think straight. She fought against the strange restraints that kept her arms immobile as the three white-clad figures held her down. They pulled her hair and slapped her, shouting at her to calm down. The needle pierced the skin of her neck and they released her.

"Nadia will be back to take you to therapy in a minute," she heard distantly. She didn't know who Nadia was. They left her a tray with food on it. It was a bowl of grayish mush. Since she couldn't use her arms, Asiah had to lean over the bowl and put her face in it. She scooted over on her bed to where she thought she could reach the bowl and leaned over. She bumped her head on the edge of the tray and the bowl fell to the dirty floor, throwing mush everywhere. She stared at the floor for what seemed like an hour, willing time to reverse so she could try again. Tears blurred her vision.

The woman named Nadia came to get her. "What have you done now?" she asked angrily. "I guess there'll be no supper for you then."

"No ..." Asiah whispered, her throat was dry as a bone.

"Oh, yes. If you're going to throw your food on the floor all the time, you won't get any at all!" The woman jerked Asiah up off the bed and tossed her roughly into a wheelchair. Asiah closed her eyes. She hated the wheelchair. It made her dizzy. After a long ride to the other end of a long hallway, Nadia left her next to a closed door. The nurse rapped on the door three times and walked away, leaving Asiah alone. After a moment the door opened and another man in a white coat appeared.

"Ah, finally! Our little science experiment!" He wheeled her into a small room with concrete walls and dim lighting. Asiah was extremely thankful for the latter. There were three other people in the room, but they weren't doctors or orderlies. They sat in chairs in a circle and didn't look at her.

"Now," the doctor said, "Rueben just told us about his mother. Thank you, Rueben. Why don't we hear from our newest member?" He looked at his clipboard. "Asiah? Would you like to talk about why you're here?"

Her eyes darted between the other patients and the doctor. Who were these people? Why *was* she here? She suddenly realized she couldn't remember how she'd gotten here.

"I ... I don't know," she rasped. "I don't ... belong here." She would have died for a drink of water right then.

"We all belong somewhere. This is your home now. What do you remember about your life before coming here?" the doctor prodded.

Asiah fought against the panic that rose in her chest. "N-nothing ... I can't remember ... anything! This is wrong ... I don't *belong* here!" She tried to wriggle out of the constricting garment she wore. Why couldn't she move her arms? She fought so hard that she fell out of the wheelchair and hit her head on the hard concrete floor. She tried to cry out, but was consumed by darkness before she could utter a sound.

༄

A blaring alarm woke Asiah. She squinted her eyes against the harsh lights in her room. She was on the bed today and her head was pounding. She stretched and realized that her arms were free. This seemed odd to her, and she couldn't remember why. She stood up slowly and the room swam around her. She didn't know if it was day or night; there was no window in her room. The walls were made of green tiles and there was only one door. It had a small, barred window in the center. She trailed her hand along the wall for support until she reached the door. Standing on her tiptoes, she peered out the window.

A man with terror in his eyes ran past her door an instant later. She thought she recognized him from somewhere. Rudy? Rueben? Two orderlies followed with long, metal rods in their hands. The man stumbled and fell. The orderlies jabbed him with the rods and the man writhed on the floor. It seemed like there was an electric charge coming from the rods. Asiah backed away from the window. What was this place? Why were they hurting that man? Why couldn't she *remember?*

Her door opened a short while later and the doctor entered. She felt like she'd seen him before ... maybe.

"Medicine time!" he said, a little too loudly and Asiah winced. Two orderlies flanked the doctor as he approached with a syringe. Her eyes went wide and she opened her mouth to shout. They must have anticipated that she would resist because the two orderlies efficiently held her arms as the doctor jabbed the needle into her neck before she had a chance to react. The doctor left and the orderlies released her, but they didn't immediately follow the doctor out.

One of the men grabbed her chin, turning her face so he could examine it. "Pretty little thing, ain't she?" the man said. He was a big man, with chubby fingers that looked like sausages.

"True enough, but you have to leave this one alone, Rogers. Doc's got her on some special drug and doesn't want her messed with," the other man said.

"What the doc doesn't know won't hurt him," Rogers said, dropping his hand from her face to fondle her breast through the thin gown.

Asiah shrieked and scooted to the far corner of her bed, hugging her knees to her chest and glaring at Rogers.

He laughed wickedly. "Feisty, too. I like 'em feisty." He had an evil glint in his beady eyes that terrified Asiah.

"Come on, Rogers, let's go." The other man went to the door and held it open. Rogers gave her a final lascivious glance before he followed his partner out.

Asiah let her breath out in a long sigh. Whatever the doctor gave her was making everything a little fuzzy again. She looked down at her open palms. She focused her eyes on the grooves and ridges of her fingertips and could have sworn she saw tiny sparks leaping from ridge to ridge. She balled her hands into fists and sat on them.

She didn't remember falling asleep, and the next thing she knew someone was tugging on her foot. She woke up with a start and saw a man in a white smock with an evil grin trying to pull her out of her corner. He was somewhat familiar ... Reicher? Ranger?

"Rogers! You in there?" a voice shouted from outside her room.

"Gimme a minute!" Rogers replied as he grabbed both of her ankles and jerked her onto her back on the bed.

"No!" She screamed, trying to kick him off. But he was too strong for her.

He knelt over her on the bed, pinning her legs beneath him and holding her arms over her head with one hand. With his other hand he pushed her gown up to her hips and licked his lips. He reached inside his trousers and Asiah realized what he was doing.

She screamed tried to buck him off but he just laughed and slapped her hard across the face.

"Good little girls are quiet," he growled, and shoved her legs apart.

Asiah closed her eyes helplessly as he moved to enter her.

She didn't know where the fire came from, just that it happened very suddenly, like someone had turned on a flame-thrower. Rogers screamed and flung himself on the floor, trying unsuccessfully to extinguish the flames. The moment he released her, Asiah scrambled back to her corner, hugging her knees to her chest as the man screamed and writhed on the grimy tiles. She heard shouts from the hallway and more men rushed in with wide eyes, dashed back out, then returned with buckets of water, trying to douse the burning man. The screaming had stopped and Asiah could smell his burnt flesh from her corner of the bed. She squeezed her eyes shut, blocking out the grisly image.

The men took Rogers away on a stretcher as the doctor appeared in the doorway.

"What happened here?" he demanded, looking from Asiah to the burnt sheets on her bed.

An orderly spoke up. "It was strange, sir. Rogers, well he ... tried to ... he was going to ..."

"Going to what?" the doctor asked irritably.

"He wanted to ... have a go at the girl."

The doctor cursed. "What did I say about that?"

"I tried to tell him, sir. Next thing I knew, I looked in and he was on fire. It was the strangest thing." The orderly looked completely bewildered.

"Did you do this?" the doctor asked, turning his attention to Asiah.

She shook her head, trying to remember. *Had* she done it? Was she even capable of something like that?

The doctor approached her and pulled her hands toward him. He examined her palms for a moment then placed his own hand against her forehead. He snatched his hand back with a frown and looked at the other orderly.

"She's got one hell of a fever. You sure you didn't see where the fire came from?"

The man shrugged. "One moment he was on top of her, the next he was on fire and screaming."

"The girl, was she ever on fire?"

"I don't think so."

"Hmm." The doctor gave Asiah another assessing look and left the room, pulling the orderly with him.

Asiah curled up into a ball as sobs began to wrack her body.

Chapter Fifteen

Chase searched the streets of San Francisco for leads for nearly a month. Each day he didn't find Asiah he fell deeper into despair. She had to be there, somewhere. He spoke to every company who employed fishermen and sailors. He spent most of his time at the docks watching ships come and go, looking for Asiah's father. He searched drug stores for Asiah and business firms for her sister. Anytime he heard an Irish accent he asked about them. He'd said her name so many times, it had become part of him. He sketched her face and carried the sketch everywhere with him. He hoped someone would recognize it as Asiah or even Merica, but so far no one had.

On the last day of September, Chase sat atop a building in Chinatown, scanning the street below and throwing breadcrumbs to pigeons. It didn't take much effort to scan for Irish people in a sea of Asians, and he was growing weary of searching. His spirits had never been lower, even when he'd fallen prey to an opium addiction less than a century ago. His ability to sense fluctuations in energy was not as sharp as a Shade's but he kept his ear to the ground in case Asiah tried to use her powers in some way. He only found one bracelet at her apartment, which he'd lost when Marysa threw him out the window, so Asiah might have the other one and could be using it to access her power. So far he had sensed nothing, which also meant that Marysa hadn't caught up with him yet. He used almost none of his powers so as not to give away his position.

He glanced down as a woman in a hat emerged from a shop. He couldn't see her face because of the hat, but something about the way she walked was familiar. He jumped from the roof, landing softly on his feet and startling a nearby pedestrian. While the woman railed at him in Mandarin he made his way through the crowd toward the woman in the hat. He could tell now that she was a brunette and he allowed himself a moment of hope. He finally caught up with her and placed his hand on her shoulder. She spun around and he almost wept with relief.

"It's you!" Merica cried in shock. "I-I'm not supposed to talk to you ... I have to go." She turned and hurried down the street.

Chase caught up in three steps, gripping her arm more firmly this time. "Please tell me where she is, Merica. She's in danger and needs my help."

"D-danger? What do you mean?" She glanced around nervously.

"Is there somewhere we can go and talk?" Chase offered. Clearly she wasn't comfortable here.

"I shouldn't. Father will—"

"Meri! Where are you, girl?" Mr. O'Connor's booming voice echoed across the street. Meri was running to him before Chase could stop her. He approached the old Irishman cautiously.

"Forgive me, sir, but I believe your daughter is in grave danger."

"Who? Meri? She's safe enough." He raked Chase with an icy glare.

"Not Meri, Asiah. You must tell me where she is."

O'Connor laughed. "Asiah? She's as safe as she'll ever be. She can't hurt herself anymore."

Chase frowned. "What do you mean 'can't hurt herself'?"

"Poor child was a danger to herself, cuttin' her wrists and all that, spoutin' nonsense about wizards and magic and stuff. It didn't help that you filled her head with all sorts o' nonsense. She's in a safe place now."

"She *told* you about her abilities?" Chase asked. They must have seen the puncture wounds on her wrists from the bracelets, forcing her to tell them everything.

"Told us a bunch o' malarkey! Had to have her committed." O'Connor had the grace to look mildly ashamed.

Chase grabbed the man's shirt and threw him against the window of a nearby store. "You had her *locked up!?*" he roared as people began to point and stare.

O'Connor struggled to speak. "Had to, laddie, the girl's lost her mind!"

Chase wanted to strangle the man for putting his own daughter in an asylum. His own incredible, perfect, and most of all, *sane* daughter. He leaned close so his face was an inch from O'Connor's. "Where?" he growled.

"I-I don't know the name. Henderson set it up. A place in Chicago." The man was near tears.

Chase released him and jabbed a finger in the man's chest. "You'd better pray they haven't hurt her, old man." Then in full view of everyone on the street, he vanished in a green flash.

A week later, Chase had visited all the asylums and sanatoriums in the Chicago area except one. He had been posing as a psychiatrist himself. Once inside each facility, he managed to steal a look at the patient rosters. He still hadn't found Asiah's name. He considered tracking down Walter Henderson and asking him where Asiah was, but he was afraid that he might end up strangling the man instead. *Who, in his right mind, puts his own fiancée in an asylum?*

All his hopes rested on the last hospital, located on the north end of town. It was an old building, built shortly after the War Between the States for recovering veterans. It was surrounded by iron fences in case any of the current patients tried to escape.

Chase approached the gatehouse and flashed the security officer a smile.

"Dr. Charles Swanson, psychiatrist," he said smoothly. "I'm here to see one of my patients."

The guard nodded and returned to his newspaper. Chase used the same line inside. A nurse told him to wait a moment and she would fetch the head psychiatrist.

Chase was shown into a dingy office near the back of the complex. After waiting for nearly twenty minutes, a harried-looking man in a white coat trudged in.

"Dr. Swanson, I presume?" the man said, peering over his spectacles.

"Yes sir, I'm here about Asiah O'Connor," Chase said.

"Right. I was told she was under the care of Dr. Walter Henderson. Have you treated her previously as well?"

"Yes, she's been in my care for several years. Her parents moved from the area recently and left her here, against my recommendation. Henderson and I have been treating her together, and I want to make sure she's receiving the proper care," Chase explained.

The doctor rubbed his chin. "She's being looked after," he said evasively.

Chase frowned. The man was hiding something. "May I see her?"

"I'm afraid that's not possible. She's in a very ... delicate condition."

"What do you mean?" Chase asked, trying to keep his voice from shaking.

The man sighed. "Look, there's a new drug that's being developed. It's going to change the way we live. It's simply amazing. I've been testing this drug on several patients, but none of them has survived the trial ... until Miss O'Connor came along."

"What does this drug do?"

"All I can tell you is that it makes ordinary people special. People like Miss O'Connor." A pensive look crossed the doctor's face.

"Why can't I see her?" Chase's voice held an edge.

The man sighed. "She killed an orderly last week. Burned the man to death with her bare hands."

Chase closed his eyes. He was afraid of something like this happening. The doctor thought it was the drug, but Chase knew better.

"I thought if I stopped administering the drug, she wouldn't be able to do that again. But now anytime anyone puts a hand on her, they get, well, *burned*. It's like her body is on fire." He shifted uncomfortably in his chair. "If I thought I could continue the trial with her, I would, it's just gotten too risky. I wish I had better news for you."

Dread pooled in Chase's stomach. "What are you saying?"

"The girl's a danger to herself and others. I've recommended a frontal lobotomy. My colleague should be administering it any moment now."

Chase grabbed the man and hauled him out of his chair, slamming him against the bookshelf behind the desk. Books and trinkets clattered to the floor as Chase lowered his mouth to the man's ear. "Tell me where she is, or I will kill you here and now," he whispered menacingly.

The man blubbered incoherently and Chase flattened his palm against the man's forehead, too impatient to wait for a verbal answer. The doctor groaned in pain and Chase released him, dashing out the door.

꧂

There were hammers pounding in Asiah's head again, and she shivered. She felt hot and cold at the same time. Sweat ran down her forehead, stinging her eyes. Her arms were constricted again and she blinked furiously trying to clear her vision. Someone stood in front of her and shone a bright light into her burning eyes. She squeezed her eyes shut against the glare. She heard muffled voices nearby and strained to make out the words.

"I'll give you a moment, Dr. Henderson."

"Thank you."

A face appeared in front of hers with sandy hair and gentle blue eyes.

"Hello, darlin'."

She blinked at the man, struggling to recall why she recognized him.

"I know they've got you drugged up, but I just wanted to say goodbye before, well, it doesn't matter." He stroked her cheek gently, then jerked his hand back, examining his fingers with a frown. "I'm so sorry about all of this. I wish things would have worked out for us." He smiled at her sadly and disappeared.

She closed her eyes for a few minutes, sure that it must have been a hallucination. No one had been gentle to her since she'd been in this awful place. She opened her eyes again and this time saw a long silver needle in front of her. It wasn't like the needles they stuck her arms, this one was longer and thicker, like a knitting needle. Surely they couldn't administer medication through something like that? She didn't scream. She knew that resisting usually meant the other kind of needle and then ... nothing. She couldn't remember what happened after the needles went into her arms. She just knew that for the past few days there hadn't been any needles, and that everyone who touched her got hurt. Her skin felt like it was on fire. Maybe it was.

The doctor held the long needle up near her eye. She shrank away from its point, suddenly afraid of being poked in the eye. He said some soothing words and laid the needle's point against the edge of her eye socket, against the bridge of her nose. The metal felt cold and foreboding. *What is he doing to me?* Her instincts told her to fight; she didn't want to go back to sleep. She sat very still, hoping whatever he was about to do didn't hurt too much. The doctor held a small hammer in his other hand, which he now raised, as if to strike the blunt end of the needle.

No!

Asiah heard a bang, like the sound of a door being kicked in. There was yelling and someone pushed the doctor away. The long needle clattered to the floor. A face appeared in front of hers: another man's, but she couldn't focus on it, yet he seemed familiar. Hands touched her cheeks and forehead with a gentle touch. Her skin tingled where his fingers touched her. She froze. She knew that feeling, but from where she couldn't recall. The man examined her face and frowned before he moved away again. "Come back ..." she tried to say, but she couldn't speak. Her mouth was too dry. There was more yelling and she heard the doctor's voice pleading. The clothing restraining her arms was ripped away and she almost cried with relief. She was lifted from her chair by strong arms. She buried her face in her rescuer's shoulder and felt the electric sensation again. She knew his scent. It comforted her.

"No ... sleeping ..." she managed to croak. He may have saved her from one needle, but she didn't know if her savior was planning on knocking her out again. That's all they did here: put her to sleep, wait for her to wake up, then put her to sleep again.

"No more sleeping, love," he whispered, his lips brushing her temple. "You're safe now."

She couldn't hold back the tears; she'd never been so thankful for anything in her life. She heard him speaking sternly to someone else then, as he carried her. She hoped they were leaving. She didn't want to stay here any longer. More shouting caused her to hide her face in his shoulder again. His stride didn't slow and she soon felt the breeze through her thin clothing. She shivered and his arms tightened around her. The breeze became a strong wind for a few seconds then subsided. She felt him walk a few more steps before she was lowered gently onto a bed.

Her savior released her and she clutched at him, not wanting to be left alone. She struggled to catch her breath as he laid a calming hand on her arm.

"I'm not leaving, love, I just need to fetch some water." His voice was deep and soothing.

Asiah reluctantly let go and hugged her knees to her chest, trying to slow her breathing.

The lights were not too bright here, and it smelled earthy instead of antiseptic. The bed was soft and not scratchy. She didn't want to sleep, but exhaustion was overtaking her. She could hear the man nearby. Surely he would protect her if they came for her again. What if she closed her eyes, just for a moment?

※

Chase struggled to contain his rage as he pumped water into a bowl behind his cottage. He was furious at Asiah's father for allowing her to be taken to such a vile place. His fury had reached its peak when he saw the doctor about to plunge the eight-inch spike into Asiah's frontal lobe. His anger had ebbed only enough for him to feel the immense relief of finding her alive, but returned when he'd seen the bruises on her face and dried blood in her hair. He didn't know what they'd done to her, and if he ever found out who had abused her, his vengeance would be swift and merciless.

Chase returned to the bed with the bowl of water and a soft cloth and sat next to her, smoothing her matted hair back from her face. She had curled up into a ball and fallen asleep. He rolled her onto her back and began wiping the blood from her face. She wore a thin linen gown with nothing underneath, a fact that hadn't escaped Chase's attention. He was torn between getting her out of the filthy gown and into something clean and not wanting her to know that he'd seen her naked. He'd vowed to keep his hands off her, but he couldn't leave her in the same dirty clothes she'd probably been wearing for a month.

He placed his hand on her forehead. She was warm, burning up in fact. He needed to cool her off and bring her fever down. He went back outside and began filling his washtub with cool water. She'd have to forgive him for this. Protecting her privacy would have to take a backseat to saving her life. He returned to her bedside and lifted her into his arms, then took her outside and gently lowered her into the tub, gown and all, effectively throwing her into waking hysteria. Asiah shrieked and clung to him with wild, red-rimmed eyes. He was almost sure he saw a look of betrayal on her face as he submerged her body in the tub.

"Shh, love, you have a fever. I need to cool you down," he said soothingly.

"No ... no water!" she said between gasps.

Chase groaned. What was he thinking? They probably used hydrotherapy techniques on her, which could be thoroughly unpleasant, from what he'd heard. Still, it was the best way to bring her temperature down. He moved his hands up to cup her face.

"Asiah, look at me," he coaxed as she looked around frantically. "Look at me, love." She did and he could see the panic in her sunken eyes. He massaged her temples with his thumbs and held her gaze while he murmured calming words to her. He felt the tension finally begin to leave her body, and let go of her to reach for the soap. Lathering his hands, Chase began washing the blood from her hair. She relaxed even more under his touch, closing her eyes and breathing through her nose. When her hair was clean he held the soap out to her, indicating for her to bathe herself. She took the soap from him but didn't move, just looked around absently.

Chase cleared his throat. "I would help you with the rest, but you'll hate me for it later, so why don't you ...?" She just stared at the soap like she'd never seen anything like it. Chase grumbled, "Fine, I'll help you, but you'd better not hold this against me tomorrow."

He lifted her thin gown and pulled it over her head with one swift motion. Trying his level best to keep his eyes averted for her sake, he lathered his hands again and began washing her feet. She sat numbly in the cold water, letting him bathe her. It was the hardest thing Chase had ever done. Heaven knew he wanted to see her body and touch her, but not like this. Not with her staring blankly ahead, immune to his touch. In a way, her unresponsiveness made it easier to get it over and done with. When he'd finished, he realized he hadn't even taken any pleasure in touching her; he simply felt a deep sadness for what she'd been through. He did notice how thin she was, like they hadn't fed her in weeks. The bruises on her face weren't the only ones she had, either. He wanted to weep when he saw the results of the punishments she'd endured. His greatest fear was that her innocence had been taken, something that could cause her permanent psychological damage.

Once she was clean, he lifted her from the tub, wrapped her in a blanket and carried her back inside to the bed. As she lay on her back, Chase ran his hands over her arms, legs and belly searching for any signs of physiologic distress. Her temperature had come down and his touch was healing her, except for the high doses of tranquilizers still in her system. He knew these would wear off soon enough, and the bath probably did her more good than anything. To his immense relief, he could find no sign that her innocence had been violated in any way, although he had to wonder what that orderly had been up to just before Asiah had inadvertently killed him.

Satisfied that she would recover with no permanent damage, Chase brought a cup of water to her lips, encouraging her to drink. She sipped it gingerly and swallowed with some difficulty. He set the cup next to the bed and pulled the covers over her, making sure she was comfortable.

He moved to get up and she made a little sound like a whimper. His heart twisted and he sighed, took off his boots, and stretched out next to her. She rolled so her back was toward him then scooted back until she felt him behind her. Surprised that she would trust anyone right now, Chase shrugged and curled his body around hers, draping his arm across her midsection and pulling her body tightly against his. He buried his nose in her damp hair and breathed in her clean scent. For the first time in over a month, he fell sound asleep.

Chapter Sixteen

Asiah woke up to the sound of birds chirping. This struck her as odd. It seemed she hadn't heard that sound in ages, and it was like a wonderful dream. She felt restricted again, and couldn't move her arms, which led her to further believe that she was dreaming the bird sounds. She noticed something else, though: she could hear breathing other than her own. In fact, she could *feel* someone breathing on the back of her neck.

She tensed and opened her eyes. The walls here were not made of green tile, but wood, and she could see the sun's rays coming through the window. There had been no window in the green tiled room. Asiah moved her head slightly to see an arm, a *man's* arm, draped across her body, holding her in place tightly. She realized she wasn't wearing the garment that restricted her arms after all. In fact, she wasn't wearing *anything!* She was covered in soft bedclothes, but had no clothes on underneath. The man's arm was pinning her against his body, but not uncomfortably like that blasted jacket.

She wiggled, trying to free herself from his grasp, if only to prove to herself that she could move freely. He rolled away, dragging the bed covers with him. She squealed and snatched them back, covering herself as she scrambled off the bed. The man jerked awake, startled by her cry. He faced her and she recognized him.

"Ch-Chase! What am I doing here? Where are my clothes? Why am I *naked* in your *bed?*" The questions poured out of her before she had a chance to organize her thoughts.

Chase stood up awkwardly, clearly uncomfortable with something, but he looked relieved as well. "Please try to relax, Asiah," he began. "You've been through a lot in the last few weeks and you probably aren't aware of any of it."

Few weeks? She wrapped the blankets more tightly around herself. "Maybe you should explain it to me." Her tone was harsh, and she wasn't sure he deserved it. Something told her that he was only trying to help her. Why couldn't she remember how she'd gotten here?

"I will. All of it. But first, I'll get you some clothes and make you some breakfast." He strode to the bureau and pulled out a shirt and some trousers. He laid them on the edge of the bed. "I'll just be out here. Join me when you're ready." He left and closed the door behind him.

Once she'd dressed in Chase's oversized clothing, Asiah joined Chase in the main room and sat down gingerly at the table. She hadn't realized how hungry she was until that moment. Wherever she'd been, they must not have fed her adequately. Chase watched in brooding silence as she scarfed her breakfast.

"What's wrong?" she asked between mouthfuls.

He seemed to snap out of it and gave her a warm smile. "Nothing, I'm just so glad you're safe." His relief still showed on his face. "I've ... missed you."

"You make it seem like I was gone for a while," she said.

His gaze became dark. "Over a month."

She stopped chewing and stared at him. "A *month?* Where could I have gone for a month and not realized it?"

Chase looked out the window, contemplating his answer. "An asylum," he said, finally.

Orange juice almost came out of her nose. "*What*? Why would I be ..." She trailed off, remembering her last conversation with her family. "They think I'm insane," she finished.

Chase just nodded, then reached forward and took her hand. The energy in his touch was comforting now. She barely remembered when it used to alarm her. "But *I* know you're not. People like us have always been shunned because no one understands what we are, even if we explain it to them. I'm sorry for everything you've been through. I truly am. If I could have gotten to you sooner, I would have."

"Where is my family now?" she asked, not sure she really cared.

"San Francisco."

"Oh." They dumped her in an asylum and left her behind. Her chest ached. She turned her thoughts to something else. "How did you find me?"

"It wasn't easy. Your parents left town before I could ask them. If I'd found out where you were earlier, you wouldn't have had to live in that place for so long." Chase looked completely miserable. "I'm so sorry, Asiah."

"Well, thank you, for doing what you did. What no one else did. I'd probably still be there." She shuddered. "Did they ... do anything to me?" she asked reluctantly.

Chase clenched his jaw. "They drugged you."

"I knew that, otherwise I'd remember more."

"Not just tranquilizers. They used an experimental drug on you. A drug that's been killing regular people. I'm not sure how you survived without your power stones," Chase said grimly.

"What kind of drug was it?"

"The doctor told me it was supposed to enhance super-human abilities, which, of course, you already have. Under the effects of the drug, you weren't able to control your abilities, and, well, people got hurt," he said, watching her carefully.

"I ... *hurt* people?" she whispered.

"It wasn't your fault, love. They tried to hurt you. You were merely defending yourself. It was purely instinctual. They thought it was the drug, when in reality it was just you. The drug just blurred your memory so you couldn't remember the control exercises we'd practiced."

She looked down at her hands. She didn't want to think about that place anymore. She remembered her other question. "Why wasn't I wearing any clothes this morning?"

Chase gave her a little smile. "It's not the reason you think. I was a complete gentleman. They hadn't bathed you in weeks in that place, so I cleaned you up and put you to bed."

Her mouth fell open in shock. "You ... *bathed* me?" She blushed furiously.

He looked slightly uncomfortable. "I knew you would be upset with me, but I couldn't leave you in those dirty rags you were wearing. I'm sorry. If it helps, I kept my eyes closed the entire time."

"It doesn't help! You were touching me! *Naked!*" she shrieked at him.

He merely lifted an eyebrow. "You've let me do it before," he reminded her, causing her to blush even more.

"That's different! This time I was ... unaware." She didn't have a good argument and she knew it.

His green eyes twinkled. "Well then, next time, love, I will absolutely make sure you are aware that I'm touching you."

"You can't ... What about Walter?" She wondered. Did he know she was in the asylum? Was he part of it?

"I saw him leaving the room, just before I found you," Chase explained. "He knew what they were about to do."

"Which was?"

"A frontal lobotomy."

"*What?*" So Walter *had* been involved. Knowing that, there was no way she could marry him now, assuming he still wanted her, which clearly he didn't. She felt even more lost. "I suppose I don't have anywhere to live, then."

"You'll stay here with me," he said, matter-of-factly. At her look of surprise he added, "You can have my bed and I'll sleep on the floor."

"You didn't sleep on the floor last night," she reminded him.

He raised his eyebrows at her. "You refused to sleep alone last night."

Her face was about as red as she thought it could get so she changed the subject again. "I'm sure you want to resume my training, but I lost my bracelets."

He waved his hand dismissively. "I'll make you some new ones. I want to make sure you're strong enough before we resume your training."

She felt strong enough, but then she couldn't remember anything that had happened in the last few weeks. "Maybe if we start with something not-too-strenuous?"

"I have just the thing." He rose and pulled a piece of parchment from a shelf. She recognized it as the scroll he wanted her to read on her first day of work. He had already unrolled it and oiled it to keep it flat. He took away her empty plate and replaced it with the scroll. "Remember this?"

"Yes. Let's hope it doesn't make me faint again," she joked. "Don't I need the bracelets to read it?"

Chase shook his head. "You didn't need them before. Give it a try." He stood behind her chair with one hand on her shoulder and gave her a little squeeze.

She took a deep breath and placed her palms flat on the parchment. The dots and swirls she'd seen before appeared before her on the browned paper. It still looked like scribbles to her and she frowned. "It's just a bunch of dots and squiggles. What am I supposed to see?"

Chase bent so his face was next to hers and squinted at the writing. "I'm not meant to read this writing. It's the language of the Ikhälea. You should be able to understand the words. Keep looking at it until your mind learns the language."

She turned her face to fix him with a skeptical look. "My mind will just *learn* it?"

He gave her a dazzling smile. "From what I'm told." His gaze moved to her lips and he planted a quick kiss there before moving around to the opposite side of the table.

Cheeky scoundrel! She gave him a disapproving glare and turned her attention back to the parchment. She stared at the scribbles, willing them to make sense. She focused so much energy on the scroll, she didn't realize the paper was starting to smoke where her hands touched it.

Chase let out a little yelp and seized her wrists, lifting her hands from the paper. The writing faded and two black handprints remained.

"I'm sorry, I didn't realize I was burning it," she apologized. "I really can't make any sense—"

"Look!" Chase interrupted, pointing at the burn marks.

The blackened areas where her hands had been revealed more dots and swirls, written in gold ink. Asiah peered at the swirls and heard a whisper in her head: *Shade* ... The word seemed to bounce around in her skull as she inspected her handprint. She turned her focus to the other print and heard more whispers. *Phantom. Darkness.* Asiah sat up and looked around the cottage, making sure the voices weren't coming from somewhere inside the house.

"I think I'm getting something," she said, and Chase's eyes widened in anticipation. "There are some words here and there that I can ... understand." She pointed to the handprints. "I think I can get some more." She rubbed her palms together and placed them on the paper again, in different locations than before. This time she focused on revealing the golden writing until the parchment smoked again, leaving more handprints. She continued placing her hands in different spots until the entire scroll was black and covered with golden swirls and dots. Chase watched her in anxious silence.

When she had finished, she sat back in her chair, suddenly exhausted. "I think I need a break," she said looking at Chase across the table. "I feel really tired all of a sudden."

He nodded. "You will tire faster without your power stones. I will get started on some new jewelry for you to wear. Shall I make some tea as well?"

"Tea would be wonderful," she said.

He returned to the table with a pot of tea and two cups. He moved his chair next to hers and sat beside her to look at the scroll. "What have you got so far?" he asked.

"Just words, no sentences yet. They seem to echo in my head. It's difficult to focus for more than a few seconds at a time."

Chase pushed the scroll across the table so it wasn't staring her in the face. He then brushed a stray lock of hair from her forehead and tucked it behind her ear, letting his fingers gently brush her earlobe. "You're very brave, you know," he said, his voice a low rumble. "Most people I've met — and I've met a lot of people — wouldn't even consider taking on the challenge you have ahead of you. You're so young, but you have so much courage." She could hear the pride in his voice. "I only wish I could be there to see what you do with your powers."

"Why can't you? You have the power to keep on living just as I do. Why can't you stay and help me? I'm sure the two of us could accomplish a lot more than I could alone," she said, not sure why it mattered to her so much what he did with the rest of his life.

"This is your destiny, not mine. I would only hold you back." His words sounded rehearsed.

"I'm not sure how," she muttered.

"*This* is how," he said and captured her mouth in a long, searing kiss. When he broke the kiss, she was out of breath. *How does he do that?*

"Your mission is too important. You have an entire planet to save. I don't care about these people; they can rot for all I care. If I stayed, it would be only for myself and for you. For this ..." He kissed her again, softly, more regretful than before. He leaned back and looked into her eyes. "Do you understand, love?"

She nodded mutely. It hurt her to hear that he wouldn't stay for her. Saying that he would distract her from her purpose was just an excuse. The truth was he had nearly completed his life's mission: to find and train her. When it was done, he could die in peace and alone, all he had probably wanted to do for centuries. He was watching her closely. She saw him reach his hand up to touch her face again and she leaned forward and pulled the scroll back to read it, causing him to drop his hand.

Focusing her attention on the gold writing, she opened her mind and let the whispers tell her what was written:

> *Let it be known that the reader of these words here written is the one True Shade, there can be no other.*
>
> *This planet to which a Shade and her sire before her, the Cleric, have been summoned is on a path to eternal darkness. It is not her world, but merely a glimmer of the past. Even so, only she may save this world from darkness.*
>
> *This task must be completed alone, but help is given to those who do not know the way. The one True Shade will be guided by the Supreme Conjurer, the one who eliminates all imposters*

before him. He can be the only one to light the True Shade's path to glory.

Beware the Phantom Shades, for they are not saviors, but enemies of the people. Born of the Banished Ones, they do not possess the true power to save our people. Their hatred of the True Shade drives them to madness.

Beware the Fallen Conjurer, for he is cursed. The Fallen Conjurer's seduction shall be a Shade's undoing. Her only lover must be her undertaking.

Squander not the gifts of the Ikhälea, for this road leads to certain doom — not only for the future of all Ikhälea, but the Shade as well. For no Shade may become one with the æthers who condemns her people to darkness.

When the whispers had subsided, Asiah sat staring at the document for a long time. Chase's voice brought her out of her reverie.

"What does it say, love?"

"Just what you've told me," she evaded.

"There must be more than that, or the scroll would serve no purpose."

"It describes my mission, but not how to complete it. It speaks of you; it refers to you as the 'Supreme Conjurer.' It also speaks of 'Phantom Shades born of the Banished Ones.' What does that mean?" She chose to avoid asking about the "Fallen Conjurer" part for now.

"I am the Supreme Conjurer." A shadow passed over his face. "My teacher told me that when an Ikhäle commits a crime the worst punishment imaginable is banishment to an underdeveloped world. That's who the 'Banished Ones' refers to. Their offspring are known as Phantom Shades. They are very powerful, but are not the chosen ones to save the planet. There is only one chosen one: that's you."

"Are there any Phantom Shades on Earth?" she asked.

Chase looked away, clenching his jaw.

"Chase?" Asiah dreaded his answer.

He sighed in defeat. "There is one that I know of."

"Why haven't you told me this before?" she admonished.

"You had enough on your mind. I would have told you eventually." He stared down at his hands.

"Does this Phantom Shade know who I am? Will she try to ... hurt me?"

"Yes," he said miserably. "And yes."

"Were you also going to tell me about all the other Conjurers you killed to become the Supreme Conjurer?" She was on her feet, eyes blazing.

Chase closed his eyes and shook his head. "I didn't mean for you to find out this way. I didn't want to kill any of the others, I just ... had to make sure they died."

"Oh, that's *much* better!" she shouted at him. "You made sure you were the only one left so you could be the one to train me!"

"Yes. I'm sorry it had to be that way, but I didn't make the rules."

"Who is the Fallen Conjurer?"

He snapped his head up. "What are you talking about?"

"The scroll said I need to beware the Fallen Conjurer's seduction."

Chase frowned, deep in thought.

"Well? Who is it? Is it you?"

He shook his head, still frowning and pointed to his chest. "Supreme Conjurer, remember?"

"You can't be both?"

"I'm not sure, but I don't think I qualify as 'Fallen.'"

"You *are* the one seducing me, though." She crossed her arms and arched an eyebrow at him.

He looked at her for a long moment, mulling something over in his mind. He let out a long sigh. "Yes, I have been treading a fine line, haven't I? Just to be safe, I promise not to seduce you further."

She laughed mirthlessly. "You've promised that before."

"I can't help it. I care about you," he said dismally.

She couldn't look at him and turned away. "It doesn't matter."

She heard him get up from the table and walk toward her. "It does matter. I've never felt like this about anyone before. I can't think straight when I'm around you. Why won't you look at me?"

His outpouring of emotion softened her heart a little and she turned around. For the first time, she could see all of his 750 years in his eyes.

"Please say something," he begged.

She took a step forward and laid her hand on his cheek. "I know you never meant to hurt me and now I understand why we can't be together, no matter how much we both want it." He closed his eyes. "But you can still complete my training and I can still save the world as I'm meant to do."

He nodded and placed his hand over hers. He turned his face into her hand and brushed a kiss against her palm. "Last one," he said, attempting to smile. He cleared his throat, bringing his emotions under control. "I'm going to go get you some jewelry. Why don't you stay here and get some rest? We'll continue your training this afternoon." He released her hand, which she hadn't realized he was still holding, and strode from the room. She saw his flash a few seconds later. She returned to the bedroom and climbed onto the bed, hugging her knees to her chest. She buried her face in Chase's pillow, breathing in his scent as the tears began to fall.

Chapter Seventeen

Chase wearily roamed the night market in Istanbul, Turkey. He stopped at a few stalls, examining various baubles, but nothing seemed to be right for Asiah. He took his time, hoping she would take some rest and feel better by the time he returned, and also because right now he couldn't trust himself around her. Every time he looked at her he wanted to scoop her up and carry her off to bed and spend the rest of his life making love to her. The scroll's words were a major blow. He knew he shouldn't seduce her because it would distract her from her purpose, but to actually bring about the end of humankind — he couldn't be responsible for that. Any hope he had of making it work with her dissipated when she translated the scroll, even if he ended up not being this "Fallen" Conjurer after all.

He ran his hands over a royal-blue silk scarf. Asiah would look beautiful wearing it, especially if it were the *only* thing she was wearing … He groaned, wondering if he'd ever be able to control his wayward thoughts. He was so close to accomplishing his life's goal, he couldn't let a little thing like love get in his way. The thought made him laugh out loud, startling the man selling the scarves. How could this be *love?* Love took years to cultivate; this was simply physical attraction. An infatuation. An obsession. He shook his head to erase the image of her face he had just conjured in his mind. Continuing down the aisle of stalls, Chase found a silversmith displaying hundreds of different bracelets, chains, earrings and rings.

He came across an interesting piece that was a combination wrist cuff and ring. The cuff was a simple silver band with a moon and stars engraved around it, and it was wide enough for a power stone, or several, to be inserted anywhere along the inside rim. A delicate chain inset with small black stones connected the cuff to a middle-finger ring over the back of the hand. The ring's black stone could also be replaced with a power stone. Chase paid the silversmith and looked down the aisle for something else to occupy his mind. He wasn't ready to go back yet. The enticing aroma of shawarma greeted him from down the way and realized he was famished. Asiah had eaten breakfast, but he'd been too anxious to eat with her.

Another hour later, Chase decided he had avoided returning home long enough. He still needed to put together her bracelet. After another quick stop at a sapphire mine in Australia, he arrived at his cottage, entering quietly in case Asiah was asleep. He heard no sound and peeked in the bedroom to check. She was curled up on the bed, fast asleep. His heart twisted as he noticed her tear-stained cheeks. He furiously fought the urge to go to her and kiss her pain away. Instead, he sat down at the table and took out the new jewelry and the sapphires. Since he had more time, he smoothed the stones into perfect sharp points for better contact and less-painful insertion. He bored a hole in the wristband and inserted one of the stones there, setting it in place by heating the silver around it. The smaller stone he set in the ring after removing the black onyx. Finger insertion was not as effective as at the wrist, where the stone would set deeper, but the ring's stone was only support for the main stone in the wrist cuff.

One power stone yielded enough energy, but Chase's mentor had warned him against relying on one stone. Two stones were better, he'd always said. It was better if they were separated more than they were with this bracelet, yet

Chase didn't think it mattered that much if she wore one or two pieces of jewelry.

Chase heard the bed creak in the other room as he put the finishing touches on the bracelet. He hoped Asiah would like it since she'd have to wear it all time. She emerged from the bedroom yawning, her hair adorably tousled. The dark circles beneath her eyes had faded considerably and some of the sparkle had returned to her eyes.

"I have something for you." He motioned for her to sit down. She did and, anticipating his next request, placed her arms across the table. He took her right hand in his. "I just need the one this time." She pulled her left arm back and propped her chin in her hand.

Chase fastened the cuff and put the ring on her finger, hesitating before pushing the stones into place. He looked at her and raised his eyebrows. She nodded and bit her lip. He thrust both stones into her skin simultaneously and she moaned. It wasn't a sound of pain, but almost one of pleasure. He thought he would give anything to hear her make that sound again.

Asiah recovered a moment later, looking slightly dazed. Her blue eyes were positively glowing. She lifted her wrist and examined the jewelry.

"It's beautiful. It must have cost you a fortune," she said, admiring it.

"I'm glad you like it. It's not easy finding jewelry in which to mount power stones that also complements the person wearing it."

"I think you did fine. Does it always feel like this when you insert the stones?"

"It gets easier," Chase said, "once you've done it about a thousand times." He smiled and she returned the gesture. "Let's go outside," he said.

In the clearing, Asiah shivered, rubbing her hands over the thin material of her borrowed tunic. "Why do we have to work out here? It's so cold today."

"Because it's safer to work with fire outside rather than inside a house full of old books and other things that burn easily."

"We could work on something other than fire," she suggested.

"Learning to control heat levels is an essential skill that provides a base for many other tasks. If you cannot use fire, your powers won't count for much at all," he said sternly, adopting a professorial manner. "In that place, they pushed you to the edge and you lost control of your abilities. That can't happen again."

"I know. I didn't know what I was doing," she said solemnly. "I can't believe I could produce a flame at all."

"People are capable of amazing things when they are pushed to their limits. Are you ready to begin?" he asked, snapping his fingers. A small flame leapt from his fingertips.

The blood drained from her face momentarily. She widened her stance and held her hand palm-up in front of her, concentrating. After a moment a few sparks flashed above her outstretched hand. She gritted her teeth. A second later her entire arm caught fire. She yelped and started waving her arm madly. Realizing that she was only making the fire worse, she stopped. Still holding her arm out, she brought her opposite hand over the flames. The flames went out as if doused with water. The sleeve of her tunic smoked slightly.

Chase approached her, clapping his hands slowly. "Well done, love. You handled that better than last time. I must say, I've lost more clothes since I met you than in the last one hundred years." He reached for her sleeve and ripped the smoldering fabric away at the shoulder. "Are you still cold?" he asked, running his fingers down her arm, checking for burns.

She shook her head and stepped away from his touch. "I already healed the skin," she said, rubbing her bare arm with her opposite hand.

Chase was truly impressed. "Multi-tasking already? I'll have you battle-ready in no time."

Asiah dropped her arms. "About that, who is this 'Phantom Shade' that's out to get me?"

Chase decided there was probably no good that could come from keeping this from her any longer. "Her name is Marysa. I don't know how long she's been alive, but it's been at least a few centuries. She's self-taught and impulsive, which gives you an advantage. Her mental powers are not nearly as strong as they should be, which is also good for you. The only real disadvantage you have is that she can transform into her mature Ikhälean form while you cannot."

"Mature Ikhälean form?" Her eyes were huge. "You've mentioned that before. Do I want to know what that is?"

"I'll show you when we go back inside. Basically, she will be nearly impossible to defeat. We must prey on her weakness: her mind. Let's try another exercise. I'm going to try and read your mind. I want to you to block my thoughts from merging with yours. To make it interesting, we're going to play with fire as well." He backed up a step and ignited both hands, preparing to hurl fireballs at her. "Ready?"

"I wish you'd stop asking if I'm ready. *She's* not going to ask," she said, irritated.

He raised an eyebrow at her feisty remark. "Fine." He threw both fireballs at the same time.

∽

Asiah stood her ground this time. She summoned a cold wind to extinguish the flames before they reached her. She felt like she was definitely getting the hang of moving air. She could put out fire at least. Now if she could just control it herself.

She extended her hands again in an attempt to spark a flame. This time, a tiny flame flared up from her palm. It was warm, but she found it wasn't hard to simultaneously cool the air between her palm and the fire so she didn't burn herself. It was a strange sensation, like she was using different parts of her brain at the same time. She focused on making the flame larger.

She felt something else happening as she focused on the fire. It felt like someone was whispering in her ear and she couldn't make out the words. She realized it was Chase trying to read her thoughts. *Oh, no you don't.* She imagined walls around her mind, surrounding the Forest and keeping it safer from invaders, and then threw her little fireball. It flew a few feet then fizzled out in midair. She frowned and heard Chase laughing in her head. Her eyes snapped to his and she glared at him.

He laughed out loud. "I win."

"You didn't win. I kept you out of my head."

"But you didn't defend your physical self. That little fireball wasn't going to stop anyone. It's true you kept me out, but you must also protect your body from physical attack. Marysa will attack you on both fronts."

Asiah frowned and with grim determination extended both arms out to the side and summoned all the strength she had and set both arms aflame from fingertips to shoulders. She brought both hands together in front of her and pushed the flames at Chase. He dodged to the side and the flames ignited a tree behind him. She dropped her arms, now both bare, and crossed them over her chest.

Stepping back from the heat of the burning tree, Chase scratched his chin thoughtfully. "Again, well done. Now put it out."

Asiah thought she should feel tired after summoning that much energy, but oddly enough she seemed to have recovered already. She prepared to summon the wind again and Chase shook his head.

"Wind will only make a fire of this size spread. Try something else."

She thought for a moment and had an idea. Keeping her arms at her sides she extended her fingers toward the ground. After a moment Chase raised an eyebrow.

"Asiah? The tree is still on fire," he urged.

She looked at him and cocked her head to the side. "Are you sure?"

He turned and looked at the tree again. It wasn't burning fiercely, but smoldering and smoking. As he watched, the embers began to hiss and snuff out.

"You pulled water from the ground to douse the flames. Not a bad solution but a slow one. Your best option would have been to pull the flames from the tree back into yourself," he said, like it was as easy as pinching out a match.

"Then where does the heat go? The energy must be transferred somewhere."

"Bring the flame back to your hands where you can best control it. Then push the heat away from yourself in all directions so it dissipates."

It sounded counterintuitive to Asiah but Chase hadn't led her astray so far.

"Now, do what you just did with the fire while I'm trying to see your thoughts."

Chase pelted Asiah with fireballs for the next two hours. She managed to learn to control the flames pretty well; however, she had trouble shielding her thoughts from him at the same time. She knew he'd bested her whenever she heard him laughing in her head. It was exasperating. After a while the fire became second nature and she found she could control it fairly easily. Closing her mind to Chase at the same time seemed impossible, though. They reversed roles and she threw fire and tried to read his thoughts. Oddly enough, it was much easier. She was able to break down the barriers in his mind without much prodding, a deed which seemed to frustrate Chase to no end. Eventually his control snapped.

"*How* are you doing this?!" he exploded when she let up for a moment.

She'd never seen him this agitated and didn't know why he was so upset. She was simply doing what he told her to do. "I'm not doing anything! I'm not even reading your thoughts! I just push through a gateway, like a circle of stones or something, and I know I'm in your head. I don't know why it's so easy. I'm sorry." She didn't really feel like she needed to apologize, but he was angry and she didn't ever want him to be upset with her, especially since he was the only one left in the world who seemed to care about her.

He sighed and rubbed the back of his neck. "I'm sorry for shouting at you. You *are* doing well. Perhaps a little too well. I guess I'm just anxious about what you might see in here." He tapped his head. "Let's go inside and have something to eat. I'm starving and it's cold out here."

She gave him her best I-told-you-so glare, then smiled. Maybe it was the power stones, but she felt very light on her feet today. It probably also helped that she wasn't drugged out of her mind or being restrained in a straightjacket.

The smell of chicken soup met her as they entered the cottage. *When did he make that?* She gave him a questioning look and he grinned.

"You're not about to tell me that you can stop time are you?" she asked apprehensively.

"Of course not! Time is constant; it cannot be sped up or slowed down, and you can't travel forward or backward in time. Even if that Einstein fellow thinks it's possible. The Ikhälea learned that long ago. That's why they keep starting new worlds."

She brightened. "You know about Einstein?" she asked excitedly. He was a hero of hers.

"I have. He's one of the most brilliant humans in centuries. I almost thought he was a Conjurer when I met him," he said as he fetched bowls from the cupboard.

Her mouth fell open in shock. "You've *met* him?"

"When I read his theories I knew he was no ordinary human. I had to make sure he wasn't a Conjurer. Let's just say it's a good thing he isn't." A shadow passed over his face.

Asiah sat down at the table as he placed a bowl of soup in front of her. It smelled delicious. She wasn't sure how to ask him about his past, but she needed to know what he'd done. "Did you really ... kill the other Conjurers?"

Chase sat down heavily. He rubbed his face with his hands and sighed. "Yes," he said finally, "but I didn't do it for sport. I had to make sure I was the only one left when I eventually found you. My great-uncle had trained several Conjurers who in turn had trained even more. All of them were power-hungry crooks, using their powers for their own gain. If one of them had found you first, you would never know your true purpose."

"Did they even know about me?"

"There are many writings about you. If any of them were wise enough to understand the literature and find you, it's likely that they would have used you for a more sinister purpose."

"Did you actually kill any of them yourself?" *Why am I asking this?* she wondered.

"Three, and it was self-defense each time. For the rest I made sure someone else got their hands dirty. I may have fought in a lot of wars, but I don't enjoy killing." He twirled his spoon in his soup, lost in another world.

"How does someone like your great-uncle train ordinary humans to become Conjurers?" she asked, hoping to bring him back from his dark past.

"Not everyone can learn Conjuring. It takes intense focus and concentration and you must give up everything else in your life to commit to it. Most Conjurers, as I've said, can't keep their gifts to themselves and end up dead. Only very focused people can live as long as I have and still maintain their sanity. Which is why I'm the only one left."

"How do I know you're not one of these rogues you've warned me about?" she kidded, giving him a sly smile.

"You don't." He ate a spoonful of his soup and his eyes gleamed at her across the table. She heard his laughter in her head again.

"Stop that! Stay out of my head!" She covered her ears, as if it could keep him out.

"I like it in your forest," he said in a low rumble.

The innuendo was not lost on her. "I didn't say you could come in whenever you like."

"Then don't let me in," he replied.

She gave him an exasperated look. "Tell me about this maturity thing," she said, changing the subject.

Chase nodded and collected their bowls as he stood up. He went to the bookshelf and pulled a worn-looking journal from the dusty shelf. He flipped through it for a moment then laid it in front of her on the table.

"Ikhälean Shades are half-human, half-Ikhäle but retain the physical attributes of the lesser-developed species until they reach maturity," Chase explained. "When the Ikhälean side reaches maturity, which takes about one hundred years on Earth, a Shade may then occasionally transform into her Ikhälean form." He pointed to a sketch on the open page.

Asiah examined the sketch. "It just looks like a person ... with wings."

He nodded. "A mature Ikhäle closely resembles a human, but with more developed features. They have reflective skin to help protect them from harsh radiation from their suns; this isn't really shown in the sketch. They also have a tapetum lucidum to help them see in the dark. Do you know what that is?"

She nodded. "It's a reflective layer of the retina in the eye. It's why cats' eyes seem to glow in the dark."

"Correct. The biggest difference in appearance is the wings. Ikhälea develop the ability to fly late in their evolution. Their wings are retractable, able to be fully concealed in the skin of the back. From what I've seen, they don't resemble the wings of any flying animal. They seem to be made of large, translucent feathers."

"Why do they need wings if they can channel anywhere they want to go?" she asked.

Chase shrugged. "No one knows, but my readings indicate that only female Ikhälea have wings."

"Have you seen this mature form with your own eyes?"

"Only twice and very briefly. Once when Marysa attacked me at your old apartment, and once in a dream," he said distantly.

"A dream?"

He looked back at her a moment, then removed a loose sheaf of paper from the journal and slid it across the table to her. "I dreamed about you."

This paper also had a sketch on it. It was of a woman sitting on a rock with her face in profile. She had long, dark hair and Asiah could just see the edge of a wing behind her hair. The woman *did* seem somewhat familiar. "This is me?"

Chase nodded. "I'm almost sure of it. It was only a fleeting glimpse in the dream, but it was on the day I met you. There's no one else it could be."

She peered at the sketch more closely. "I'm ... naked."

He grinned sheepishly. "Yes, as you were in the dream. I just sketched what I saw."

"You need to stop seeing me naked," she muttered.

He gave a quiet, derisive snort and she glared at him.

"Why doesn't Marysa stay in this form all the time?" she asked, resisting the urge to read his thoughts.

"This is generally avoided as primitive species, like humans, are likely to see them as a threat. I've read that most Shades who show their Ikhälean side to humans end up dead before their mission is completed."

"Then why show it at all?"

"Shades are dangerous beings in their human form, but in their Ikhälean form, they are a deadly force. Their speed, strength and telekinetic powers increase tenfold, making them hard to capture and nearly impossible to kill. This is why Marysa can so easily best me in her Ikhälean form."

"I thought her mind was weak? And how do they end up dead if they are so hard to kill?"

"Her mental powers aren't much stronger, even in transformation. She may be more powerful than me, but I doubt that her psychological powers would be able to rival yours, even before you reach maturity." He beamed at her. "I said they are *nearly* impossible to kill. Resourceful humans find a way, usually by waiting until the Shades resume their human form. It requires a lot of energy to stay in the Ikhälean form when Ikhälea are away from their home planets, or so I'm told."

"I don't feel like my mind is that strong," Asiah said doubtfully.

"Let's sit by the fire and practice closing your mind to intruding psychic forces," he suggested. "You'll be surprised by how strong you are."

They sat on the rug as before, across from each other, except this time Chase's knees touched hers so he was within arm's length.

"I'm going to place my hand on your forehead and push my way into your thoughts. Direct contact is much harder to resist than when I was standing ten feet away from you. You will not feel anything if you let me in, however, it can be quite painful if you resist. I want you to resist, and if you are strong enough, you can do so without feeling any pain. Understand?" he asked.

"I think so," she nodded.

Chase placed the palm of his hand against her forehead and closed his eyes. She only had a moment to consider shrouding her thoughts before a lightning bolt slammed through her skull. She threw her arms up to bat his hand away but he held firm. She was blind, her vision obscured by white flashes of light. She knew she wouldn't last much longer if she didn't do something. Balling her hands into fists she pushed every ounce of energy she could conjure into a blocking force against him.

The pain stopped instantly. She opened her eyes to see Chase examining his hand in bewilderment. Had he pulled his hand away or had she stopped him?

"What happened?" she asked, wiping sweat from her brow.

"You burned my hand is what happened," he said, confused.

"Did that ... work?" she wondered.

"I'd say so. I don't know what you did but suddenly the forest was on fire and my hand was burning." He reached forward and touched her forehead with his fingertips. "You're sweating."

She nodded. "It was hard, resisting you."

"Not that hard, apparently. No one has ever been able to resist me like that before."

"Would that make you ... irresistible?" She smirked.

"Obviously not," he grumbled.

She rubbed her temples to ease the dull ache returning to her head. "I don't think I can handle any more mind reading exercises tonight."

"Agreed." Chase stretched his arms over his head and leaned his head back. Asiah's eyes fell on the thin, white scar on his neck.

"Did Marysa do that to you?" she asked hesitantly.

He dropped his arms and traced the scar with his fingertip. "Yes, when I wouldn't tell her about you."

"When I found you, it wouldn't stop bleeding for the longest time. Why was it so hard to heal?" she asked.

"Two reasons: first, she attacked me in the way we just practiced, by trying to break into my thoughts. It took most of my energy to resist her. Second, she used an Ikhälean blade. As I showed you before, wounds from such weapons never truly heal. That is why I had to borrow some of your energy to heal it as much as I could. This is another wound from the same knife." He lifted his tunic, revealing another small scar at the edge of his ribcage.

Asiah reached forward and gently brushed her fingers over the scar, wishing he hadn't had to suffer because of her. To her surprise, the scar began to fade. She looked up to his face and saw that he was just as surprised. "I thought it would never fully heal?" she said.

"Apparently, you have the magic touch," he said, rubbing the spot where the scar had just disappeared completely.

"What about these other scars? From the same blade?" she asked, pointing to the myriad of marks crisscrossing his torso.

"No, those are from regular weapons during the wars. If wounds heal naturally without the aid of my healing ability, they leave scars. I never healed them because I wanted to remember each wound."

"More sadistic souvenirs," she said. "Lift your chin." She placed her finger under his chin and tilted it up, then traced her finger along the scar on his neck. It, too, faded at her touch. "You can keep the rest, but I don't want to think about how you were hurt because of me every time I look at you." Her voice shook slightly, and she wasn't sure if she was more angry at Marysa for hurting him or at Chase for putting himself in harm's way for her.

Chase caught her hand as she pulled her fingers from his neck and brought it to his lips, pressing a kiss to her palm. "I told you I would never let any harm come to you. I meant it before and I mean it even more now."

She snatched her hand back, annoyed that he was distracting her again with his tantalizing lips. "You don't have to fight my battles for me, you know. I never asked for that. I'm not going to let this woman kill you for my sake."

Chase looked wounded. "I'm not that easy to kill. And I *will* die for you if it comes to that, and you have no say in the matter."

Asiah stood up, irate. "Why would you do that? Why does it matter so much to you what happens to me?" she shouted.

"It's my job to keep you safe!" he shouted back, coming to his feet. "My life's purpose!"

"That's not true. Your purpose is to train me and leave me behind. Tell me why you suddenly care so much about my well-being," she demanded.

"Because I'm in love with you!" He took a step forward, standing over her. The moment the words were out of his mouth he closed his eyes, realizing what he'd just admitted, and ran his hands through his hair.

Asiah's anger evaporated into shock. "You're ... *what?*"

Chase rubbed his hands over his face and sighed. Finally, he raised his eyes to meet hers. "I love you, Asiah."

She shook her head, trying to understand. "But you said ... we couldn't ..." she trailed off.

"I know. But it doesn't change the way I feel." He looked at her with his heart in his eyes.

She didn't know what to say. Did she love him? She wasn't sure, having never been in love before. She'd certainly never felt like *this* before. He was still waiting for her to say something.

"I-I'm sorry, Chase, I don't know what to say. I didn't expect you to say that." She looked down at her hands so she didn't have to see his heartbroken expression.

He sighed and walked away, disappearing into the bedroom. He reappeared holding a pillow and blanket under his arm. "You should get some rest," he said without looking at her. "We still have a lot of work to do. I'll get you some new clothes in the morning so you don't have to wear my old rags." He tossed his pillow on the floor in front of the fire, causing her to back up a step.

"Chase—" she began.

"Don't," he warned. "Now get some sleep."

She nodded and headed for the bedroom. She closed the door quietly and crawled into bed. She went to the boulder in the lake in the Forest, trying to calm her nerves. Eventually, she drifted into a troubled sleep.

Chapter Eighteen

Chase lay awake for hours, unable to get his emotions under control. So she didn't love him. It just meant she was stronger than he was. He told her they could never be together and she took it to heart. She knew how important it was for her to close her heart to him. Hell, *he* knew how important it was, he just couldn't stop himself from falling for *her*. He'd long known of the danger of falling in love with the Shade once he found her. Tojen spoke of the flawless beauty and allure of such creatures and how men's hearts were lost to them almost instantly. Chase hadn't fallen for her beauty; he'd seen many attractive women over the years. He had fallen for her innocent smile, her brilliant mind and her vivacious spirit. The fact that she was the most beautiful creature he'd seen in seven and a half centuries was just a bonus.

It tortured him to think she was sleeping in his bed this very minute and he could no more go to her there than cross the entire universe. He rolled onto his back, staring up at the ceiling and wondering if she was still awake thinking about him. He snorted. She was probably fast asleep, dreaming in her beautiful forest: a safe haven where he wasn't welcome. He closed his eyes and forced his breathing to slow.

Chase wasn't sure how long he'd slept. When he awoke the sun had not quite risen yet and he shivered beneath his thin blanket. The fire had gone out and the cold from outside was creeping in. He scratched his jaw and decided a hot bath and a shave would be good for lifting his spirits, if only a little.

    He went outside to the wooden tub behind his cottage and began pumping water into it until it was almost full. He heated the water with his hand so that steam rose into the cold morning air. Disrobing quickly, Chase stepped into the tub, letting the hot water ease the tension in his body. His shaving kit was on a tree stump next to the water pump and he reached for his straight razor. He noticed it was much easier to shave his throat without the scar in the way. Apparently wounds from Ikhälean blades always left a scar, but Asiah had the ability to heal the wound completely, not that Chase needed another reminder of how special she truly was.

    He finished shaving and stood up in the tub to rinse off. Using a small bucket, he dumped water over his head several times. He shook his head to clear the water from his ears, flinging water everywhere in the process. He reached his arms over his head, stretching, and heard a gasp behind him. He froze. *Oh no ...* Without turning around, he looked over his shoulder just in time to see Asiah scamper back inside.

    Chase dropped his arms and buried his face in his hands. How could things between them get any more awkward? If it weren't so cold outside he could stay out here all day and avoid the difficult conversation he knew was in store. He sighed and reached for his towel. There wasn't any point in delaying the inevitable. He'd have to face Asiah sooner or later. Drying himself quickly, Chase pulled on his trousers, grabbed his shirt off the stump and headed inside.

    Asiah was flitting around the room, preparing breakfast. She didn't look at him when he entered, but instead seemed to find renewed purpose in brewing the tea, even using her power to do so. Chase cleared his throat, and Asiah focused more intently on heating the kettle.

"I supposed we're even now," he began, trying to keep the mood light.

She remained silent and blushed furiously, obviously more uncomfortable than he was.

"You can't avoid me all day you know. We have a lot more to learn," he tried, taking a practical approach.

"I'm not ... avoiding you," she said, her voice a little higher than usual. "Would you like some tea? I'm making tea. It should be ready soon, if you want some." She still wouldn't look at him.

Chase smiled; he adored her nervous babbling. It was somewhat satisfying to know that he unsettled her as much as she did him. He moved into her line of sight and stood in front of her as she poured hot water over the tea leaves.

"I would love some tea," he said, willing her to look at him.

She glanced up and her eyes widened as she noticed he was only wearing his trousers. She blushed even more and set the kettle down shakily. With her eyes still glued to his bare chest she stammered, "I ... I ..."

"Asiah," he interrupted her, "I'm up here." He pointed to his face and her eyes snapped to his. He graced her with his most charming smile.

She sank into a chair at the table and covered her face with her hands. "I'm so sorry! I didn't know you would be bathing. I just went to get some water and there ... *you* were."

He sat down across from her and pulled her hands away from her face. "I'm not embarrassed and you shouldn't be either. Like I said before, we're even now. Alright, love?"

She still had trouble looking him in the eye, but seemed to relax a little. "I'm not sure we're even. You *bathed* me. I only saw your ... backside. And then you put me in your bed naked." She blushed again at her own words.

He grinned at her. "You can bathe me next time if you wish. I'll not stop you. And I promise the next time you're naked in my bed will be by your own choice."

If possible, her face reddened even more. "I think the eggs are almost ready." She popped up from the table and busied herself with the eggs she had just boiled. It was clear no more would be said on the matter.

Chase pulled on his tunic to put her out of her misery, even if he did like the way she looked at him when he was half-clothed.

Still drained from having not slept the night before, Chase sat with his back against the big oak tree in front of his cottage watching Asiah practice various skills. She lit matches one by one at twenty paces, then lit one match and lit the rest by moving that match down the line. She made a tower of matches without using her hands and by lighting one, set the whole tower ablaze. She made rocks float and move at various speeds and in certain patterns. When her control strengthened, Chase had her levitate water droplets then electrify them with sparks of electricity. She had trouble producing an electric spark at first, but soon was shooting tiny lightning bolts from her fingers.

While Asiah was in deep concentration, Chase took the opportunity to let his thoughts wander. If their circumstances had been different, he could see himself spending the rest of his life with her. It was a cruel twist of fate that he'd fallen so hard for her. Tojen had warned him that the Shade would be a temptation that most men wouldn't be able to resist, and like most men, Chase couldn't resist her. Except he had to, or the world could be doomed. He snorted. Ancient prophecies and writings often had a very gloomy approach to things. Just because two people fell in love couldn't possibly mean the end of civilization, could it? It didn't matter anyway, Asiah didn't love him. She was attracted to him, he could tell by the way she looked at him, but physical attraction wasn't enough. If she wasn't supposed to save the world, he'd run away with her and make her fall in love with him.

As if she'd been reading his thoughts, she stopped what she was doing and walked over to where he was sitting against the tree with his legs stretched out in front of him. Placing her hands on his shoulders, she straddled his legs and lowered herself onto his lap so she was facing him.

"What are you doing?" he asked, bewildered.

"I didn't respond very well last night when you said you were in love with me," she replied, looking into his eyes.

His mouth went dry and he slid his hands up to grip her waist. "No, you didn't," he choked out.

"Well, maybe this will satisfy your curiosity," she whispered, and lowered her mouth to his.

Chase couldn't believe *she* was kissing *him*. He knew he shouldn't reciprocate, but the taste of her sweet mouth was driving him wild. He ran his hands up her sides until his thumbs brushed her ribcage. He pulled her closer so he could nuzzle her neck. A spark of electricity made him flinch and he chalked it up to the fact that she had just been practicing with sparks and had let one go involuntarily. He went back to kissing her neck and she shocked him again, harder this time.

He woke up with a start. Asiah was standing over him with her finger pointed at his forehead. She shocked him one more time and he jumped to his feet.

"What the devil are you doing?" he asked angrily, rubbing his forehead. He wasn't sure if he was more upset that she'd been shocking him in his sleep or the fact that he'd only been *dreaming* she was kissing him.

"Trying to get your attention. You were sleeping. How am I supposed to know what to do next when my teacher falls asleep?" She looked mildly annoyed. "Why are you looking at me like that? Do I have something in my teeth?" She covered her mouth with her hand.

Too late, Chase realized he'd been staring at her lips, willing her to repeat what she'd just done in his dream. "No, nothing. I'm sorry I drifted off. I didn't sleep well last night."

She had the grace to look ashamed. "Then *I'm* sorry. That's probably my fault." At least she knew what she'd done to him.

An awkward silence followed, during which they didn't look at each other.

"Look," Chase said finally, "we're going to have to get past this tension between us if you're to complete your training. Then I will be out of your life and you can move on. Until then, we're just going to have to work through this."

He could see her disappointment in her eyes as she nodded her understanding. "What's next, then?"

Glad for a change of subject, Chase thought about his next lesson. He decided some physical exertion might help ease some of the tension. "How about some hand-to-hand combat? And if you knee me in the ballocks again, you're sleeping outside tonight."

∽

Asiah still hadn't gotten over the mortification of seeing Chase in his bath that morning. Every time she looked at him she remembered how he looked in the cold morning air, steam rising from the bath, enveloping his perfect body in a thin, misty veil. She'd never seen a man naked before, and she was sure that most men weren't built like he was. She was almost sure that he was taunting her when he came inside only wearing his trousers, a few droplets of water still clinging to the hair on his muscular chest, as if he knew how uncomfortable she was. Her embarrassment tripled when he caught her staring at his torso and wondering where the little trail of hair extending down from his navel ended.

She made a promise to herself that every time she caught herself thinking about him in that way she would zap herself with an electric shock, her newest mastered skill. Eventually, she thought, she could train herself not to think about his body anymore, just like Pavlov's dog. Maybe then she wouldn't have to confront her feelings about him, either.

A week went by. Chase pushed her so hard in her training that she had little time to think about anything else. He started waking her before the sun was up to run through the woods and she didn't get to go to bed until almost midnight because Chase had her reading various writings about her people who lived on other planets. He told her that the key to proper energy manipulation was knowing one's own body inside and out, and the best way to know one's body was to push it to its physical limits. On the second night, as she headed for Chase's bed, he stopped her. He made her sleep on the floor by the stove because it would "heighten her awareness of her own body." She took that to mean he didn't want to sleep on the floor anymore.

When they weren't training, Chase kept his distance, never standing or sitting too close to her, and he rarely touched her. He stopped calling her "love" which she actually missed more than anything else. She also missed the way he used to brush her hand with his or when he used to tuck a stray lock of hair behind her ear. She knew this couldn't all be from the fact that she didn't respond to his declaration of love like he expected. *He* was the one who said they couldn't be together and the scroll had confirmed it. Still, she didn't like the cool and aloof Chase as much as the one who kissed her senseless every chance he got.

The more she improved, the harder Chase pushed her. By the third night, she was so tired that sleeping on the floor felt like a blessing. She knew she was getting stronger and she could even see the difference in her muscle definition.

She had learned most of the skills she needed: controlling fire and electricity, levitation, telepathy, channeling, and healing. Now she was learning to use her powers together or when Chase was attacking her. She couldn't believe how far she'd come in just a week. She learned that her mental capabilities were much stronger than Chase's, a fact that he seemed to resent, but he never discouraged her.

On the ninth day since Chase had rescued her from the asylum, Asiah realized how much she missed her family. They may have abandoned her in an insane asylum, but she was starting to think that they might not have known any better. She *did* sound crazy when she told them the story, especially when she told it in a desperate attempt to keep her family from moving to California. She woke up before Chase for once and dressed quickly. She peeked into his bedroom through the cracked door and saw him sprawled across the bed on his stomach. The bedclothes covered him from the waist down except for his toes which hung off the end of the bed. He wasn't wearing a shirt and Asiah took an extra second to admire his muscled frame. She wrote a quick note and left it on the table so he wouldn't worry about her. Outside she turned her focus to the west and channeled to San Francisco.

When she arrived in the City by the Bay she had no idea where her family was. Chase had mentioned finding them in Chinatown when he came looking for her. She went to the congested neighborhood and focused her mind on finding her family. She thought she sensed their presence east of her location. After asking a few shopkeepers and people on the street, none of whom spoke very much English, she found their apartment building. She went inside and up a flight of stairs at the top of which was a door covered in peeling brown paint. She placed her palm against the door and searched for a familiar presence. Taking a deep breath, she knocked.

The sun was up when Chase shot straight up in bed. Something wasn't right. He leapt from the bed and threw open the bedroom door. Asiah was nowhere to be seen. He checked out back and ran around to the front of the cottage, shouting her name until he was hoarse. He went back inside and paced the room. He picked up the blanket from the floor where Asiah had been sleeping and buried his face in the soft wool, breathing in her scent. Tossing the blanket aside, he went to the table and dropped into a chair. Maybe she was practicing channeling. She wouldn't have gone far; Chase explicitly told her to stay within the confines of the energy fields he'd placed around his property. If she used her powers outside the fields Marysa would be able to find her. He couldn't let that happen.

It was then that he noticed a handwritten note on the table.

Chapter Nineteen

The look on Aileen's face was priceless. Once she had recovered from the initial shock of seeing her youngest daughter show up at her door, she sobbed into Asiah's shoulder, apologizing profusely for sending her away. Patrick had told Aileen about seeing Chase vanish into thin air on the street and how they thought Asiah might have been telling the truth all along. They were making plans to return to Chicago to retrieve her, but they hadn't scraped together enough money yet. Asiah spent the next hour telling Aileen and Meri all about the wonderful things she was learning, and when Patrick came home from his night shift at the shipyard, she told them all again.

Their disbelief was evident, but Asiah showed them some of her skills by lighting the fire and boiling water for tea as Chase did at one of their early meetings. Rather than shun her as a freak of nature, her father embraced her with tears in his eyes.

"I never thought me little Cricket would learn such a valuable skill! You've no idea what this means for our family! We'll be able to make tons o' coin with this new talent of yours, girl!"

Asiah's excitement dimmed as she realized what he meant. "Father, these abilities of mine are not parlor tricks or gimmicks, they are for me to use to help people. To make the world a better place," she explained.

"Nonsense! One girl canna' save the world with magic tricks! But she can bring home bread for her family's dinner," he said matter-of-factly. Apparently working at the shipyard was not as lucrative as he'd claimed it would be.

"Well, yes, but—" Asiah realized it was useless to argue with her father and changed the subject. "Why don't we all go do something today? The weather is nice, what about a picnic?"

"I think it's a lovely idea!" Meri piped up.

They went to Golden Gate Park with a basket full of corned beef and soda-bread sandwiches. Aileen spread a blanket on the ground and they enjoyed the autumn breeze for a few hours. Asiah hoped Chase wouldn't mind too terribly that she took a day for herself. She lay on her back with her hands under her head, staring up at the sky as her father sang a sea shanty from his fishing days in Ireland. Everything almost felt normal again.

She sensed rather than heard the disturbance across the field from where their blanket was spread. Asiah sat up, suddenly apprehensive.

"What is it, Cricket?" Aileen asked.

Asiah slowly got to her feet. Something was definitely wrong here. "I don't know, Mam."

She was knocked off her feet a moment later. She didn't see what knocked her down, but she could feel the power behind it — and it wasn't human. Asiah jumped back to her feet and looked around furiously for the source. She didn't have to look long; a woman with bright red hair strode across the field with long, purposeful strides. Her dark eyes bored into Asiah and she knew this woman must be Marysa.

Panic overcame her momentarily. She had no idea what to do. She'd been preparing for this, but now that the moment was here, she couldn't think straight. Marysa must have sensed as much because she knocked her down again. Asiah forced herself to focus. Chase said her mind was stronger than this woman's, and she needed to use that strength now.

Marysa stopped about fifteen feet from Asiah. Her family sat frozen with mouths agape, staring at the woman with black stones piercing the skin of her throat.

"If I couldn't feel the electromagnetism of your aura, I'd never pick *you* as the True Shade. You look so ... pathetic," Marysa jeered.

Patrick seemed to come out of his shock. "Now see here, missy, I dunna' who you think you are, but that's m'girl you be insultin'."

Asiah found her voice. "Father, take Mam and Meri and *get out of here*." The other people in the park had already begun to flee at the sight of the woman in the black cloak.

Patrick didn't budge. "No, Cricket, I won't stand by and let this woman talk that way to you." He moved in front of Asiah.

"I'll talk to your 'Cricket' any way I want to," Marysa said, and a bolt of dark lightning shot from her fingers, hitting Patrick in the center of his chest.

He didn't even have time to cry out before the bolt hit him, making his body twitch unnaturally. He crumpled to the ground and didn't move.

"Patrick!" Aileen cried, dropping to her knees at his side. "Oh, my love, wake up, please wake up!"

"You shouldn't have done that," Asiah said through gritted teeth, and threw her own lightning at the Shade.

Marysa easily deflected it and advanced on Asiah. Using mostly defensive, blocking techniques, Asiah stole a look at her parents. Aileen had her head on Patrick's chest, tears streaming down her face. Meri was shaking his shoulders, trying to rouse him, and Asiah's rage heightened. *No ... he can't be dead!*

With renewed vigor, Asiah fired more bolts at the woman and tried also to see her next move by reading her mind. She was able to penetrate the woman's psyche only for an instant, and what she saw terrified her. She watched, paralyzed by fear, as Marysa sent another bolt at Aileen which rebounded onto Meri.

"NO!" Asiah screamed, running to her mother's side. She hunted frantically for her mother's pulse, unable to find a heartbeat.

"This is too easy," Marysa said casually. "And now it's your turn to die." She extended her arm toward Asiah.

Asiah closed her eyes in defeat. Some Shade she'd turned out to be. She couldn't even protect her family.

She heard Marysa cry out and opened her eyes. Chase was on top of her with his hands around her throat. They struggled only for a moment before Asiah heard a sickening *crack*, and Marysa went limp underneath him. He stood shakily and watched Marysa's motionless form intently. The woman's body began to twitch and Chase backed away slowly toward where Asiah knelt next to her lifeless parents.

"Get up, love, we need to go," he said quietly, not taking his eyes from Marysa's body.

"My parents, I need to help them," she said absently, looking back and forth between Aileen and Patrick. Meri was also unconscious, and Asiah hadn't even checked to see if she was alright.

"I'm sorry, there's nothing we can do for them now. Let's go," he said firmly. He grasped her arm and pulled her up from the ground. He still watched Marysa closely and Asiah saw the woman's skin was darkening to a shimmery gray color.

"Ch-Chase," Asiah stammered, suddenly very afraid.

He didn't respond; he was mesmerized by the creature now standing before them, spreading her great wings and glaring at them with ethereal black eyes.

The creature lunged at them and Asiah's scream echoed across the deserted park long after Chase channeled them to safety.

"We have to go back!" Asiah screamed hysterically the moment they landed in front of the cottage. Chase gripped her shoulders, but she fought him off. "I have to help them!" She backed away from him, preparing to channel back to San Francisco.

He strode forward quickly and ripped her bracelet off before she could disappear. He tossed it aside and held onto her arm so she couldn't go after it. Blood began cascading down her forearm from the wound, but she didn't seem to care.

"Let me go! I *need* to go back! Please!" she cried frantically.

Chase held her wrists firmly, trying to calm her down. "I'm so sorry, Asiah." He didn't know what else to say.

"Why won't you let me go?" she cried, tears streaking down her face. "I have to help them!"

"She'll kill you!" he said, more forcefully. "If you go back there, she *will* kill you. You're in no condition to take her on right now. I know you're in pain, but you must protect yourself from her."

Asiah sagged to the ground, sobbing. "Please, they need me."

Chase lowered himself to the ground and pulled her onto his lap, laying her head on his chest and wrapping his arms tightly around her as she cried. Sobs wracked her body and she curled her fingers into his tunic, holding on for all she was worth. It began to rain, but he didn't move to go inside. He knew she would cry herself out eventually. After a long while her body finally became still and he heard only the occasional sniffle and the sound of raindrops on fallen leaves.

He stroked her wet hair. "I'm so sorry, love," he said again. "I wish I'd been there sooner."

"It's my fault," she whispered miserably. "If I'd just stayed here, Marysa never would have found me … or them. It's my fault they're dead."

Chase held her tighter. "You mustn't say that, love. It's not your fault she attacked them. It's my fault for not being there with you. I should have been more clear about the dangers of using your powers anywhere but here. If I could bring them back, I would."

"They didn't deserve to die that way. Not after everything they've been through." Fresh tears began to mix with the rain on her face and she began to tremble.

"They are at peace now. And I know that they loved you very much." Chase wasn't sure he believed the second part, but he knew Asiah would want to hear it.

She tried to speak in between gasps. "They were all I had ... in the world ... and now ... I'm all alone ..." She dissolved into sobs again.

Chase turned her on his lap so he could look into her eyes. "You are *not* alone, Asiah. *I'm* here and I love you. I wish I could show you just how much." He leaned in and kissed the tears from her cheeks.

"Then show me," she whispered.

He drew back, searching her face. "What?"

Her eyes were round and pleading. "Show me how much you love me. Make love to me, Chase."

"You don't know what you're asking, Asiah," he warned, squelching the urge to indulge her right then and there. Her emotions were too raw, and Chase couldn't believe he was actually considering it. What kind of scoundrel did that make him?

She threaded her fingers into his rain-soaked hair. "Maybe not, but I need to feel something right now that's not grief or sadness. You're the only one who can help me now. Please, Chase, I need you." She pulled his head down and kissed him tenderly.

Chase pulled back, searching her face. "Are you sure?" He knew he shouldn't do this, but he wanted more than anything to take away her sadness, even if it was just for tonight. But how much would she hate him for it in the morning?

"I could never hate you," she whispered, reading his thoughts. "You're all I have left in the world. I'm sure I want this because ..." she trailed off, biting her lip. "Because I love you."

Her eyes were so dark and haunted that he couldn't say no. Hearing her say the words he'd so longed for was all he needed to make his decision. Abruptly he stood, scooped her up in his arms and strode toward the house. Inside, he set her on her feet and kicked the door closed behind him. He backed her up against the wall and thoroughly kissed her, willing her to forget all the events of the day and focus only on this moment. She didn't disappoint him and twined her arms around his neck, surrendering fully to his touch.

He leaned back and ran his thumb over her swollen bottom lip. "Mmm, I could do this forever," he said with a seductive smile. He backed up a step to tear off his jacket. His tunic and belt followed and he treated her again to the sight of him without a shirt on. Her eyes widened momentarily in appreciation. He stepped close again and began swiftly undoing the buttons on her shirt. He bent his head so his lips brushed her ear.

She placed his hands over his, stopping him.

"What is it, my love?" he whispered and caught her earlobe between his teeth.

She dropped her eyes to his chest, uncertainty on her face. "I'm just ..." she began.

He tipped her chin up, forcing her to meet his gaze. "Tell me, sweetheart," he coaxed gently.

She looked like she might cry again. "Afraid," she finished. "I've never done this before." She waved her hand back and forth between them.

He sighed in relief. "I know of your innocence, love." He pressed a kiss to her forehead. "And I promise," he kissed her right cheek, "that you could never," he kissed her left cheek, "do anything wrong," he kissed the tip of her nose, "and you will enjoy every minute." He kissed her lips, deeply and passionately.

She moaned against his mouth and he deepened the kiss, tangling his tongue with hers. He picked her up again, walked to the table, and set her on the edge so her legs dangled off the side. He stood between her legs and tilted her head back so he could kiss the soft skin of her throat. His hands drifted down and resumed unbuttoning her shirt. He pushed it off her shoulders, leaving only her rain-soaked camisole. He slipped its straps off each shoulder, replacing them with a kiss. He moved his hands to the tiny buttons of her camisole and slowly began unfastening them, straining against his instinct to rip the thin material from her body.

She leaned back to fix him with an impatient glare and he laughed out loud.

"You *are* a mystery, love," he chuckled. "One moment you're batting my hands away and the next I can't undress you fast enough. Believe me, I could tear your clothes off in an instant if I wanted to, but I want to do this right so you can fully appreciate it." He finally made it to the last button and paused again.

She made a little sound of disappointment and he smiled as he bent to kiss her collarbone. "Trust me, Asiah." He brushed his fingers against her belly and trailed them up to skim over her barely-covered breasts. He continued nipping at the soft skin of her throat as he filled his hands with their fullness. She let out a soft moan and he smiled against her neck.

He nudged her back until she was lying on the table and pushed her camisole open all the way. This time when his mouth found its way to her nipple and captured it to caress it with his tongue, she didn't stop him. Instead, she combed her fingers through his wet hair and held his head in place. She was like a drug and he couldn't get enough. He wanted to taste every inch of her body. She was so responsive to his touch, he couldn't remember why they hadn't been doing this all along.

Chase finished his oral assault on her breasts and pulled her upright again. Instead of helping her down from the table he picked her up and tossed her over his shoulder. She gave a small yelp of surprise as he strode to the bedroom. He dropped her unceremoniously onto the bed and went to fetch a candle, which he laid on the table by the bed. A flame sprang from the wick with a flick of his fingers, casting a soft glow around the room.

Suddenly self-conscious, Asiah hugged her knees to her chest. "I'm not sure we need that much light."

Chase chuckled and climbed onto the bed, raking his wet hair back with his fingers. "I'm afraid you'll have to live with it, my sweet. I want to see every inch of you." He reached out and gently eased her out of her damp camisole.

"If you insist," she with a nervous laugh.

His smoldering gaze raked her body. "I do." He attacked her then, pushing her roughly onto her back and plundering her mouth with his tongue. He removed his trousers before he started working on the buttons of hers, stripping them off before she even knew what was happening. A look of shock and fear came over her face and she began to tremble.

Chase softened his kiss and placed his hand flat on her belly, rubbing his palm in circles around her navel to calm her. After a moment he felt her tension drain away. His hand drifted down to the apex of her thighs and he looked into her eyes, gauging her reaction to the intimate touch. She bit her lip and nodded slightly. He smiled seductively and lowered his mouth to hers. His fingers found a particularly sensitive spot and she gasped. His hand stilled and she arched her hips up, begging for more.

"Don't ... stop," she breathed.

His laugh was a low rumble in her ear. "I don't intend to, love." He nibbled her earlobe and continued his caress. "My god, you're so ready for me," he whispered. He continued stroking her while raining kisses along her jaw, neck, face or anywhere his lips could reach.

She rocked her hips against his hand and he almost lost himself in the enjoyment of pleasuring her. He couldn't remember how many times he'd imagined this moment and how every imagining fell so completely short of the real thing. His beautiful siren was no longer in control of her voice, sighing and moaning uncontrollably. She arched her back suddenly and held her breath.

"Let go, my love," Chase whispered in her ear. "I want to see you come undone."

She cried out and Chase slid his fingers inside her. She rode wave after wave of pleasure as her body convulsed around him in spectacular release. He couldn't believe how uninhibited her climax was or how badly he needed to be inside her. Finally, she relaxed onto the bed, breathing heavily.

"Did you enjoy that?" he asked.

She nodded, dazed.

"I knew you would, love." He moved down to kneel between her legs. "I've been waiting for this for a long time." He leaned over her, sliding his hands under her back. He pushed himself inside her, just a little, then stopped. He looked into her eyes, searching. "Do you trust me, Asiah?"

"Yes," she whispered.

He kissed her then and thrust himself fully inside her. She cried out at the pain of losing her innocence. Chase stilled and held her close as she cried softly.

"I'm so sorry, my love, I should have warned you about the pain." He kissed her tears away.

She took a deep breath. "It's not so bad," she sniffled.

"Use your power, love, and you'll feel better, even without your stones. I can't hold back much longer, I want you so much," he said breathlessly.

"You have me," she whispered.

His gaze smoldered and he began to move inside her, slowly. It was the most amazing and intimate feeling he'd ever known and he didn't want it to end. He felt her begin to tighten around him and he moved faster, completely immersing himself in her touch.

"Chase ... I think I'm going to ..." she moaned in pleasure, "again." He was sure she could never be more beautiful than she was right then. He etched her image permanently into his memory so he would never forget this moment.

"As am I, love," he ground out. He looked down at her, meeting her gaze.

She watched him intently with nothing but love in her eyes.

He leaned his forehead against hers. "I love you so much, Asiah," he whispered.

"I love you, Chase."

He thought his heart might explode with joy. "Yes ... oh, god ... *Asiah*." He gasped her name as he poured himself into her and felt her go over the edge again. She threw her head back and screamed, her fingers digging into his back. He continued to move with her as they found their pleasure together.

Finally, he collapsed on top of her, his breathing ragged. He didn't know how long it took for his heart to finally stop pounding. He rolled onto his side, pulling her with him, and held her close until their breathing slowed.

"It's never ... been ... like *that*," he panted into her hair.

She tentatively asked, "How many women have you ...?" Even though her face was buried against his chest, he could sense her embarrassment.

He sighed contentedly, "I don't remember, love, but it doesn't matter. None of them could hold a candle to you." He tightened his arms around her for a moment then sat up to pull the bed covers over them and blow out the candle. He lay back down and pulled her against his chest again. As he drifted off he thought he heard her voice echoing in his head, pleading:

Never leave me, Chase.

Chapter Twenty

When Asiah woke up, Chase was wrapped around her like a vine. She blinked in the sunlight coming through the window. Careful not to disturb him, she looked at his serene face and carefully extracted her arm so she could brush a stray lock of hair from his forehead. She forced herself to focus on him and the way his face lit up when she'd said she loved him; she wasn't ready to think about what happened in the park yesterday. Tears stung her eyes and she gently slipped out of Chase's arms, then collected her clothes and headed out back to the wooden tub behind the cottage.

She quickly washed up, not wanting to spend too much time in the cool, autumn air with no clothes on. She returned to the cottage and saw the blackened scroll on the table. The impact of what she and Chase had done last night hit her all at once. She sank into a chair and listened to the whispers of the scroll again. One passage in particular made her blood run cold.

Beware the Fallen Conjurer, for he is cursed. The Fallen Conjurer's seduction shall be a Shade's undoing. Her only lover must be her undertaking.

What had she done? What if she'd just ruined everything for one night of passion? Chase didn't know if he was the Fallen Conjurer, but what if he was? She rubbed her temples. She was so distraught over the loss of her parents that she hadn't been thinking clearly last night. All she'd wanted was to feel like someone loved her, that someone was there for her. Chase had shown her just how wonderful it could be between them, and Asiah didn't regret a moment.

But this morning her thoughts returned to her family. Chase had said she couldn't go back because Marysa would kill her. Was it true? The woman certainly had been able to best her physically, but Asiah *had* managed to penetrate the woman's mind, if only for an instant.

Asiah looked down at her hands, vaguely remembering Chase tearing off her wrist cuff the night before and tossing it into the woods. She grabbed her blanket that was still on the floor by the stove and wrapping it around herself, went outside to look for the bracelet.

She found it on the ground at the edge of the trees in a mud puddle. She gingerly picked it up and wiped it on the blanket, trying unsuccessfully to remove the dirt. The chain that attached to the ring had broken and the ring was nowhere to be seen.

The cold outside seemed to creep into her heart and she welcomed it. Wandering into the woods a little way, Asiah settled herself on a flat rock, facing away from the cottage and staring off into the dense trees. Chase may have successfully distracted her from her grief last night, but this morning her head was clearer. She knew that what she'd have to tell him would break his heart, and she didn't have a choice. She couldn't stay here with him. Even if there were still things he needed to teach her, she'd never learn to concentrate her focus when he was around. He'd told her before that his time on Earth was nearly at an end anyway, so why shouldn't they part ways before it became too difficult to say goodbye? Chances were that Marysa or some other enemy would eventually try to harm Chase to get to Asiah, and she would never forgive herself if he was hurt on her account.

Asiah closed her eyes and turned her focus inward and spent a moment remembering her parents. She knew that they had loved her, in their own way. Perhaps it was better now that their hard lives were over. She couldn't think the same about Meri. Her twin sister had so much potential; her work on this Earth was nowhere near finished. Asiah didn't even know if she was dead or alive. The bolt of electricity that rebounded off her mother had hit Meri, and Asiah didn't know if it had actually killed her or not. If there was a chance her sister was still alive, she needed to find her before Marysa did. The evil Shade obviously had no problem killing innocent people.

Asiah walked through the Forest in her mind, letting the cold from the real world reach into her sacred space. Tendrils of frost clung to the leaves on the trees and the soft undergrowth became crunchy and brittle beneath her feet. She walked across the frozen lake to where the boulder was and climbed atop, finally letting her grief wrap its icy fingers around her heart.

Chase didn't know when he'd decided that he would stay on Earth with Asiah. He felt like he'd heard her voice in a dream, asking him to stay. He knew the dangers of starting a relationship with a Shade, but the æthers be damned if dying was better than living forever with Asiah at his side. He wasn't sure how to tell her just yet. He sipped his tea as he looked out the window to where she sat on a boulder at the edge of the woods, wrapped in a blanket.

He'd panicked for a moment when he'd woken up without her next to him. Fearing that it had all been a dream, he'd made a quick search of the house before he noticed her meditating in the forest. He didn't disturb her. She'd been through enough and if she needed to take some time to clear her head, then she should do it. He was just glad she hadn't tried to go back and find her family.

Chase had hoped he wouldn't have to leave the bedroom for the rest of the day, or even the rest of his life. If he'd known this is what awaited him when he found the Ikhälean Shade, he never would have been so depressed his whole life. Asiah made love with more passion and fervor than any woman he'd ever known. And this was after she'd suffered a major tragedy. He couldn't even imagine what it would be like if she were having a good day. He sincerely hoped he would find out someday. His siren had no idea how alluring she was, either. The way she screamed his name when she reached her climax made him want to weep. It must have been her Ikhälean blood that made her such an uninhibited lover.

He made her breakfast and built a fire in the stove while he waited for her to come back inside. When she hadn't moved in over an hour, he decided that she shouldn't sit outside in the cold any longer, no matter what the reason. He approached her from behind, his boots crunching loudly on the dead leaves so as not to surprise her. Even so, when he touched her shoulder, she jumped.

"I'm sorry, love, I didn't mean to startle you. It's cold out here. Come inside and eat something."

She nodded solemnly and turned toward him. Her cheeks were tearstained and her lips were turning blue.

"Bloody hell, love, you're going to catch your death out here!" he said, wrapping her in his arms.

She let him lead her inside, remaining quiet. She sat down in the chair he held for her, but didn't eat, instead staring morosely at the food in front of her.

"Asiah? Have some tea, love. You'll feel better soon," he prodded gently, taking a seat across from her and gesturing to her steaming teacup.

She raised her eyes to his and his heart sank. He could see her next words written on her face before she said them aloud.

"Chase ..." she began, and bit her lip as her eyes filled with tears. "I have to go," she whispered.

He reached across the table and took her hand. "You don't have to go, love. Please don't say that," he pleaded.

"I do. What happened last night ... was wonderful." She gave him a brief, wistful smile. "But it can't happen again." She pulled her hand from his.

He struggled to control his emotions. Asiah was still distraught, that must be why she was thinking so rashly.

"I don't mean right away, of course, but as soon as we deal with ... that *woman*." She trailed off, grinding her teeth.

Chase could feel her rage. "Look at me, Asiah." She reluctantly met his gaze. "No matter what happened last night, I will help you defeat her. But I don't think you're thinking clearly enough to make any decisions about us right now. Let's just get through this together, alright?"

She looked regretfully out the window for a moment, then nodded. "Alright. But until then, you can't ..." She trailed off again, looking utterly miserable.

"Right. I'll leave you alone," Chase said, unable to keep the bitterness out of his voice.

"It's better this way, you know, because of what the scroll said," she said tonelessly.

Chase picked up his teacup and stood up. "I'm sure you're right," he said tightly. "Why don't you eat something and we'll figure out our next move." He walked to the bookshelf and started rummaging through the volumes, unable to look at her anymore and not wanting her to see the hell he was in. He heard her sigh and start eating, which was a good thing. He knew Asiah wanted to find out if her sister was alright, but he wasn't sure it was safe to go look for her just yet. The most important thing would be to first get Asiah to focus on her priorities and center her mind. She would be useless against Marysa if she didn't have a clear head.

Asiah finished breakfast and cleared the table. Chase noticed that she still looked completely miserable. It was absolutely killing him that he couldn't comfort her. Suddenly, he had an idea. He went to his trunk and pulled out a small vial of sand.

"Come outside," he said, grabbing his jacket off a chair and pulling it on.

"But, it's so cold," she complained.

"And you almost let yourself freeze out there this morning. Come on, you need to get some aggression out and I know just the thing."

Outside, Chase pulled the vial from his pocket and emptied it onto the ground. Then, one by one, the grains of sand seemed to multiply and float upward as he placed them in a particular pattern. He rotated each grain to refract the light so each cast a different color. After a moment, an image of Marysa stood before him, complete with her red hair and onyx necklace. He turned his attention to Asiah. As he expected, her jaw was clenched and her eyes were ablaze with rage.

"What is this?" she asked Chase, not taking her eyes from the floating sand.

"Motivation," he responded. "Attack her, as if she were the real thing."

"Doesn't seem like a fair fight," she muttered, and Chase smiled to himself. Asiah put on her bracelet and closed her eyes momentarily as the stone pierced her skin. Then, with a warrior's yell, she threw everything she had at the sand: lightning, fire, wind, and a sort of shockwave that Chase had never taught her. The sand shimmered and shifted, but never really changed or disappeared. Chase watched Asiah grow frustrated and put even more effort into her assault. He continued to move the sand around, so she never got a clean shot off. Finally, she turned her rage on him. He fully expected this, but thought she would use her power. Instead, she charged him, ramming her shoulder into his gut and knocking him down. She leapt onto his chest, raining blows down on him with both fists, none of which hurt very much. He let her continue until she slumped on top of him, panting. She buried her face in the folds of his jacket and began to cry. He tentatively reached his arms up to surround her and, when she didn't stop him, held her tightly as she sobbed.

She went still after a few minutes. "Feel better?" Chase asked.

She pushed herself up and wiped her eyes. "Actually ... I do."

"Sometimes it helps to just let all your frustrations out at once," he said, propping himself up on his elbows.

"I suppose so." She didn't move off of Chase, and he didn't mind. "Yesterday, what happened after you attacked Marysa? It looked like you won. I heard her neck break and she went limp, until—" She paused, looking thoughtful. "That was her Ikhälean side, wasn't it?"

"Yes. If a Shade is near death, her Ikhälean side takes over, as long as she has reached maturity," he explained.

To Chase's disappointment, Asiah slid off his chest and sat cross-legged on the ground next to him. "Did you know that would happen if you tried to kill her?"

Chase nodded. "That's why I got you out of there. Neither of us stands a chance against her in that form."

Asiah shuddered. "I don't ever want to see that again."

"Neither do I. If her power alone isn't enough to scare you, it's said that the Ikhälean side has its own consciousness as well."

"What does that mean?"

"It means that the Ikhäle that lives within her has independent thoughts and can act autonomously if that side of her is active."

Her eyes grew wide. "So how does she control it?"

Chase shook his head. "That I do not know. I suppose it's something that is learned at the time of maturity."

"What about me? Didn't you say that I have an Ikhälean side?"

He chucked her under the chin with a smile. "Yes, but you are far from maturity, love."

"Am I going to ... look like *that*?"

"Not exactly like that. The image of you I saw in my dream was different. She was terrifying. You will be breathtaking."

She blushed. He loved it when she blushed. "I don't know, I'm a little afraid of the whole sharing-a-body-with-an-alien-consciousness thing," she said.

"You will be fine. If anyone can handle that sort of thing, it's you."

She looked down at her hands. "So what are we supposed to do, then? Since neither of us can defeat her?"

"We must find a way to immobilize her so you can enter her mind. That is the one place you are stronger. If you were a mature Shade, we would have no problem. But you won't be for about eighty years or so and we don't have the luxury of time. This needs to end now."

"Do we search for her? Lure her here somehow?" She looked doubtful.

"It would be best if we were on familiar ground. I would say luring her here would be best. Hopefully she doesn't burn down my house." He smiled wistfully. "I don't like moving."

"How do we do it?" she asked.

"Simple: I'll just disassemble the electromagnetic fields that have been shielding our location from her. She'll find us soon enough. Her goal is to kill both of us, and I'm sure she doesn't have any more pressing matters to attend to at the present time. We must be ready, though. As soon as the barriers are down, she could be upon us. Stand up."

Asiah did as he bade. Chase conjured the sandy form of Marysa again.

"Once more, now that your mind is clear," he instructed.

Without hesitation, Asiah threw a powerful bolt of lightning at the spectral form. A loud *crack* echoed across the clearing, and where there had been sand before now stood a mass of twisted glass that vaguely resembled a human.

Chase nodded his approval. "I think you're ready."

❦

Asiah and Chase ate their lunch quietly. The plan was to take down the electromagnetic fields after they ate and wait for the witch to show up. Chase was going to remain out of sight and hopefully take Marysa by surprise so Asiah could get her hands on the woman and invade her psyche. It was the best plan they had. Asiah hoped the anger that fueled her this morning to turn the sand into melted glass would serve her well. The last time she had met Marysa she felt weak and helpless. She knew that couldn't happen this time. It would mean her death and Chase's, too.

The thought of Chase giving his life for her made her gut twist. She'd only just come to terms with her feelings for him. She knew that distancing herself from him would be the best course after Marysa was dead, but the thought of losing him made her stomach hurt. She decided that she wouldn't give it any more thought until they dealt with Marysa. After that, she could decide between love and duty. She sat up suddenly as she noticed a blue scarf folded neatly on the table.

"What's this?" she asked, running her fingers over the silky fabric.

"I got that for you in Istanbul. I thought it would match your eyes."

She picked it up and wrapped it around herself. "What do you think?"

"It's beautiful. Perfect for you."

She blushed. He smiled.

After lunch, Chase stood in the middle of the clearing with his legs spread in a wide stance and his hands pressed together in front of his chest. His eyes were closed and his head was bowed. If Asiah didn't know any better, she'd think he was praying. Without opening his eyes, he lifted his head and extended his arms to the sides, murmuring some words under his breath. She felt the ground tremble slightly and then everything went quiet. The birds in the woods stopped chirping and even the breeze ceased to blow.

"Here goes nothing," Chase muttered and raised both hands over his head. A bolt of green lightning flashed skyward from his hands. The gray sky was momentarily illuminated with an ethereal green light. "If that doesn't alert her to our location, I don't know what will." He dropped his hands and fixed her with a dark look that made her shiver. He strode purposefully to where she stood and shoved his hands into her hair. He lowered his mouth to hers and kissed her hard, making her head spin and her knees weak. "Keep your mind clear and trust yourself, my love," he whispered, and walked resolutely into the house, leaving her alone in the clearing.

Chapter Twenty-One

The sound of Asiah's cry nearly stopped Chase's heart. He'd turned away from the window only for an instant. *So much for the plan*, he thought as he dashed outside.

In the clearing in front of the house Marysa was standing behind Meri, holding her Ikhälean blade to Asiah's sister's throat. Asiah's face was white as a sheet as she dropped to her knees in the clearing. Chase could hear her panicked thoughts in his head. His blood turned to ice and he forced himself to remain calm. They hadn't considered the possibility that Marysa would use Meri against them.

"Let her go, Shade, and I will promise you a quick death," he threatened.

Marysa laughed her evil, raspy laugh. "Never! Unless you propose a trade: one sister for the other?"

"Mine is the only life I will trade," he said.

"Asiah! Help me!" Meri shrieked.

"Quiet!" Marysa hissed, pulling Meri's arm more painfully behind her back. "You would fall on your sword for her? Right here and now?" Marysa asked, interest piqued.

"You know I would," he ground out.

"Chase, *no*," Asiah moaned.

"Then do it, and the girl goes free ... for now," Marysa jeered.

"Release her first, then I'm yours," Chase growled.

She cackled again. "You must think me a great fool, Sorcerer. I hold her life in my very hands. Why would I give that up?"

"Your fight is with me – the girl is innocent." Chase took a step forward, playing his last card. "You show great cowardice hiding behind a defenseless woman. At our previous meeting you said you could best Asiah with a wave of your hand, yet now you fear to face an untrained Shade and a mere Conjurer. No, I don't think you a fool, just a coward." He prayed it was the right move.

It was. Marysa's eyes narrowed. From what little Chase knew of the Ikhälean people, accusing one of cowardice was the greatest insult. Even if Marysa was only half-Ikhäle, something inside her would take offense at his accusation.

She shoved Meri to the ground and sheathed her dagger, freeing her hands. Without warning she hit Asiah with a bolt of dark lightning, throwing her against the trunk of the oak tree. Asiah fell to the ground and didn't move. Meri cried out and ran to her sister's side.

Chase saw red, but he knew better than to attack Marysa outright. She was stronger than he was physically. He needed to attack her mind. He needed *Asiah* to attack her mind. *Wake up! I need you!* he thought furiously and threw a bolt of lightning to keep Marysa busy. He followed the lightning with fire and edged toward where Asiah lay while Marysa defended his assault. At last he reached her side. He uprooted a small tree behind Marysa and swung it at her, knocking her down and giving him a chance to rouse Asiah.

"Wake up, love." He shook her gently while Meri looked on, then more vigorously. She was breathing, yet still unconscious. He heard wood splintering and whirled around to see thousands of wooden shards streaking toward him. Meri screamed. He blocked with fire and set the splinters ablaze and pushed them back at Marysa. He nudged Asiah again with his foot while preparing his next move. "Wake her up!" he snapped at Meri, who nodded and began shaking Asiah again. Asiah moaned and he turned away from Marysa for an instant. He heard the crack of the wood against his skull an instant before everything went black.

Asiah was dizzy and felt like she'd been punched in the stomach by a prizefighter. The sky swam above her and she could hear Chase moaning distantly. She pushed herself into a seated position and leaned her back against the tree, trying to get her bearings. She heard Meri's voice nearby, but couldn't understand what she was saying. Why was she in pain? Where was Chase? She looked around and saw him lying face-down on the ground nearby. Blood trickled from a wound on the back of his head.

"Ch-Chase ..." she gasped. The pain in her abdomen increased when she spoke.

"Asiah!" Meri cried from her other side. "Look!" She pointed across the clearing and Asiah struggled to focus her eyes.

"On your feet, Sapphire Shade," a voice screeched from far away.

Asiah turned her head slowly in the direction of the voice. Her eyes took a few moments to focus, and she barely made out a redheaded woman in a black cloak standing in the clearing. Asiah turned back to Chase.

"Leave him! Stand and face me or I will kill him now," the woman called.

Asiah paused with her hand above Chase's wound, ready to heal him. Something told her that this woman was sincere. She looked at Meri and the two exchanged a look. Meri leaned over Chase, inspecting his wound as Asiah pushed against the tree to help herself stand and took a shaky step forward.

The redhead cackled. "This will be too easy. Why don't you take the first shot? I'm feeling generous today." She crossed her arms over her chest and eyed Asiah across the clearing. It was now or never.

Summoning what little strength she had, Asiah threw fire from one hand and lightning from the other. Chase had taught her that two forms of attack at once were much harder to defend. But Marysa quenched the fire and somehow absorbed the lightning without a problem. Asiah groaned in exhausted frustration.

Prey on her weaknesses, she heard Chase's voice say in her mind, even as he lay unconscious behind her.

Asiah turned her attention to the woman's mind, shoving into the woman's psyche. Marysa resisted and pushed her right back out with a sneer. Asiah needed physical contact. She stepped forward and Marysa pushed her back down with an unseen force. She got up and stepped forward again. Several times she repeated this, inching closer to the woman as she fought against an invisible wall of power. She was beginning to tire, but pushed on ruthlessly. For Chase, for Meri, for herself, and for the world. She pulled herself up one last time and found herself face to face with the cackling witch. Asiah shook with fatigue, and forced herself to meet the woman's evil glare with steady determination.

Marysa drew a long finger down the side of Asiah's cheek. "So perfect," she whispered, "and such a shame." She unsheathed her dagger quick as lightning and drew back to plunge it into Asiah's heart. Inches before it landed, the dagger flew from her fingers and lodged in a nearby tree. Chase's dagger appeared at Marysa's throat as he restrained her arms behind her back.

"Now, Asiah." Chase nodded at her over Marysa's shoulder.

She lifted her hand to place her palm against Marysa's forehead. Before she could touch her, the woman vanished in a flash of light, reappearing an instant later behind Chase. He whirled around, dagger drawn, but not fast enough. Marysa caught his arm that held his dagger and twisted it forcing the blade's point toward Chase's heart. Asiah barely registered the triumph in the woman's eyes before she saw the knife plunge into his chest to the hilt. Chase's eyes went wide in shock and he fell to his knees.

"No! No ... Chase!" Asiah cried and dropped to her knees in front of him, unsure what to do. *Heal him now!* her brain screamed at her. She jerked the dagger out and threw it aside as he groaned in pain. She placed her hands over the gaping wound to heal him. He put his hands over hers and pulled them away, shaking his head.

"Destroy her," he whispered.

"You'll die!" she insisted. "Please, Chase. Let me help you."

"I'll be fine. Do it now, love," he said with a grimace.

She knew he was lying about being fine, and there was nothing she could do about it. This needed to end now. Marysa laughed again. Oh, how she hated that sound. Asiah spun around and was on top of the woman in a flash. Blind rage fueled her and she held the shocked woman down with strength she didn't know she had. Sealing both palms against Marysa's forehead, she thrust herself into the Phantom Shade's mind.

∽

The breeze was the first thing she noticed. It was a warm, tropical breeze, scented with frangipani and coconut. She looked down and wiggled her toes in the warm sand. In front of her, the turquoise ocean stretched for miles and gentle waves splished and splashed on the white sand. Turning to her left she saw Marysa. She sat on a sandy dune looking out to the sea. She was wearing a simple red dress that fluttered in the breeze. Asiah turned around and surveyed the land. It was a small island, ringed in white sand with a thatch of dense jungle in the center. A diminutive building stood to the side of the trees, most likely the knowledge library. On the far side of the island, a rocky jetty led to another tiny island, on which a single wooden chest rested: Marysa's memories.

It made sense that she would build a tropical getaway in her mind, being from Russia. But Asiah couldn't understand why the place was so limited. An island in the ocean indicated a need for solitude, and Asiah felt a twinge of pity for the woman. She didn't know what kind of past Marysa had had, but it must have been harsh if the woman's own escape was a place as desolate as this. The Forest was endless in Asiah's mind. She knew she could explore a different part every day and never see it all. But this tiny island could be covered in less than an hour.

Asiah turned and walked slowly toward Marysa.

The woman didn't look up when Asiah reached her side. "I underestimated you," Marysa said in a flat tone, a strand of red hair floating across her face.

Asiah sat down on the dune next to her. Strangely, she didn't fear this woman anymore. Even in Marysa's mind, Asiah knew that she was in control here, not Marysa. "Yes," she nodded, "but this doesn't have to end in death. You can still live out your life on Earth in peace. We only want to be left alone to accomplish our mission."

Marysa scoffed, "You have a duty to this pathetic planet. Letting me live is not part of that duty. You and I cannot coexist."

"We have been, though, for twenty-one years," Asiah said.

"And we would continue until your maturity. Only then would the balance of energy be truly upset." Marysa's voice held regret. "You really are the chosen one. I see it now. For years I believed I was the one destined to save the planet. Then I read the prophecies about you and I knew what I believed wasn't true. But there was a way for me to gain the power of the True Ikhälean Shade, and that was to kill you and take your power stone. Phantom Shades do not get to become one with the æthers, only the True Shade gets that honor. And the Supreme Conjurer, not that he deserves it," she said, somewhat venomously.

Asiah knew most of this already from Chase's teachings. She remembered that he was hurt and she still needed to help him before she lost him forever. "So what now?" she asked the redhead.

An evil gleam returned to the woman's eyes. "You rot in hell!" She was on her feet in attack position before the words were out of her mouth.

Asiah shook her head. "Not today." She flicked her finger in the direction of the library. The small building exploded. Brick, mortar, wood splinters and obliterated books shot hundreds of feet into the sky. The dust cleared and a black crater was all that remained.

"What have you done?!" screeched Marysa.

Asiah shrugged and leveled the jungle with another wave of her hand. Trees were flattened and little pieces of destroyed leaves floated down around them like green confetti. Next, she turned her attention to the small chest on the outer island.

"No! You can't!" Marysa screamed and Asiah smashed the chest into a pile of dust. A wave rolled in from the sea and swept the chest's debris away. Lifting her arms, Asiah pulled the wind and currents from the ocean into a massive, swirling storm of wind and water surrounding the island. She gathered more water and pushed the walls higher until she could no longer see the sky above the whirlpool surrounding them. Blinded by vengeance, her power flowed easily through her and she knew she could do anything.

"Stop it! You'll destroy everything!" Marysa pleaded, her voice all but lost in the roaring sound of the wind and water.

"That's the idea," Asiah said grimly. "You've taken away everything that I love, and now I'll take the same from you." She leaned her head back, looking up into the tunnel of water, and closed her eyes as she released the swirling ocean. An eerie silence ensued for a brief moment as leagues of salt water plunged toward the barren island. Marysa screamed one last time as Asiah released her hold on the woman, condemning her to drown in the flood.

Asiah opened her eyes, gasping for air. She'd stayed a moment too long and was momentarily swept away by the raging current in Marysa's ravaged mind. She pulled her hands away from Marysa's face. The other woman was staring blankly at the sky, seeing nothing. Her body wasn't dead, but she would never use her mind again.

Asiah's strength was shattered and she shook violently with fatigue. She suddenly remembered Chase and looked around frantically for the man she loved. He had dragged himself to the oak tree and was leaning against it, blood covering his torso and trousers. His eyes were closed and he was pale and motionless. Meri knelt next to him, holding his hand. Her eyes were full of despair.

"Chase!" Asiah called weakly, and crawled toward him. It felt like he was miles away, and it seemed to take ages to reach his side. "Chase, talk to me, please." She cupped his face, praying there was still a chance to save him. She looked at Meri. "Inside ... something to stop the bleeding. Hurry!" Meri nodded and ran inside the house.

Chase groaned softly and his eyes fluttered open. "Asiah, love ..." he managed.

"I can heal you. I've done it before," she said, although she feared that her waning strength wouldn't allow her to do so.

"Not this time, my love," he said, lifting his hand with some effort to stroke her cheek.

"Don't say that!" she cried, tears beginning to streak down her face. "I can help you!"

"I saw what you did to her mind. Bloody brilliant." He tried to smile. "You don't have the strength to walk, much less heal me. If it were any other blade, maybe ..." He leaned his head back against the tree and swallowed weakly, exhausted from the effort of speaking.

"Chase," she wept, "don't leave me, please." She didn't know what to do. There had to be something that could save him.

"I was going to stay with you forever," he whispered. "And spend the rest of our lives together. Until this cruel twist of fate." His breathing was becoming shallower.

"You can, Chase. I want you to stay with me. I *need* you to. Please ..." She pressed her hands to the wound and put all the strength she had left into healing him. She gritted her teeth and pulled her hands away. The wound hadn't healed at all; she was too weak to save him. She raised her eyes to his in a panic.

He looked steadily into her eyes. "If I can, I will find you again someday ... in the æthers. You won't forget about me, will you?"

"Never, Chase," she whispered brokenly.

He closed his eyes and smiled. "Good. Don't ever forget how much I love you." With a last burst of strength, he pulled her close and kissed her gently with his final breath.

Asiah felt the tingle of his touch fade upon her lips. "Chase?" she whispered, brushing his hair back from his serene face. "No ... no ... Chase." She buried her face in his neck and sobbed, holding him tightly until she gave into exhaustion and fell fast asleep.

Chapter Twenty-Two

The sun was setting when Asiah awoke. She was lying in Chase's bed alone. At first she thought she'd just had the most horrifying nightmare. Could it all have been a dream? Where was Chase? She leapt clumsily from the bed and dashed into the kitchen, not daring to hope.

Meri sat at the kitchen table, staring blankly at its worn wooden surface. "He's gone," Asiah's twin whispered. "Just ... gone."

Asiah gripped the edge of the table to steady herself. "What do you mean?" she asked Meri, already dreading the answer.

Meri looked up at her, her face drawn and pale. "Chase – he just disappeared. You were holding him, exhausted, and then he was just gone."

Asiah sank into a chair. It hadn't been a dream. Her heart shattered all over again.

"Asiah, I'm so sorry." Meri shook her head and reached for her sister's hand.

"How did I ...?" Asiah began, gesturing to the bedroom, trying to think about anything but Chase.

"I couldn't leave you out there, with *her*." Meri nodded out the window.

Asiah saw Marysa, still lying on the ground, staring blankly up at the darkening sky. "She killed him," Asiah whispered.

Meri nodded miserably. "I carried you inside and put you in the bed. These were all that was left behind," she said, pointing to Chase's silver bracelets on the table. His bloodstained dagger was next to them.

Asiah swallowed and picked up one of the bracelets, fresh tears stinging her eyes. The memory of his last kiss flooded back to her and she couldn't hold the tears back. Meri came around the table and wrapped her arms around Asiah. After several moments the flow of tears ebbed and Asiah sat numbly staring at the table, vaguely remembering that she still had a sacred duty and Chase's death would be in vain if she wasted her life pining for him. She pulled herself to her feet shakily and paused to catch her breath. Clearly, she hadn't recovered fully from today's battle. Still leaning on the table, she reached out and picked up Chase's jeweled dagger, now hers.

Marysa was still lying where Asiah had left her, staring unblinkingly upward. Marysa's dagger was lodged in a tree and Asiah collected it, shoving it roughly into its sheath. She wanted to slit Marysa's throat right then and there, but she knew the woman was suffering a new type of torment, being trapped in her own mind under a stormy ocean of psychological debris. As the evening chill descended, she left Marysa outside and went back into the house. She made a fire and put the kettle on, trying to keep herself busy. If she let her mind wander, she would think about Chase and she would break down again. It helped having Meri there. Her sister didn't speak, but her silent presence was comfort enough.

The twins slept in the bed Chase had shared with Asiah the night before, and she allowed herself only a moment to think about him when she inhaled his scent on the sheets before she fell into an exhausted sleep.

In the morning, Asiah found some paper and made a list:

1. Pack up Chase's belongings
2. Make arrangements for Mam's and Father's burial
3. Find a safe place for Marysa to live

4. Go to Ocea
5. Figure out how to save the world

It was a ridiculous list, but she needed something to help her focus right now. She knew she could easily fall into a pit of despair and forget what needed to be done. After breakfast, Asiah pulled one of Chase's trunks into the center of the room and opened the lid. It was full of junk, none of which looked useful to her.

"This is going to be a lot of work," she muttered to herself.

Over the next few days, Asiah and Meri collected all of Chase's knives, trunks, scrolls and old books from the shop on North Avenue and brought everything to the cottage to take inventory. Asiah closed the shop and gave the keys to the neighboring tenants.

She put Meri to work emptying the trunks. Her sister proved to be a big help, especially to stave off the loneliness that threatened to creep into Asiah's broken heart. Meri had also just lost her parents, and the twins only had each other left in the world.

By week's end, all the things Asiah wanted to keep were in three large trunks. They were packed to the brim with books, scrolls, Chase's weapon collection, various vials of strange liquids that Asiah would have to examine later and a few of his clothes to remember him by. She had no need for most of his household possessions and opted to leave them behind. In the process of repacking his things, Asiah had found several ledgers accounting for bank notes and bonds that were in accounts all over the world, and she added another item to her list:

6. Make sure Chase's money is safe

She knew she wouldn't need any money on Ocea, but someday she would return to Earth and surely she would have need of it then.

Asiah spent a lot of time at the end of each day sitting on the boulder in the middle of the lake in the Forest in her mind. She stared into the depths of the lake, looking for a sign that Chase had made it to the other side, to the æthers. She didn't really know what the "æthers" were, but Marysa seemed to think a place there was worth killing for. On the other hand, Chase thought their love was worth giving it up. He said he would look for her there someday. She didn't know when she would be able to join him. There was a lot more training for her to do, and after that, Asiah had to figure out how the people of Earth had doomed their own existence, if that was truly the case.

She truly hoped that somewhere in Chase's old writings there was something about that. He had told her that the Dark Ages were the turning point. Wars over religion dominated that time period. Could it be that religion was the root of all evil? Wouldn't *that* be rich. If that were the case, she definitely had her work cut out for her. If Chase was also correct about her progression to maturity, she had about eighty years to figure things out before she would be ready to save the planet, anyway. And she had no idea if it was enough time to become ready to take on a gargantuan task like that.

After her meditations each night, Asiah stood outside looking up into the sky. She located the tiny planet called Ocea each night and memorized its location in the heavens. She practiced channeling as much as possible, eventually travelling around the world and learning to land properly. She didn't know how far this planet was, but it must be farther than one trip around the globe. She thought about trying to go to the moon, but knew from her studies that it would be cold and there was no atmosphere. Chase said these things didn't matter, that she could still survive in any conditions if she needed to, yet it was too great a risk to take at this time.

November brought colder weather and Asiah decided she'd better leave Chicago before winter was upon her. She hadn't decided what to do about Meri yet. Asiah had no one else left, and she had no idea if her sister was ready to understand everything Asiah had to do and where she had to go to do it. Luckily, it ended up being fairly easy to talk to her sister about it.

"Take me with you," Meri said one afternoon after Asiah returned from a few hours of channeling around the world.

Asiah was confused at first, assuming Meri wanted to channel around with her.

"Meri, I need to practice first—" Asiah began.

"Please," her sister interrupted. "Please, there's nothing for me here. I want a new life, a new adventure. That's what you're doing right? Leaving Earth? I want to come with you."

"I never said I was leaving Earth," Asiah said warily, amazed at her sister's blind acceptance of these strange circumstances.

"I know that's what's happening. You told us about these 'people' of yours that live on other planets. If you're not crazy, which I'm still not sure of," she smiled sheepishly, "then that's where you're going, isn't it? You can't leave me here alone."

Meri was more intelligent than most, despite her trouble in school, but Asiah never knew her to be so open-minded.

Asiah considered a moment. It would be much less lonely if her sister were there on Ocea with her. "I suppose you can come with me. It's going to be very different."

Meri's face lit up. "I hope so! This place is so dismal. Anything could be better. I think we both need to live in a place that doesn't constantly remind us of what we've lost."

"You know we won't see Monty or Maryn again — probably ever."

Meri nodded. "They'll be okay on their own. It's safer if they stay far away from this ... evil that seems to be following you."

Asiah nodded in agreement. "It won't be safer for you."

"I'd feel safer if I was with you than left behind on my own."

Her sister's words warmed her heart. Perhaps her parents couldn't accept her new circumstances, but Meri didn't seem to have a problem. "Alright. We'll need to make arrangements for Mam and Father before we go. We should also send letters to Monty and Maryn so they know what's happened to our parents, but don't tell them where you and I are going."

Meri wrote the letters while Asiah visited the morgue in San Francisco where Aileen and Patrick's bodies had been taken. She made arrangements for their burials, using some money that she'd found among Chase's belongings. She hated to use his money for something so personal, even if he was no longer alive to object, and she vowed that she would pay it back as soon as she was able.

Asiah took Marysa to the same asylum where she had been held for that one awful month. She left her at the gate, not wanting to risk anyone recognizing her as the almost-lobotomized girl who'd stayed there recently. She stayed nearby long enough to make sure that Marysa was found and watched with grim satisfaction as two orderlies carried her inside on a stretcher.

Finally, she bounced around the globe collecting bank notes and savings bonds in Chase's name. She had to use a bit of telepathic persuasion to get the money, and she felt extremely guilty about it. There even were a few stocks he owned and she took the paperwork for those as well. After she had all his money and financial paperwork safely in a small trunk, she returned one last time to the cottage in the woods. She didn't feel safe leaving Chase's money behind in a time of economic depression since she had no way to fully ensure it would be secure while she was gone. If she brought it with her, it would still be worth the same amount when she brought it back to Earth in the future, or possibly more depending on economic changes.

She returned to find Meri making dinner. Chase's food stock was amazing and Asiah had already taken most of it to the local soup kitchens in Chicago. She'd left only enough for them to eat dinner before they departed to the distant planet.

While Meri finished preparing the meal, Asiah checked the stone in her bracelet. She removed the cuff gingerly, not enjoying the sensation of the stone leaving her body. She made sure her sapphire was secure and slid it back on to her wrist. She was about to fasten the clasp when she noticed the edge of an inscription. There hadn't been one before and she was confused. She removed the bracelet and examined the swirly letters engraved inside it.

You were worth the wait. Love, Chase

He must have added the inscription later. She almost cried. She glanced at Meri, but her sister hadn't noticed what she was doing. Asiah knew she needed to be strong now, especially for Meri, and she held back her tears.

They ate in silence. Asiah and Meri were both too anxious to talk. After supper, Asiah led her sister outside where she scanned the sky to make sure she still knew where her planet was. She hadn't channeled with other people yet, but she knew she could do it. She planned on three trips: one alone to make sure she knew how far she was traveling and that her sister could survive the conditions, one with the trunks, and once more with Meri. Meri gave her hand a little squeeze as Asiah prepared to make the first journey. Asiah smiled at her sister and stepped away from her to focus her thoughts. With one last deep breath, she launched herself into outer space.

Epilogue

February 2003
Langley, Virginia

Ben was having a miserable day. His girlfriend of four years had decided that this morning would be the most opportune moment to end their relationship by telling Ben that she'd been seeing someone else for the past three months. If that weren't enough, one of his teammates had been transferred to a desk job yesterday and he was left with a mountain of paperwork.

He stared at the slow-drip coffee machine in the break room bleakly.

"Hey, Torricelli!" a voice called from the hallway. "Spencer wants to see us."

"Thanks, Sawyer, be there in a minute," he replied dully.

"He said you'd say that, and that I should tell you to get your ass in there pronto," Sawyer said, then disappeared down the hall.

Ben groaned. This was all he needed today. He rarely got called into the formidable deputy director's office for good news. Leaving his empty CIA mug next to the coffee machine, he straightened his tie and headed for the office at the end of the hall.

Spencer's aging assistant waved him in, and he swallowed his trepidation as he entered the spacious office.

"Ah, Torricelli, about time." The old man gestured to one of the leather chairs surrounding the conference table in the corner. Sawyer and Ben's other teammate, Clarence "Soultrain" Mason were already seated at the table. A pretty brunette stood next to Spencer's desk, and Ben assumed she was an aide or an analyst, like most of the women that worked there. There was no way she was an agent. Ben sat on the edge of the chair, waiting for the hammer to fall.

"I called you in here to introduce you to your new teammate." Spencer gestured to the brunette. "This is Asiah O'Connor. She's the best profiler the Bureau's had in years so we had to snatch her up. They say she can get into anyone's head. Asiah, this is Benjamin Torricelli, Sawyer Jacks, and Clarence Mason."

Ben took a moment to look at the girl more closely. He couldn't believe his eyes. She was *gorgeous*. Huge blue eyes, long legs, perfect figure, full lips. Was the CIA recruiting from modeling agencies now? He couldn't seem to find his voice.

"Welcome to the Agency," he managed, standing and extending his hand.

She grasped his hand firmly. "Thank you, Agent Torricelli. I look forward to working with you. I've heard great things."

She smiled and his mouth went dry. Ben could only smile weakly and nod.

Spencer broke the silence. "Agent Jacks is your team leader and will be handling your training for the first few months here. Your team is known around here as Whiskey Squad."

O'Connor raised an eyebrow and Spencer shrugged. "What else were we supposed to call it when we got to 'W?' I'll let the four of you get acquainted. Why don't you go do that over that pile of paperwork on your desk, Torricelli?"

"Yes, sir." He looked at his new teammate and gestured to the door. "Ladies first."

She nodded and walked into the hall ahead of him. He hurried to catch up with her brisk pace.

"Where are you going in such a hurry?" he asked when he caught up.

"Your office. Paperwork, remember? It's this way, right?" She veered off to the left and Ben heard Soultrain chuckle behind him.

"Well, yes, but do you want to grab some coffee or something first? Believe me, the paperwork will still be there when we get back."

She stopped walking suddenly and turned to him, causing him to stumble slightly. "What about what Deputy Director Spencer said?"

Sawyer stepped up next to Ben. "What about it?" he said with a shrug.

"Listen, gentlemen, I'm here to work hard and get the job done. Your lackadaisical attitude is not going to fly with me. Paperwork first, coffee later." She marched off again in the direction of Ben's office, which he shared with Soultrain.

"Oh, she's going to be *loads* of fun," Soultrain said and strolled off down the hall after O'Connor.

Sawyer turned to Ben. "Dibs!" he said with a grin.

"All yours," Ben winced at the painful reminder that he was single as of this morning.

"We should probably go help them," Sawyer sighed.

"You go on ahead. I don't care what she said, I'm getting coffee."

End of Book 1

Thanks for reading!

Asiah's story continues in *Secret Shade*, available now!

Follow Ann on Facebook and Twitter!

Facebook: https://www.facebook.com/asiahoconnor
Twitter: @ann_serafini

Made in the USA
Middletown, DE
03 December 2025

22075126R00149